Ethereal

Prelude

Eight years before:

Wade Miller, his wife Angie, and four-year old son Timmy looked around at the various other "Estates of Willow Run." They were finally settling on a house. This one was, according to the real-estate agent, exactly what they had specified, a roomy, semi-detached house with a large back yard and not too many neighbors.

Angie had misgivings. The area seemed a bit isolated, somehow timeworn, although the houses were relatively new. It was like a place where only those who lived there would go there. She found it depressing.

Wade was equally uncertain. Several years of living in a rental apartment had prepared him to make some sacrifices, but he was not entirely certain this was the investment his agent assured him it was.

Timmy was delighted. A house of his own, a bedroom of his own, a back yard, *a back yard!* It would be like the "Hundred Acre Wood" where he would have adventures and excitement, exercise and fun! Timmy was enthusiastic.

Wade was hoping that the large back yard, merging into an "erosion-control community resource" which looked to him like a ditch, would allow him to have a garden area, where vegetables could supplement their food budget, and flowers could brighten their day.

Angie worried about being so close to neighbors, and who knew anything about them? Maybe they wouldn't get along. Maybe they would be noisy.

Timmy looked forward to making friends and having pets and outdoor games.

Despite the uncertainty of the adults, the boy's enthusiasm made them not want to disappoint him, and they knew apartment living was not for active four-year olds.

They signed.

And then …

Wade's garden never seemed to prosper. Too much sun, too much rain, too little time also. After several efforts, Wade threw in the towel and let the garden project wither.

Angie had her troubles inside the house, with noises and unexplained air currents. Half the time she was spooked by nothing she could really put her finger on.

But Timmy loved it. He spent nearly his entire time outdoors, whenever he could. His wondrous woodland was weeds and saplings, and the garden area was either mud or dust, but it was his kingdom, and he explored every inch of it, making it his own.

Neighbors came and went. Moving in, and occasionally in less than six months, finding reasons to move out again.

Wade settled into a day-to-day lethargy of acceptance. He had tried, and failed. More failure was not needed to prove the point. Besides, he had his work, and Timmy's delight in having his own place to play made the sacrifices worth it.

Angie kept an eye on the community, as much as she could. It was hard not to feel isolated here, but at least it was a quiet neighborhood, whenever it wasn't spookily too quiet.

Eight years went by like that. Evidence of how time flies, when a boy is having fun.

1. A Neighbor

Day One

"Wade, I'm worried."

"What about, Angie?" Wade put his beer down on the table beside his recliner.

Angie looked at it in annoyance. It was probably too late now to worry about stains. The table already looked like a doily convention from its circular watermarks. "Our new neighbor. All I know is that the "For Sale" sign is gone, and I'm hearing movement next door."

"Well? They've got furniture to rearrange. What would you expect?"

"I'd expect to see a moving van! I'd expect to see a truck parked out there and people carrying stuff in! As far as I know, the only thing they may have carried in is the sign from the front yard!"

Wade chuckled softly, but he could see that Angie was not going to be mollified. It occurred to him that he should have married someone named Molly.

"Well?"

"Oh, sorry," Wade picked up his beer and finished it quickly. "I'll go see our new neighbor and uh ... welcome him to the neighborhood."

Angie rolled her eyes.

Taking a deep breath, Wade lumbered his way out of his favorite seat, and headed for the porch.

Their house was a duplex, with a common porch covering both

doorways and a little sitting area on both sides. It was a great situation for having good neighbors, but after six tries, Wade was still waiting for the good neighbors to show up.

He knocked on the other door. Actually, it was a screen door, as the front door was standing wide open. The only light came from the window.

"Hey, buddy! You need a hand with anything?"

Wade heard some grunting and shuffling near the back. He couldn't make out whatever was being said.

"Well, anyway, I'm your neighbor, next door. Name's Wade. If you need something, just give a shout, okay?"

More indistinguishable noises. It sounded like the guy was having a wrestling match with a refrigerator, and losing.

"Okay, then. I'll see you later!" Wade beat a retreat. It was time for another beer.

"Well, did you talk to the neighbor?" Angie asked.

"Sure!" Wade said, "I couldn't help him with anything, though. I think he was having trouble with the fuse-box, or something."

"The fuse-box! I hope he doesn't burn us down!"

"Or something, I said. He wasn't in a good mood, so I didn't stick around."

Angie rolled her eyes again.

Wade got himself a beer.

⸺⸺ ⋅⧫⧫⧫⋅ ⸺⸺

Wade was standing in the kitchen, staring at the cabinet over the refrigerator. It seemed to be sagging. He opened the cabinet door, and saw what looked like an enormous ham, wedged into the cabinet. He stared at it.

Timmy came running in barefoot, from the back yard. "Hey, Dad! What's new?" The back yard wasn't exactly safe to run barefoot in, but Angie bought band-aids by the pound.

Wade grunted, "Neighbors."

"Huh?"

"Next door. New neighbors."

"Oh," Timmy said, then paused, "I'm gonna go see 'em!"

Wade was staring at the ham, trying to figure out where it had come from, because it looked like it was coming through the wall. Belatedly, he responded, "Well, don't you go pestering them! I don't think they like pests."

He heard his own screen door slam. "… Nobody likes pests," Wade continued softly. He reached for a large knife.

Wade figured if he couldn't get the ham out one way, he'd just carve it out a slice or two at a time. He carved off enough to feed about four grown men, and laid it on a platter. It had a kind of plastic cover on it so he peeled that off. Then he sliced up some potatoes, carrots, and onions over it, and put it in the oven. Angie didn't like onions.

Wade closed the cabinet door. Maybe now the ham would shrink up a bit, and he could drag the rest of it out of the cabinet. That could come later, though. While the ham was cooking, he'd have some time for a beer or two.

Timmy showed up after supper had cooled. Wade gave him a plate of leftovers. There wasn't a lot of it. The ham had been remarkably delicious!

Timmy sat down and tucked in. Wade was pleased to see him enjoying the meal. There were a lot of things that he didn't do well, and cooking was on that list.

Timmy seemed distracted by something. He kept looking down at his foot.

Wade looked at it. His right foot was unusually clean. Sparkling clean, almost, except that the sparkles came from glittering reflections on the surface of his skin. His other foot was still soiled from playing in the back yard.

"So what'd you do over there?" Wade asked casually. He really didn't care, but he was still curious about his strange new neighbor.

"It's a really cool place! They keep the lights off, except for some strings of Christmas lights, I think. And there's real neat furniture around, soft and comfy, and every time you come into the room the furniture's been moved! They were putting on a puppet show! It was so funny, with all these squeaky voices and scary monster noises! I had a great time! I think they must have a dog, too. I didn't actually see it, but it came over and was licking my foot while I was laughing myself silly! What a great place!"

"Puppet show, huh?" Well, that explained the sparkles. They probably came from some puppet costume. "Any other kids there?"

"I think so," Timmy looked a little puzzled, as if he were having trouble remembering precisely, "I didn't get a chance to talk with them though."

Timmy stretched and yawned, "The show started as soon as I got there. I guess maybe they must have three or four little kids, probably younger than me."

"All right," Wade said, "go get cleaned up, and go to bed." That way, if Angie scolded him about whether he had told Timmy to brush his teeth, and take a bath, he could say, "Yes, I did! I told him quite clearly."

What the heck. Tomorrow was Saturday. He could get a bath tomorrow.

Wade opened the cabinet on Saturday morning, to see how the ham might have shrunk.

He stood there for a minute and scratched his chin. The ham was as big today as it had been yesterday.

Wade grabbed his knife again, and sawed off several good-sized slices to sizzle up in the skillet. While they were cooking, he made up pancakes too.

Timmy was waiting at the table when the breakfast was ready. Wade set him out a good plateful, and Timmy dug into it with gusto.

Smiling, Wade began munching on his own heaping platter. Oh, that was so tasty!

Soon Timmy was off and running again. Ah, the impetuousness of youth!

Even Angie enjoyed a bit of ham before she headed out to meet with her whatever-it-was group.

"I'll bring home some orange juice, Wade!"

He nodded as he savored another bite. Orange juice was a good idea, he thought. He wondered what had made her suggest it.

When Timmy came home, late in the evening, he was yawning already.

"I have food for you, buddy!" Wade called.

"No thanks, Dad. I'm not hungry. I'm really not. We had fun, and I guess there must have been snacks and punch and stuff. Anyway, I'm not hungry. I'll just go up to bed."

"Get cleaned up first, y'hear?" Wade made sure to get that in. He watched as Timmy climbed up the stairs. For some reason, now Timmy's left leg seemed funny looking. Maybe it was clean too.

✦

Day after day, Wade carved yet more ham off the unending supply in his cabinet. He tried different ways to prepare it, trying to mask the fact that it was the same meat day after day. But no one seemed to object.

Every way he prepared it, the meal was delicious!

Timmy was almost always at the neighbor's house, but at least he was staying clean now. Except for the sparkly appearance, the boy never seemed to have any dirt on him at all.

The visits seemed to be very good for the boy. He was light-hearted and happy all the time, skipping across the room like a dancer, and going up or down the stairs with the same joyous energy. He seemed to almost glow with delight!

And then one day, Wade opened the cabinet, and the ham was gone. Nothing was in the cabinet at all, including one side of it, an opening through the wall that led toward the adjacent house. Except ... except for a long, curling piece of paper. With the curious stick-like figures of script on it, it almost looked like a scroll of parchment.

"Dear Neighbor/Doctor,

I will be leaving your neighborhood now. My rest and recuperation is at an end, for I find myself cured!

Yes, cured! I had come here at my last hope, anguished and in pain, with the throbbing, aching, swollen tentacle growing in a place no tentacle should be!

In my shame and pain, I thrust the painful protuberance into a wall-cavity, seeking only to conceal it from my attention and sight. How I was relieved one day, when the pain and pressure was suddenly reduced!

And how I was so delighted when your spawn came to me, so willingly surrendering his sweet flesh to my fevered appetites! I did not dare to consume him entirely, at least not all at once.

Instead, I arranged for his sweetness to be supplanted by a simple other-dimensional substitute. He was so deliciously happy, he did not even notice that his mass, and his very flesh, were being consumed, and that his body was slowly disappearing.

Yes, he surrendered his legs, and then his arms, and delicious tiny nibbles of his goodness that only brought joyful giggles and tear-filled laughter. Oh, those delicious tears! Oh, my! I am so grateful.

I AM SO GRATEFUL!!!

And then to discover that my ailment too, was being alleviated. My pain diminishing. My disfigurement disappearing … oh, Sir, you have no idea how pleased I am that I found myself in your blessed graces.

I could not in fairness to your delightful kindness and generosity, take away that essential part of you that I found so wonderful, and leave you nothing of it in turn.

Accordingly, in taking my leave of you, I return to you

a part of the delightfulness that you extended to me, a complete and utter stranger to your realm.

I give you back your precious Timmy, although by this time of course, all of his tasty flesh has been completely consumed. I found enough of the genetic material to make two clones of him, so that you will have that delicious essence in full repayment, and I have completed the other-dimensional entity which mirrors his joyful exuberance and delight for all the joys of life.

You will also, no doubt, notice that this poor substitute for the original is not entirely the same. For that I apologize, as my workmanship is in sorry condition, with these last few centuries of neglect as I was distracted with other nonessentials.

Your spawn will not be able to enjoy the normal span of years that a human can ordinarily expect. My poor imitation ability has simply made him immortal and ageless.

And now I must return to my own realm, inspired and energized, by you and your acts of inestimable kindness.

Good bye to you, and if by any chance your sweet, oh-so-sweet child should weep at my departure, by all means taste those delicious, delectable tears. I have never before enjoyed the like.

Good Day, Sir!"

Wade read through the scroll, again and again, turning to stare at the hole in his wall, and then back to the incomprehensible document.

"Timmy!" He bellowed at the top of his lungs.
There came a clattering and galumphing down the stairs. Light-footed, indeed!
Timmy came into the kitchen, and sat down at the table.
And then another Timmy came in and sat down.

And then another Timmy came in and tried to sit down, but tended to float upward from the seat. His brothers reached out and gently held him in place. This Timmy was a sparkling, ethereal, glowing entity, with a smile of endless sunshine and joy.

"Hi, Dad!" they said.

Wade looked at the document again, and then at his sons. A kind of a sound came out of his lips, but it was not of a language anyone understood.

"We've discovered that this one," the boy on the left raised his hand, "who we will call Oliver, is left-handed." Oliver shrugged his thin shoulders.

"And this one," the boy on the right raised his hand, "is right-handed, so we will call him Dexter." Dexter smiled his Timmy smile.

"And I am what's left of the original Timmy," Timmy the sparkly one said, as he rose up through the table and flew around the room. "I'm not a ghost, but I'm not quite sure what else I am. I think I'm going to have a lot of fun, though!"

The other Timmys nodded in smiling assurance that it was true.

2. Later

Two months later, the bank evaluator, Walter Hargreaves, changed his recommendation on the troublesome property. Instead of continuing the neglect and trying to sell it as is, the bank would hire a contractor to make repairs that had been languishing for years.

Hargreaves could not say specifically what caused his change of heart. He had been administering this property for several years now, and he had never gone out on a limb like this before. He just "had a feeling".

The contractors had seen the house before as well. Roger Cannon, and his two cousins, Luke and Eddie, took a bit of time in formulating a plan. Not just some new carpeting and a paint job, but a bit of a redesign to modernize the house and make it more comfortable and more appealing. Looking at the sketches prior to submitting them for approval, they agreed that this was going to be a satisfying project.

Wade listened to the construction work next door, and felt strangely impelled to do a little more fixing up around his place. Obviously, the doors had needed some adjustments, and he had already acquired some furniture and set it up.

Maybe it was time to replace some appliances, or make a modification to the kitchen. He'd have to think about that. They were going through more food. Maybe he could plant some beans and tomatoes in the garden.

Theodore McMasters and his wife took the open house tour, rather pleased that they had decided to go just a little bit farther in their search. Corinne had wanted to stay in the same local area, because of her involvement with her church activities. This almost hidden area was quiet and close by, allowing them to continue in the same school and even have a shorter commute!

It had a good vibe to it, Corinne said.

<hr>

Six months later, Timmy was frustratingly bored. All the fun he had thought he was going to have had settled into a day-after-day sameness of doing essentially nothing.

Since his "accident", Timmy had yet to set one foot in school again, or anywhere else.

His sparkly ethereal nature aside, Timmy had a problem related to getting himself "fit to present"; his clothes kept falling off of him.

Shoes were the worst. Timmy could barely lift anything as heavy as a grapefruit. Every time he would get dressed, and try to go somewhere, he would step out of his shoes at the very first step, and it usually wasn't long before everything else was strewn in his wake as well.

There just wasn't much of him to hang things on. They kept slipping off. Angie found some cheap shorts, which weighed only ounces, and thin tee shirts to wear that the other boys could not even handle without destroying.

Timmy's clothes had to be left out where he could get them. If they were shoved in a drawer, they might as well be locked in a safe. Angie got used to picking them up where she found them, and putting them on an open shelf in the upstairs hallway.

That made his going for a visit somewhere very problematic. On opening day of school, his attendance there was not even a point of discussion. It was enough of a hassle to try to get a second Timmy registered for attendance. The whole round of explanations and fabrications about "Timothy Oliver" having been in Arizona for his health with Wade's imaginary sister for a few years was trying and exhausting enough.

So Timmy stayed home, while Oliver and Dexter took up his former life at school. To be fair, they were him too. But for the ethereal Timmy, staying home all the time took a bit of the luster off his glow.

But even staying home had few comforts for the predominantly ghost-like boy. He could not lift anything with any appreciable weight to it. The best he could do was for example, to set the table for the others precisely one glass or fork or spoon at a time.

He could move quickly, so that became a bit of an art for him, but he could not lift very much. And none of it meant anything to him anyway, as he could not eat a bite of even the sweetest, lightest dessert, or take even a sip of liquid. His ghostly essence could not be mudded over with mundane reality.

His family got used to seeing him, in his always-accidental nudity. But he seldom got any relief from being housebound.

The arrival, at last, of what could be that "good neighbor" the family had been seeking for a long time, was merely the occasion of a stern lecture from everyone to Tim, not to screw up this new arrangement.

Naturally, Timmy was outrageously intrigued by the new arrivals. A father with a good-paying job; a mother involved with numerous community activities; … yawn.

But, an eight-year old girl, who tended to spend just a bit too much time alone, *right next door to an ethereal wunderkind,* was entirely too much to ask of Timmy's patience and forbearance. Naturally, he began spying on her.

And naturally, eventually, she caught him at it.

It was a cool afternoon. Oliver and Dexter were off at the ball-field playing baseball, for as long as light permitted. No one had yet suggested a glow-in-the-dark baseball.

Timmy discovered that the neighbor girl was playing outside, on the common front porch. Because his side was the one with sunshine at the moment, that's where she was.

He peeked his head through the wall to look over her shoulder as she arranged her dolls and partied with them. She also had a hand-mirror and brush for making everything tidy at her impromptu soiree.

She was using the hand-mirror as if it were a microphone, while she recited the names of guests at her party. She seemed to have a lively imagination.

As Timmy studied the various dolls and their arrangement, he became aware that the girl had adjusted the mirror such that she could see his face sticking out of the wall behind her. He withdrew hurriedly.

And then he heard her soft and plaintive lament, "Well, boy, don't be shy. Why don't you come out and play with me?"

He stuck his head out again. She had not moved, and her reflection in the mirror smiled at him.

Looking around, Timmy saw no one else visible anywhere on the street. It might be safe to venture out just for a moment. He passed through the wall and hunched down near the little girl so that they would both be unnoticed behind the low, latticed wall of the porch.

She glanced at him and turned to her dolls. "This is Elizabeth, Mary, Belinda the Ballerina, and Grouchzilla. I'm Hannah. Thanks for coming out."

"What's wrong with Belinda's feet," asked Timmy, looking at the doll.

"She dances on her toes. That's what ballerinas do."

Timmy nodded. "Grouchzilla. I like that. My name is Timmy Miller. Do you live next door?"

"Yes. We've only been here a couple of weeks. They fixed this house up and painted it and everything. I like it."

"It's good to have neighbors again."

Hannah considered. "Mom said I shouldn't bother any of you. You don't mind if I sit out here, do you? It's warmer here in the sunlight."

"Warmer? Oh, I guess it is." Said Timmy, who was rather immune to hot and cold. "No, it's fine if you want to play on this side. We don't mind."

"You must not mind the cold, either," observed Hannah. "You didn't bring any clothes with you."

Timmy looked down. Sure enough, the tee shirt and play shorts he had been wearing a moment ago were now abandoned on the other side of the wall through which he had just passed. "Oh, I'm sorry. I guess I should have come out through the door."

"Why? How would that have made a difference?" Hannah asked, quite calm considering she was talking to a naked boy who had just walked through a wall.

"Well, I can keep my clothes on, usually, if I use the regular doorways. I tend to forget sometimes though. And it's a lot of work for me to get the door open."

"Why, are you a ghost? Mom said somebody had told her a boy was murdered over here, but she didn't think it was true."

"No, I wasn't murdered. But something happened. My regular body got copied into two other regular bodies, which are my twin brothers. At one time there was only one Timmy, and now there are three of us. They go to school and seem normal, but I have trouble with being all the way here."

Hannah reached out suddenly and passed her hand through the space where his knee was. It was just empty air.

"Oh, sorry. I wasn't ready. Try it again."

Hannah reached out, more slowly this time. She touched Timmy on his knee, and spread her hand across his leg for a moment.

"Wow! That's really strange. Sometimes you're there, and sometimes you're not there."

Timmy nodded. "It can be a problem. That's why I don't go to school. I have trouble staying in touch with things."

"Staying in touch with things like clothes?" Hannah asked.

"Yes, and books, and jackets. Shoes are really difficult. I guess I'd have trouble even using a piece of chalk."

Hannah considered. "But you're not a ghost?"

"Not any kind of ghost I ever heard about. Most people have trouble seeing ghosts. I have trouble *not* letting people see me."

"Why don't you want them to see you?"

"Like this?" Timmy opened his hands. "It's a little embarrassing." He looked at her. "It isn't bothering you, is it?"

"I don't think so. It was kind of surprising, but you're a nice boy, with good manners. I like you."

"Thanks. I like you too." He looked up and down the street again. "I'd better go back in. It was nice visiting with you."

"Wait," she said, "can we play again later?"

"I don't know. My mom wouldn't be happy to find out you've seen me like this."

Hannah touched his leg again. "I won't tell her." She looked thoughtful. "Hey, is your house like mine, only opposite? I was thinking, my bedroom is upstairs, toward the back. Do you think you could come to see me there?"

Timmy looked over his shoulder, visualizing the house. "My bedroom's on that side too. I share it with my brothers. I don't think I should let them know if I come to see you."

"Oh," she pulled her hand back and looked down. "Well, don't let them know about it. Just pop in when you can. Maybe tonight after supper?"

"Maybe … okay!" Timmy smiled. "I'd like that! I don't get to go many places. Just going next door will be a fun adventure!"

"For me too!" she smiled at him, "See you later!"

Timmy disappeared back into the house.

Suddenly everything was so quiet, Hannah almost doubted that the encounter had been real. But the boy was so cute!

She had seen his brothers, racing out from time to time, letting the screen door slam and boisterously yelling back and forth. They had looked at her as well, but they had not *seen* her. To them, she was probably no more than a tyke just out of diapers.

They might not have even noticed if she was a boy or a girl.

But *this* boy; well, he seemed different. More curious, *lots* more shy, and maybe patient enough to actually look at, and even talk to a girl that was *years* younger than he was.

"What do you think, girls?" she asked her companions. All seemed just a bit glum and non-committal, except Grouchzilla, who didn't like it, of course.

She gathered up her dolls and went back inside. The sun had gone away too.

Timmy listened. All was quiet in the adjacent house. Either Hannah's room was empty, or she was being quiet. At least he thought she might be alone.

He hesitated. His mother would not approve. He would already be in trouble if she found out that Hannah knew about him.

He could hear voices in other parts of his house, but his room was currently empty. Summoning his courage, he poked his head through the wall. Hannah was sitting in front of her dresser, and she looked over at him and smiled.

He stepped through and smiled back at her. Now that he knew where all her stuff was, he could slide back into his room over there in that corner, and he would be under his own bed. That was where he usually slept, anyway; the floor space under a set of bunk beds.

He could come out from under his bed at any time and no one would say anything about it.

He looked over to Hannah again. She was staring at him closely. He realized that he was indeed, standing, and that he had just stepped through a wall. He was, therefore, naked once more.

"Oh, gosh. How many times will I have to say I'm sorry?"

Hannah smiled. "Don't worry about it. Come on in. We'll have tea together!"

"Thanks!" Timmy had grown accustomed to being seen in this condition by members of his family. His brothers, especially, tried to make him squirm in discomfort. It was good to find someone who seemed willing to accept his limitations.

She led him to a corner where a tiny table was the meeting place for her dolls. Moving Grouchzilla away, she gestured for Timmy to have a seat at the table.

He sat on the floor, and looked around the room. All in all, the renovations to Hannah's house had made it quite nice.

Hannah moved Elizabeth and Mary to the same side, and sat on a small round pillow herself. She sat up straight, as proper tea manners required.

Timmy nodded, and looked across the table at his hostess.

"Tea, Mister Timmy?" Hannah picked up a toy teapot and a tiny cup. She pretended pouring an imaginary tea into the cup.

"Don't mind if I do," said Timmy. "I seldom indulge, but since it's an occasion, thank you!" He accepted the cup and pretended to drink.

"That's about all I usually eat or drink anyway." He said.

"You don't eat?" Hannah was sipping from her own cup. "How do you stay alive?"

"I wish I could answer that. We call it "The Accident" like it was a car accident or something. Actually what happened, happened here in your house. We had a new neighbor, and I kept coming over and hanging around. I can't really remember much about it, but he must have been some kind of magician or something. Dad got a letter from him."

"Anyway, after he left, I didn't weigh anything anymore. I guess that's why I don't eat, because if I ate, then I'd weigh something."

"If you don't weigh anything, how do you stay sitting down? Wouldn't a breeze blow you around?"

"A breeze? No. But I have to concentrate on staying where I want to. If I push too hard, my legs would go through the floor, and then there would be my naked bottom half sticking out of your parents' ceiling."

Hannah giggled, visualizing it.

Timmy laughed softly too, and then grew serious. "I know this is a crappy way to present myself, Hannah. I don't know what I can do. I hate the choices I have. If I can't come to you like, well, like this, I probably wouldn't be able to see you at all. As it is, I never get to see anybody, anyway."

"I'm glad you came, Timmy. This way, I get to see you!"

Timmy smiled casually, before the true meaning behind her words penetrated.

"Wait. You mean …?"

"Uh-huh. The way you look right now, you're like art, with that glowing, and sparkling like a dusty sunset. I've always been interested in art, but all I usually do is make fancy colorings in coloring books." She looked toward the door. "My folks are giving me a big book of old-time artists, the classics."

She looked at his face again. "That's what you remind me of, a classic painting! You shouldn't be ashamed, anyway. I think you're beautiful!"

It was a little hard to tell, but Timmy was blushing furiously. "Um. I think you're saying I should just relax and be natural." Timmy shifted his head left and right, while looking upward. "I don't feel too relaxed, but I like being with you."

He looked down. "Tell you the truth, I don't even know why I have this thing. I don't pee any more. I don't go to the bathroom at all. This thing could fall off of me and I wouldn't miss it."

"Well, you look funny with it, but you'd probably look even stranger without it. Let's talk about something else. Give me your hand."

Timmy put his hand out.

Hannah opened a bottle of nail polish and began putting polish on his fingernails.

"That might be a bad idea," Timmy said, watching closely. "If my brothers see this, they'll make trouble for me."

Hannah stopped for a moment. "Well, it's an experiment. I'm wondering if this polish can go through the walls when you do. I'm betting it can't."

"I don't know." Timmy said. "I've never done it. I can't carry water through a wall, no matter how wet I seem to be."

"Well, it's good for relaxing, anyway. Give me your other hand."

Timmy submitted his left hand too. He looked at the nails of his right hand. Who ever thought this was a good idea, anyway?

Then Hannah wanted to do his toes as well. Timmy realized that his nakedness would never be more exposed to view than in this ridiculous posture. He didn't care.

He put his left foot in her lap and let Hannah paint his toenails. Then he submitted his other foot as well.

Hannah put the polish away.

Timmy stood up and walked around, looking at his feet.

Hannah smiled. "I don't think it makes you look girly at all."

Timmy smiled, "Well no, not like this, I guess."

Hannah laughed.

"Hannah? Everything okay?" A voice called through the bedroom door.

"Everything's fine, Mom. I'm just playing with my dolls."

"Okay, sweetie. If you want a snack or anything, just come on down."

"Okay, Mom. I'm fine."

She looked at Timmy. "Hungry?"

He smiled. "No." Timmy looked around Hannah's room.

Hannah came over to him. "You're tall. How old are you? I'm nine, or I will be."

"I should be going on thirteen. I don't think I am. My brothers are getting bigger than me. I think they're growing, and I'm not."

Hannah touched his arm, gently. "How could that be?"

Timmy looked at her hand, and her face. Hannah had very pretty eyes, with long curling eyelashes.

"When the accident happened, I was almost twelve. We were told that the kind of copy I am won't get older. The document said I would be ageless."

"Ageless? You'll stay twelve? How long can a person be twelve?"

Timmy shrugged. "The document also said immortal. I don't know how long I'll be like this. But I guess that as long as I'm … like this, this sparkly thing, then I guess that's how long I'll stay twelve years old."

Hannah stared at his face. "I hope I stay here a hundred years, and live next door to you!"

Timmy put his arms around her, and pulled her close to him.

"You're nine? Pretty eyes, nice hair. In three years, *you'll* be twelve. Then in three more years, you'll be fifteen, then eighteen … Wow! As good as you look now, I'm … Wow!"

"You're what, lucky?" Hannah laughed softly.

"Yeah! Whatever happens, I'm lucky to have found a friend."

Hannah squeezed him gently, too.

3. Another Day

Timmy swooped up through the roof, looking out over the back yard and across the distant lines of trees. He saw that it was going to be another quiet evening, with a potentially clear night.

That would be good for stargazers.

It would be good for him too. Stargazing was his new hobby.

He melted back into the roof, and slid over to Hannah's room. Listening as best he could, with the thick insulation in his way, he could detect no sounds from her bedroom.

Near the center of the room, where there was a light fixture, he stuck his head out of the ceiling to look around.

Hannah was at her dresser, studying. She was already wearing her nightgown.

"Psst!"

Hannah looked up, and smiled. She beckoned him to enter.

Timmy drifted on down through the ceiling, and landed lightly on his feet. He bowed politely and approached.

Speaking softly, he asked, "What are you reading?"

"Just some spelling homework. I'm almost done."

Timmy went over and lay down on Hannah's bed. It was made up like a princess bed, with posts and curtains. He looked up at the ceiling and put his hands behind his head.

After a few minutes, Hannah closed her book and came to sit at the edge of the bed.

Timmy shifted his eyes to look at her, but remained where he was. "You seem very relaxed. You're not being as shy as you used to be." He smiled.

"I like it," she said. "You used to act like a scared puppy." Hannah reached out and gently brushed her hand along his chest. "I'm not going to hurt you, you know."

"Aside from the fact that you can't," Timmy said with a smile, "Thanks! I wasn't afraid, you know. I just didn't want to be … well, annoying, I guess."

Hannah twisted a bit, and brought her knee up on the bed. She ran her hand along Timmy's shoulder and arm. "You feel solid enough now, and very smooth. You have nice soft skin."

"That tickles, kind of," Timmy said, "I like it though."

"You don't have any hair under your arms." Hannah observed. "Mom always shaves hers. Your body is very smooth."

"I have hair on my head, don't I?"

"Yes, you do have that." Hannah passed her hand through his curls. They were exceedingly fine, almost like spider webbing. "I like that you are smooth though." She stroked his cheek.

There came a soft tapping at the door. Timmy sank through the bed.

The door opened, and Hannah's mother looked around. "I thought I heard voices."

"I was reciting my spelling words."

"Oh. I'm sorry. Good night, then."

"Good night, Mom."

The door closed again. Timmy peeked out from under the bed.

Hannah was looking at him. "You're such a scaredy-cat!" She said quietly.

"I thought I was a scared puppy." Timmy responded in a soft voice.

"No, you *used* to be a scared puppy. Now you're a scared kitty."

He slid out onto the floor and sat up, pulling his ankles in. "Your mom shaves her armpits, huh?"

"Yeah. It's kinda gross, actually. What'cha want to do?"

Timmy shrugged. "We'll have to be quiet."

"You'd better come up here." Hannah said. "If she comes back, you'll sink through the floor and Dad will have a heart attack."

Timmy smiled and pushed off from the floor. He glided through the air to sit beside her.

"You fly good."

"Yeah. It would be fun to be able to do it outside, maybe chase some birds around."

"Don't you go scaring the birds! I like birds. I like hearing them singing in the morning."

"Sometimes they sing all night long." Timmy said. "I go outside at night once in a while, when it is dark and no one can see me." He put his chin in his hands. "Don't worry. I won't hurt them. I like them too. Besides, I don't think I'd want to go skinny-dipping in the sky in front of the whole neighborhood."

"Just in front of me, huh?" Hannah teased.

"Just in front of you. Yes." Timmy looked over at her. "It doesn't seem as bad, if it means I can be with you."

"You know something? This is fun, visiting with you. I wonder why people always make such a fuss?"

"I don't know. Remember I'm only twelve."

"Well, sheesh! I'm only nine!" Hannah rolled her eyes.

"Okay, let's forget about it then. Just pretend. What were we talking about?"

Hannah thought. "Nothing. Being shy. Not being shy." She looked at him.

"Maybe just between us, we can forget being shy if we don't know why?"

"I don't want you to be shy." Hannah smiled at him. "I want to keep you, like a pet."

Timmy smiled. "Not a cat or a dog, but still a pet?"

"Why not? I won't even have to feed you."

"I'd like being your pet."

Hannah began rubbing the skin of his shoulder again. "Like that?"

"Like anything. You can pet me. I like it when you touch me."

"Roll over, and lay down straight. Make some room for me."

"Roll over? You said 'roll over', right?" Nevertheless, Timmy complied. He lay down on his stomach, with his legs parallel to the bed.

"Good puppy!" Hannah stretched out alongside him, with one hand supporting her head, and the other stroking his back, down to, and then up and over his rump, like with a cat, the way it arches its back. She did one side and then the other.

"I could lay here like this for a long time." Timmy said softly, almost sleepily.

Hannah leaned closer for a moment. "Good doggy," she said softly, "play dead for me now."

Timmy relaxed even further. Eventually they both fell asleep.

4. School

The door opened. "Hannah! Time to get up. It's a school day."
The door closed.

Hannah woke up. Timmy was still with her, snuggled so closely to her that he almost seemed to be a part of her. Even though he mostly felt like air, he was keeping her warm.

She raised her head to where she could see his face. He was so peacefully angelic. She kissed him on the cheek. "Wake up, sleepy puppy."

Timmy opened his eyes. "What? I'm still here?"

"Yeah, you are!" Hannah whispered. "Let's get up. I have to pee!"

They untangled themselves, and Hannah started toward the bathroom. She looked back. "Well, come on!"

"Sorry, I don't have to pee. I'll just wait for you here."

He sat on her bed and watched with great interest as she got ready. He hadn't cared at the time, but now he wished that he could go to school too.

Soon, Hannah was dressed and ready to go out the door. She stopped with her books in hand and looked at him. "Give me a kiss, Rover. I'm going to school."

Timmy stepped up and kissed her on the cheek. "Have fun!"

"Not 'til later!" She kissed him again and went out the door.

Timmy stood there in the silence for a moment. Then he looked around the room, shrugged his shoulders, and went over to his corner and slid through the wall.

◆◆◆◆◆

When Angie came home, it was after dark and there was a note on her door.

> *Dear Neighbors,*
>
> *Thank you for all the kindnesses you have shown us since we moved in. I know we haven't gotten together formally yet, what with everyone having such chaotic schedules, the rush of Holiday preparation and everything, but I wanted to invite your family, and especially your young sons, to participate in our local Church choir and its regular practice.*
>
> *You see, I am the choir director there, and I would like to both expand our membership and also get a few more male voices in the choir. A good mixture of boys and girls always enhances the beauty of their combined voices.*
>
> *Our daughter Hannah, whom you may have seen in our comings and goings, has pleaded with me to invite your boys to join us. We would be very pleased if that should prove to be possible.*
>
> *Perhaps we could all meet soon to further discuss this, and other things as well. Please feel free to knock on our door at any time to set up a family-to-family meeting.*
>
> *In any case, we look forward to meeting all of you, and to many years of neighborly relations.*
>
> *Corinne, Theo, and Hannah McMasters.*

Angie read the letter over several times, and then brought it to Wade's attention.

"A choir?" Wade furrowed his brow, "Our boys? Somehow I don't think they're going to like this idea. They're more into sports."

"I know, but we should try to meet, at least. These people sound very nice. After the trouble we've had with neighbors, I want to keep everything working well for all of us. Maybe they'll stay a while."

Wade considered this, and nodded ruefully. Then he went to get a beer.

It happened that two days later, schedules aligned such that the families were able to get together.

The McMasters came in and looked around with the appearance of people familiar with the house, but curious as well, for their side of the structure was a mirror image of this one. The differences, and the feeling of déja vu, were mixed together.

Angie played hostess, inviting her guests in to sit at the dinner table, which had been expanded, as it should be for Thanksgiving dinners and such. Theo, Corinne, and Hannah sat at one end, and Wade, Angie, Oliver, and Dexter sat at the other.

"Where's Timmy?" asked Hannah.

"Timmy?" Wade looked at her, "What do you mean?"

"Your *other* son, of course. The third one."

"You, ah, you *know* him?"

"Well, I know he doesn't go out of the house much, but we both have back yards. We've talked over the fence back there. He's my friend."

"Ah, yes, of course. Odd that he didn't mention that. Well, anyway … Timmy! Come on down! We have company."

Angie smiled at her guests in a wide-eyed semblance of terror. Oliver and Dexter looked at each other and shrugged.

Timmy walked very carefully down the stairs. He was wearing a pair of shorts and a tee shirt. For him, that was about as formal as he could get. His feet were bare.

As he came around the table, Hannah pulled out the chair next to her for him to sit on.

Very cautiously, Timmy sat down.

Hannah smiled at him.

"Hi, Hannah!" Timmy said softly.

"Hi, Timmy." She smiled.

"Now, anyway, I wanted to invite you boys, all of the family actually, to come and participate in choir with us. It's a way to meet people without everything being stuffy and formal. For folks who don't like church much, it's a better way to get together." Corinne said brightly.

Wade exercised his eyebrows. He seemed dubious.

Angie was looking around at everyone, as if waiting for a chandelier to fall.

"Does this involve singing?" Oliver asked. Dexter nodded.

"Of course! Children have such lovely voices! I try to get as many involved as I can."

"We should probably participate at least once," Angie said, "just to give it a fair start."

Wade looked at her as if she had suddenly grown another head.

"I'd like to go." Timmy said softly.

His family looked at him.

"But you never go anywhere." Oliver said.

"That's why I'd like to go."

"That, might almost be worth seeing …" Dexter mused. He looked at Oliver.

"Well," Mrs. McMasters began, "Well, I'll be going, of course, along with Hannah. Theo usually has to work when we're practicing, but he always shows up for the performances on Sunday." She smiled at her husband, who dutifully smiled back.

Wade looked from one of them to the other.

"I could take the boys along, for practice, if you'd like. It wouldn't be any trouble." Corinne continued. This was her project, after all.

"Um, I don't know," Angie tremulously suggested, "these boys can sometimes be a little rambunctious. They don't like to sit still for very long."

"Oh, it's really short! Most of our practices only last a half-hour. Forty-five minutes at most. Everyone has family obligations, of course!" She said enthusiastically.

"I think this could be a bad idea," Wade said slowly.

"I still want to go." Said Timmy, "I think it would be fun to sing in a choir."

"Timmy may be right, Dad," Dexter suggested, "Singing, at least, is something Timmy should be able to do. I'm sure we would all enjoy it."

Wade looked at his son with narrowed focus.

"We'll be there to help, of course," Oliver offered in support. He nodded to Dexter.

"How about if I pick you up at six-thirty? Um, I mean, we can all go in my car." Corinne tried to keep the momentum going. "Would that be okay? Six-thirty Saturday?"

"Yes, please?" Timmy said.

"Sure, we're okay with that, right, Dex?" Oliver said. Dexter nodded slowly.

"Oh, dear!" Angie said.

Wade held up his hands.

"Well, then it's settled! Hannah and I will give you boys a ride Saturday, and we'll just see what kind of joyful noises we can make, and how much fun we'll have!"

Slow nods of agreement around the table seemed to settle their fate. Hannah and Timmy were smiling at each other, and Oliver and Dexter were grinning.

Corinne and Angie each had smiles indicative of varying degrees of terror.

Wade glanced at the kitchen. The call was nearly audible.

"Well, very well, then," Corinne bustled, "I suppose we've taken up enough of your time tonight. We'll go on and make preparations for a fun evening, then. Come along, Hannah."

"I'll be right along, Mom. Timmy wanted to show me his room, right Timmy?"

"Oh, uh, yeah! Right this way. Okay, Mom?"

"All right, Timmy. Be very careful, sweetheart!"

Timmy and Hannah extricated themselves from the group and slowly went up the stairs.

Dexter and Oliver dashed for the outside, Dexter saying something about his baseball glove.

Corinne and Theo, all smiles, made their way slowly to the door, like a nervous cowboy exiting a hostile western bar.

"We'll be seeing you, then. Good Night!"

Wade stared around at the emptiness. "Angie? Could you bring me a beer?"

Hannah closed Timmy's bedroom door behind them, after seeing Oliver and Dexter heading out.

"Whew! What an ordeal!"

"Yeah, I thought I was going to sneeze, or something, and all my clothes would fall off!"

Hannah smiled, and then looked thoughtful. "You know, I've never seen you sneeze. I bet you never even get sick."

"Not since the accident, no." Timmy responded. "Hmm. I don't sneeze. Well, that's another one!"

"Another what?"

"Another way I'm different from everyone else."

"The only difference that I care about is that you're cuter and sweeter than anyone else!"

"Sweeter? Now, that's one thing I can't be. I don't have a taste or smell at all."

"Of course, you can be a stinker in your own way." Hannah whispered.

Timmy blushed somewhat, in his mildly noticeable fashion.

"So this is your bedroom." She said, looking around. "Not bad."

"It's actually Oliver and Dexter's room. They have the bunk beds. I sleep *under* the bottom one, down there." He pointed.

Hannah bent down to look. "Eww. It's dark under there. What about spiders?"

Timmy smiled. "We get along. I don't even mess up their webs. But nobody looks for me, either. That gives me … more time for other activities."

Hannah smiled, "I understand." She grew serious. "Say, are you okay with this idea? I know I pushed it with mom, and I never really talked to you about it. Will you really be able to participate?"

"I don't see why not, if I have a little help. I should be able to sing, anyway. I don't know if I'll be any good, but I should be able to stand there and sing. That sounds easy enough."

"What about your clothes?"

Timmy looked down. Hannah was right. A tee shirt and shorts would not be appropriate at a choir practice.

"I don't have a very big selection." Timmy went to the bedroom door and pushed down on its lever, then slowly pulled it open. Hannah watched as the door moved as if a turtle were pushing it. No wonder he sometimes just ran through them!

"Some doors I can manage. Dad changed them to levers, instead of knobs. Car doors, I can't even budge."

Out in the hall, Timmy indicated an open shelf. "That room is for Oliver and Dexter's things mainly. This is where we keep my clothes and other stuff. It's easy for me to get them here; no doors between here and where I need to be wearing clothes."

"Several doors between your house and mine, though." Hannah mused.

She looked at the shelf of clothes. It was basically just a line of tee shirts and a line of shorts. They were arranged like books. He could draw one from column A and one from column B. That's how he dressed, winter and summer. There weren't even socks.

"No socks?" Hannah looked over.

"I can't wear shoes, so wearing socks would only get them dirty. My feet stay clean without them." He shrugged.

"Hey! I've got an idea!" She said. "I'll get you an extra choir robe to wear. They're light, and you should be able to wear it to the practice and back, without having a problem!"

"Oh, that's a good idea! I think you're right, as long as it isn't heavy. I can't do heavy."

Hannah reached out and retrieved a pair of shorts from the collection. They were very light, no heavier really than the matching tee shirts. The shorts had a partial liner and weak elastic at the waist. There was no fly or zipper.

She realized they were actually exceptionally cheap but colorful beach trunks for children younger even than she was.

She folded them up and put them back in place. It was hard to imagine having no more selections for clothing than this!

"And I'll open the doors for you and everything. I like it! It's going to be fun!"

She stopped, at the head of the stairs, just to give him a goodnight kiss, and then they proceeded down the stairs.

"Good Night, Mr. and Mrs. Miller! See you tomorrow!" Hannah said near the front door.

"Good Night, Hannah!" called Angie.

Hannah opened the door for herself. It was a heavy door. "Good Night, Timmy!"

"Good Night, Hannah!" Timmy said, a little louder than really required.

Hannah left then. In a moment, they could hear the adjacent door open and close.

"Night Mom!" Timmy said.

"Timmy, wait!" Angie called. "Come here, sweetie."

Timmy went into the living room. Wade was looking at the TV, but it wasn't on.

"Timmy, this girl, Hannah. You talked to her in the back yard?"

"She was playing with her dolls, Mom. I just sorta said Hi, to be neighborly."

"And did she see you, ah …"

"I know I hafta wear clothes, Mom. I wouldn't want her to think I was weird. And besides, she's a *girl!*"

Angie appeared to be relieved. "Well, she seemed to like you."

"Uh-huh. Like I said. She's a girl." He shrugged, as if that alone explained everything.

Angie smiled. "All right, have a good night, then."

"Don't let the bed bugs bite." Wade said.

"They can't bite me, anyway." Timmy said as he walked silently away. He always walked silently.

As soon as possible, Timmy made his way over to Hannah's bedroom again.

She observed him with wry amusement, as he sauntered so

nonchalantly toward her. She was wearing her ballerina outfit. "You're so bad! I should have brought some shorts over for you to wear while you're here."

"You didn't bring anything with you when you came to my side. Someone might have noticed if you were carrying something away."

"I know. I'll get the clothes when I bring you your robe. I'll have a bag with me to carry them in. In the meantime, try these."

She held up something that looked like a doll's costume.

"What's that?"

"Dance tights. We're going to dance tonight!"

"You're kidding, right? Are these for Belinda? Look how small they are!"

"They're stretchy. Come on, put them on."

"You want me to wear girl's clothes?"

"You'd rather be naked?" Hannah handed him the tights, and he accepted them.

This was a new experience for Timmy, but he was game to give it a try. The tights were extremely light. Oddly, it was easier for him to slip them on than he had thought it would be.

He stood up again, after wriggling into the tights.

Hannah had a top for him. This was a pullover with a snap fastener at the crotch.

Timmy got into it, but he could not fasten the snap.

Hannah did that for him. Then she led him in a number of moves and stretches she had been taught.

"Let me show you some videos of the things we're going to practice. Okay?"

"Sure!"

Hannah went to her door. "Mom! I'm going to do a few dance exercises. That will be the noise you hear!"

Corinne's musical laughter echoed up the stairway, "All right, Sweetheart. Don't hurt yourself!"

"Now we can make noise, or at least I can. Ready?"

Timmy nodded.

First they did the arabesques, the basic poses and position from which to launch the other moves.

Awkward and embarrassed at first, Timmy soon mastered the beginning steps and was actually enjoying his activity.

They continued for a lengthy period.

Hannah called a halt. "Aren't you tired?"

"No, not at all. There's more, isn't there?"

"Oh, there's a lot more. But we don't have to learn it all in one night. All of the things my mother is inflicting on me, I'm going to torture *you* with. Dancing, singing, art projects. Now I have a companion in my misery."

"Torture? Hannah, if this is torture, you're going to get tired of it before I do. I'm having fun! I haven't had anything to do since the accident, and now you're helping me do everything! It's wonderful!"

"I'm glad you like it. Now I have a boyfriend who likes to do everything I like to do."

"Boyfriend?"

Hannah looked at him, biting her lip as if to take back the words she had blurted out. She seemed concerned that she had pushed him too hard.

"You want me to be your boyfriend? Hannah, I will love to be your boyfriend, your scaredy-cat, your play poodle or anything else you want me to be. You are the best thing that has ever happened to me in my whole life."

Hannah came to him then and hugged him in relief.

"All right, then. The next thing we have to do is work out a schedule. We're going to be very busy!"

5. A Choir Robe

Hannah stopped over the next day with an extra robe. There were only three sizes, so she brought the middle size for Timmy. She also brought him a coloring book.

"Wait a minute? Coloring?"

"I got one for me too. I want you to do this one, and I'll do mine, and then we'll compare to see how much we think alike."

"Oh, that's even worse. First you want me to color in a coloring book like a kid, and then you want to compare them, like it's a boyfriend-girlfriend kind of thing. Is that what you think?" Timmy looked exasperated, posing with his hands on his hips.

"Yes, I do."

"Okay, that's what I thought you thought." He relaxed and smiled. "I haven't done this for a while. But I'm willing to try. Thanks for thinking of me."

"Let's put your robe on your special shelf."

"It's not like I'm going to forget about it." He looked at her curiously.

"Well, I thought I'd borrow a couple of your outfits for when you come to visit me." Hannah whispered. "We can do that now."

"Oh! Hey, I like that!" Timmy looked at her, and looked around to see that no one else would hear. "Who's supposed to see them besides you?"

"Silly! It's not who sees your clothes that I'm thinking about. I'm thinking about what *doesn't* need to be seen when you come to visit!"

"Nonsense! I have it on good authority that I am *beautiful*." Timmy struck another pose, and then he giggled. "I'm teasing you, of course. That's a very good idea."

✦✦✦

Saturday came, eventually. Timmy had practiced the songs a few times when Hannah had brought over his robe and some recordings. At least he knew the words.

The robe was light and easy to control. Timmy felt confident that his trip would be uneventful.

His mother was less certain, warning him again and again that he would need to keep his wits about him and not get distracted.

"I know, Mom! I know! Sheesh! It's a church. I'm not gonna flash everyone."

"All right. I guess I've worried enough. Try to have fun, then, but practice your good manners." Tenderly she kissed him. Of course, tenderly was the only way he could be kissed, but it's the thought that counts.

Hannah took over at that stage, escorting Timmy out the door and into the car. She opened doors for him and generally treated him as if he were the Pope.

Not so Oliver and Dexter. They loved their brother, after their fashion, but his constantly getting the attention, when they were the ones who excelled at athletics, induced them to work at putting Timmy in his place. In this case, his place was between them in the back seat.

Although they had their seatbelts fastened, they still seemed to be trying to crowd Timmy in the middle. Timmy, by the way, was *not* wearing a seat belt.

Hannah looked over her shoulder and scowled. These two were not elevating her general opinion about boys. It was hard to believe that they shared their entire life experience, up to "the accident", with their physicality-challenged brother.

Timmy was so different! The difference translated as, well, niceness.

She thought about this. Maybe it was because most boys liked to roughhouse, and Timmy, of course, never did *that!*

They arrived at the church. Mrs. McMasters bustled about, making sure the door was open, and that arriving choir-members were being properly channeled into the right locations.

Hannah escorted Timmy again, but Oliver and Dexter seemed to hover very close. Hannah did not have the feeling that they were concerned about Timmy at all.

And it was in going up the stairs to the choir loft that they struck. Oliver "accidentally" stepped on Timmy's robe, and then "fell" against it, collapsing it down to the floor, with Timmy standing suddenly unclothed among a line of young boys and girls. Unable to rescue his own robe, Timmy sought shelter the only place he could, inside the robe of Hannah, herself!

She could feel his presence within her clothes, within her body. But that did not upset her. Her anger, bordering on rage, was directed at Oliver and his sniggering conspirator Dexter.

"Get away from us right now or I will punch you in the eye!" Hannah said in a low and menacing voice.

Oliver, surprisingly, looked rather alarmed. His concern was well founded, for Hannah was in a position to send him plummeting backwards down the stairway, and possibly injuring him more than a simple girl-punch should do.

Assessing the situation quickly, and having already carried off his prank, Oliver quickly backed away a step or two.

Timmy hurriedly shimmied under and into the robe again, and climbed up on the other side of Hannah. Remarkably, no one seemed to have noticed the altercation, their eyes primarily having been on where to put their feet as they ascended.

"Come on, Timmy. Let's stay away from those jokers. I knew they were plotting something." Hannah and Timmy finished entering the choir area, and made their way to the front row.

Hannah kept a watchful eye on the other two, and a hand around Timmy's waist.

Dexter and Oliver decided to keep their distance. Not only was

Hannah being suspicious of them, they knew she would be able to relate what had happened in a way their mother would believe. Any further attempts to embarrass Timmy were likely to recoil on them instead. A few hurried whispers between them convinced them that their plan was blown, and that denial would be their only defense. They were no further trouble.

Now, however, the trouble that *could* have been anticipated was about to commence; the tryouts and practicing for the choir. Corinne McMasters, choir director, called for everyone's attention.

Dexter and Oliver, along with a few others, were washouts. This was not surprising. In every recruiting drive, there would be an occasional clinker, a person unable to recognize their own failure to find the proper pitch, or too self-conscious to even be audible, or a child only present at the insistence of an adult for whatever reason, and not his own.

Corinne was used to this. She was slightly disappointed that it had included the two Miller boys, since they were at least individuals to whom she might have had ready access.

She had no way of knowing they had only come along as part of a long-planned prank.

It was also prudent to begin by selecting trials for those who appeared to be approaching puberty, as their voices could be uncontrollable or become so in short order. Dexter and Oliver had the look of being somewhat ahead of Timmy in that regard.

Basically, Corinne had learned to begin from the rear, so that self-selected volunteers intent on failure could accomplish it quickly, and the real work then begin.

Accordingly, she ended by calling on those new arrivals in the front row, including Timmy.

He had been serious in his preparations, where his brothers had not. They had never intended to become part of a choir, preferring to continue their sports activities uninterrupted.

He did not have sports to distract him, and he was really motivated to get into some kind of activity that could get him out of the house. Singing seemed a real possibility. And so he had prepared.

When Timmy began singing, he pushed the sound out with

enthusiasm. Hearing his own voice echoing back to him set up a reverberation feedback within his otherworldliness that caused the whole structure to vibrate with his voice, like those melodic stalactites set up with acoustic stimulation in caves for tourist entertainment.

Timmy's voice rocked the house, one might say.

Doors to church offices down below began opening, and faces peered out in mysterious wonder at the suddenly new phenomenon. The Bishop walked out and craned his head up to see.

Timmy was feeling it, and Corinne let him continue. She could tell that everyone within earshot was recognizing the birth of a new talent. She wanted the celebration of the discovery to be its own reward for their efforts to grow and find new expression.

Timmy ended his portion, and grew silent. No one moved for a moment, and then the Bishop himself began applauding. The rest of the congregation followed suit.

Hannah and her mother were beaming, as Timmy looked around in startled confusion. He had wanted to do well, but he had not expected anything like this!

6. Thumps

Wade heard several thumps from upstairs. He looked around the room. Timmy was lying on the floor of the living room applying himself to his coloring book. It was a bit of effort for him, but not outside of his ability. At least the light pressure he was able to exert made a smooth and pleasing level of saturation to the work. Many kids pushed too hard and made garish contrasts.

Wade turned off the TV. Timmy had been making an effort to keep his clothes on for longer stretches of time. Wade presumed he was hoping the neighbor girl might stop by at any time. The mental effort to keep his surface intact and apply himself to other tasks at the same time was satisfying to see.

"Timmy, buddy, would you get your old dad a beer?"

Timmy looked up and smiled. He put down his crayon and started getting up. "Sure, Dad! Coming right up!" Walking carefully, so as to stay on the floor, Timmy moved into the kitchen without bumping into anything and knocking his clothes off.

Even brushing against the leaves of a potted plant had been enough to do it before, snagging his shirt or pants and sending them to the floor when the bubble of concentration burst.

Timmy stepped up to the refrigerator, his former nemesis. Wade had built a contraption on the side of the 'fridge to give Timmy enough leverage to get the door open. It took about ten pounds of force to open the door against its magnets, and Timmy couldn't pull that hard.

With the lever, Timmy was able to open the door, get a cold beer, and let the door close by itself. He was proud to be able to do things for himself, and in this case, for his Dad.

He wrapped both hands around the can of beer. It was always necessary to maximize the amount of surface area of an object he touched in order to control it. Cold though the metal was to most people, Timmy did not feel it, and he did not want to drop it.

He carried the beer carefully and proudly back to his dad, and set it gently on the table with a smile.

"Thank you, son. Now, as quickly as you can, go up and tell your brothers I want to talk with them."

Timmy looked up, bounced on his feet, and sailed upward through the living room ceiling. His tee shirt and shorts fluttered down to land on Wade's head.

Sighing, Wade plucked the items off his head and sat them on the arm of the chair. Then he popped the top of the beer.

✛✛✛✛✛✛

Timmy waited until the boys were down the stairs, and then he slipped under his bed and partially slid into the bedroom of the house next door. Hannah was rummaging through her dresser drawer.

"Ahem," Timmy softly cleared his throat.

Hannah looked over and smiled at him. "Come on in!"

Timmy came out the rest of the way, like a mechanic getting out from under a car. He stood up and walked over to Hannah.

"Hi!" he said innocently.

Hannah pulled a pair of his shorts out of the drawer she had open, and handed them to him.

"Oh, okay," he said, accepting the garment with a sheepish grin. He slipped into the pastel printed shorts and squirmed into position.

"Clothes do make the man, they say," Hannah observed.

"I feel more comfortable now," Timmy said. "I'm actually surprised."

"I didn't think it would matter, either," Hannah observed, "but these are cute. Did you know they make you look younger?"

Timmy laughed. "Yeah. I think they're for smaller kids, all right. The size is okay. They must be for bigger little kids, if that makes sense. Mom got them mail order from China, I believe. But they are light enough for me to wear without walking out of them."

"*My* mom was so happy about how well you sang! She's been bubbling all over since we got back home!"

"I don't know what happened, really." Timmy said seriously, "I usually try not to make noise and call attention to myself, for obvious reasons, but there in the church, it just felt good to be making noise. It was like the building was encouraging me to sing."

"I guess they build them that way. It would make sense for them to do that."

Timmy nodded. "It felt good, but then everyone was looking at me. I didn't know what to think."

"I think Mom wants to spring you as a surprise for the Holiday special performance. We always get a good crowd then, and she'll want the choir to be the talk of the day."

"It almost was already! I'm glad you were there when my robe fell off. I guess you noticed that was the only thing I was wearing."

"What I noticed was the look on Oliver's face when I threatened to punch him! He couldn't wait to get away!"

"I'm glad you were there to protect me."

Hannah closed the drawer she had open, and took him by the hand. She led him into her bathroom. "I wanted to talk to you about that," she said, dropping the volume of her voice. "When you jumped into my robe with me, I don't think you were trying to do anything but hide. But did that feel different to you in any way?"

Timmy looked puzzled. "Different? I can't remember. I remember being scared, and you were awesome!"

Hannah went over to the toilet, and pulled her shorts down so she could pee. "Thanks! He made me mad, and I knew he was picking on you deliberately."

Timmy hopped up on the sink cabinet and drew his leg up to wrap his arms around it.

Hannah's father, Theo, had come up the stairs with a package for her. He opened her door to call out to her just as she started speaking.

"I could feel you in there with me. It was different from touching you. Kinda like when someone is sitting beside you on a couch. You're touching all along your leg. But this was like being touched inside. I don't know how to describe it."

Theo was hearing the voice, but could not make out the words. He walked quietly over to the bathroom. The door was only partially shut.

"I guess I know what you're saying, but I don't have an answer. I can't remember much about it."

Theo pushed into the bathroom, seeing Timmy and Hannah about the same moment. "You little pervert! What are you doing in here?" He said angrily.

Timmy flashed backwards through the wall, leaving his shorts collapsing on the sink counter.

"What the …" Theo said. He looked at Hannah.

"And what are *you* doing in here, Dad?" Hannah said testily, "A little privacy, if you don't mind?"

"I don't …"

"Just wait outside, please. I'll come out and explain everything. Go sit down, please."

Hannah wasn't quite as proudly confrontational as she was acting. But she had defended Timmy once already and it looked as though she would have to do it again.

Hannah picked up Timmy's shorts and walked out with them. Her father was standing near her dresser. She went over to him, showing him the shorts she had picked up, and placed them in her drawer again. "Please sit down, father."

Theo did not know what to think, or what to do. His world had just changed in a radical way, and he was not beginning to process it yet. He sat down.

"You have noticed, I think, that Timmy is different. When you and mom met him, a few days ago, you will remember that he was walking very slowly and carefully. That he was wearing shorts like these, and a tee shirt. No socks, no shoes; you remember?"

Theo nodded his head slowly.

"When Timmy got to the table, I pulled out the chair for him." She waited for her father to nod an acknowledgment.

"While we were there, and while you were watching him, did you see Timmy pick up, touch, or move anything?"

Theo shook his head no.

"Timmy walks through walls. He can go through floors, and he can float in the air. Actually, he can fly! I'll bet you didn't know that!"

Theo began to purse his lips as if about to say something.

"There's still more." Hannah paused, "when Timmy walks through a wall, he can't bring any clothes with him. The clothes fall off on the first side of the wall. *He* can go through the wall, but he can't carry anything through with him. Not *anything*."

"That's why I brought some of his clothes over here. When he comes to visit, he can get dressed again, and we can talk and visit for as long as we wish."

"You mean he's been ... sneaking over here and ..."

"Stop thinking like that, Dad! Timmy has been stuck in his house ever since his accident. He wasn't even *allowed* to go to school!"

"When we started talking, I realized how lonely and terrible it has been for him. He's so nice! And he can't go anywhere or do anything! His brothers go *everywhere*, and then they come home and act like he's ... *nothing!* But *he's* the one who is so miraculous! They are ordinary, but *Timmy* can walk through walls!"

"Walk through walls?"

"You saw him do it!"

"I'm not sure just what I saw. I know I saw a boy in your bathroom with you, while you were *on the toilet!* I know that isn't right!"

"Concentrate on what's important, Dad. Every time Timmy comes over here, he shows up naked. What's a little bit of peeing in comparison to that? Timmy is my friend, my very special friend! I don't know if he's a ghost, or a poltergeist, or just an imaginary friend of some kind, but he is a friend, and he's my friend. He's like the brother *you* said I could never have."

"He shows up naked?"

Hannah stared at him. Her father only seemed to be catching one word in three.

"Hang on. I'll show you." She pulled out the shorts again and walked over to the common wall; the place where Timmy had first stuck his head out. She rapped on the wall three times, then three times more.

After a moment, Timmy stuck his head through and looked around. He saw Mr. McMasters and looked nervous.

"Come on in." Hannah said.

"Are you sure?"

"Come on in, and stand still, please."

Timmy stepped through the wall. He was naked.

Wordlessly, Hannah handed him his shorts, and he put them on. Then she took his hand and led him over to her dad.

"Timmy Miller, meet Theodore McMasters, my father. Father, this is our neighbor, Timmy Miller, my best friend."

"How do you do, Sir?" Timmy offered his hand to shake.

Theo reached out gently to take Timmy's hand, and held it in his own.

"Now, Dad, would you like to knock this kid's block off? Go ahead! Take a swing at him."

"Swing at him?" Theo said.

Timmy looked alarmed.

"Yeah! Go ahead! You got mad at him, remember? You want to smack him around?"

"No, not really. I don't want to hurt him."

"Dad, you can't hurt him! Look, I'm a girl, and even I can beat the pants off of him physically!" Casually, she swung her arm out and through the boy, colliding with and dislodging his shorts once more. They fell against the wall.

Once again, Timmy was standing there naked.

"Oops." Hannah picked up the shorts and handed them to Timmy.

Delicately, Timmy pulled his hand away from Theo's, and straightened out the shorts to put them on again.

"You see, Dad? It isn't something evil or nasty. It's just the way things are. Timmy, miraculous Timmy, can walk through walls! But his clothes fall off when he does."

"Sorry, Mr. McMasters. I didn't mean to cause trouble."

"I …I don't know what to make of this."

"Don't make anything of this, please Dad! There isn't anything to make. We're working things out just fine. Timmy has a friend now, and he isn't so lonely, and I have a friend too, who is like a brother. Everything's just fine." She looked at Timmy and smiled.

"You know, Dad, I think Mom is convinced that Timmy is an angel! You should have been there to hear him sing! Mom is just walking on air about it! Um, actually that's Timmy's job, but you know what I mean."

Theo reached out and touched Timmy again, to reassure himself that the boy was indeed real. He gently stroked the boy's cheek and placed his hand on his shoulder.

"Remarkable! What kind of scientific marvel are you, my lad?"

"Oh, be careful, Dad. Science doesn't know about him yet. We're hoping to keep it that way."

"Why? This is a wonder of the ages!"

"Dad, that never works out well. You know that."

Theo grew contemplative. "Yeah. You may be right. You're a very bright girl, Hannah."

"Not as bright as Timmy. Just look at those sparkles!"

Theo laughed. "All right. We'll help to keep his secret, but …" He looked around.

"Don't worry, Dad. I'll make sure Timmy keeps his pants on."

Theo laughed again. "Wow! What a world! We're going to have to do some research, I guess. Oh, speaking of which, here's that book you requested. That's the reason I came up."

Theo looked at Timmy again. "I'm glad I met you, Timmy. I may have some more questions for you, once I figure out what I want to think."

He went out of the room shaking his head.

"That went well, considering." Hannah mused.

"A brother?"

"Sister?"

"No, I guess brother works better. Why a brother?"

"Tim, Dad caught us together in the bathroom! You're a boy and I'm a girl. He's not totally clueless!"

"I think your dad's pretty smart."

"Most people are smarter than you might think, they just have trouble getting their thoughts out clearly. Your dad doesn't say much, but he sees a lot."

Hannah smiled and put her arms around his neck. "Brother Timothy, let's look at my new book!"

***

Wade looked somberly at his two sons. His two normal sons.

His two troublesome sons. The typical boys, as compared to Timmy, who was never any trouble.

He chuckled inwardly. Dexter and Oliver looked at each other.

"Boys, you're missing something, and it's something important. You two would make any father proud, but I have three sons. I know you have a thing about Timmy, but I think it's misplaced."

He grew thoughtful, "Timmy's a good lad, but he's not all there." He looked at them. "That's a joke. You can laugh now."

Dexter and Oliver made a pathetic, insincere kind of chuckle.

Wade stared at them. "Anyway, I'm getting older. It's something to think about. You're getting older too. Soon you'll be in and out of High School, and maybe college if you're up for that. I'll be sitting around in a rocking chair, waiting for people to come visit me."

"Of course, Timmy will be around too. The question is, will he be getting older like the rest of us? It's still a little early to tell, but we have clues. Timmy never needs a haircut. He never needs to get his fingernails trimmed. He probably will never need to shave, but you two aren't too far away from that."

"Timmy may be unchanged when I am in my rocking chair. There's a possibility he may be unchanged when *you* are in *your* rocking chairs! Now, think about that for a minute."

"I know you think that you don't have room in your lives for someone like Timmy. But I'm telling you, if you're smart, you don't want to keep him out of it."

Wade picked up his beer can, holding it as he looked at them. "Are you smart?"

Oliver said, "Dad, if this is about the choir practice …"

"Don't." Wade said. Oliver gulped.

"You three boys are like these beers. You look the same, but Timmy's container makes a different sound." He tapped the can, and it made a tinny, empty sound.

"You two are full of it." He continued. "You're full of yourselves and your own self-importance. That's why you make a different sound than he does. You're not so different from Tim, and for a good reason, you all started from the same material. But Timmy has room for love, and you don't because you're full of something else."

"Now I want you to be nicer to Timmy, and be nicer to his friends, too. You are his friends, you know. Just ask him. He loves you." He drew a deep breath. "His problem is he can't be like you. And I know you can't be like him either. But you can be his brothers. Give him help when he needs it, and let him be a part of your lives too. You'll both be a whole lot richer for it."

He looked at them.

They looked at each other.

"Anything to say?" Wade asked.

"Dad, you're right. We'll …"

"Don't say it if you don't mean it," Wade said.

"We'll be thinking about what you said." Dexter went on. "Timmy seems to have found some interests to keep him busy, so maybe he won't be looking so … vulnerable, to us … I think that's what triggers our … attitude."

"Being bullies?"

They squirmed. "Not intentionally, no."

"All right. If you can recognize that you're stepping over the line, that means at least that you know where the line is. Keep what I said in mind. I don't want to have to make up all this crap again, because it might come out different next time, and I don't want you boys to be confused. Go on. Go play, and have fun. But be nice."

7. A Discovery

Hannah and Timmy were lying together on the floor of her bedroom, looking at her new book.

"That one," said Hannah, "that's you."

It was a picture of Cupid, looking like a lad of about fourteen or less, showing full frontal nudity, for what it was worth without a magnifying glass. (Cupid and Psyche in the Nuptial Bower, 1792-1793 by Hugh Douglas Hamilton)

"Okay, but … wings? I don't have wings."

"You fly."

"But I don't have wings. There are wings in the picture."

"True. The rest of him looks like you though. Especially when you've lost your pants."

"I thought we were doing away with the shyness stuff."

Hannah looked at him sideways, smiling. "You think I'm being shy?"

Timmy smiled. "Your father knows I'm here, you know." He looked back at the picture. "What about the girl? Does she look like you?"

"The hair's not dark enough." She studied the painting. "She's smaller than he is, but her arm looks weird, like she doesn't have any muscles."

"She has muscles!" Timmy chuckled.

"Oh, you! I'm only nine! She looks like maybe thirteen. Anyway, I don't have that kind of "muscles" yet. My chest is flatter than yours."

Timmy looked down at his own chest. It was pretty flat.

"I wonder what else is in the book." Hannah said.

"There are women in the book. The old painters always had women and children around who would take off their clothes. But I'm not going to say that any of them look like you."

"I hope I don't get fat. All of these women seem to be fat." Said Hannah.

"And most of these Cupids seem to be really small, almost children."

"Well, you said that's what the old painters had, women and children who would take off their clothes."

"I think the women took the clothes *off* the children." Timmy suggested. "The women probably got paid, but I don't think the children got paid."

"No sense paying them, they don't have pockets."

"I don't have pockets." Timmy admitted.

"Who would have to pay you to take off your clothes?" Hannah asked.

"No one, I guess."

"If I *did* get fat, you'd be small compared to me, like these guys."

"You mean you think I'm not going to grow, and you will?" Timmy inquired.

"You already said that's the way it would be."

"I guess the next time I hide in your robe, I won't have to have my head sticking out."

"Nope, you'll have …" She sat up and looked over at him.

"What? Why'd you stop?" Timmy looked into her face.

"I was remembering. We started to talk about it before, and Dad chased you away."

Timmy wrinkled his brow, but he was not remembering.

"I was asking about when you hid with me under my robe. There really wasn't room for both of us under there. I think part of you was *inside* me."

"That doesn't sound right. I hope your dad didn't hear *that*."

"No, nothing like that. I mean that both of us were standing in the same place. Our bodies were mixed together."

"No wonder you thought that was weird. I've *never* done that before!"

Hannah smiled, "Lad, we have research to do!"

"Uh-oh!"

"Here, get behind me. Put your arms inside my arms. We'll turn the pages of the book together."

This was easier said than done. Timmy had a natural reluctance to invade someone else's personal space. Inside their skin was about as personal as you could get! Timmy sat behind Hannah on the floor, wrapping his legs around her, and reached inside her shoulders, pushing his arms into her arms as if putting on a sweater. He could feel her shudder as he moved along.

Leaning his head over her shoulder, he asked softly, "How's that?"

"Really strange! I could feel your hands moving along, as if you were sliding your hand along my skin, but it was inside my arm. Both arms, actually. It was kinda ticklish, but a little scary too."

Timmy adjusted his hands to coincide with her hands, like pulling a stocking straight and free of wrinkles. He relaxed and let Hannah control the positions of her hands. He wasn't trying to move anything, just touching along the surfaces and feeling the sensations.

Hannah reached out and turned the page of the book in front of her. Timmy's hands and arms followed along as if *her* arms were inside *his*.

"Wow! That feels different to me now." Timmy said, "I can really feel the edges of the page, and how it pushes back when you curl it."

Hannah turned another page. "I can't feel your hands moving with me when you're just following along. It's only when you move them around that I can feel them."

Hannah turned a few more pages. Neither of them was looking at the pages, though. "I'd like to try picking up the book now." She closed the front cover.

"Hang on a minute," Timmy said right next to her ear. He shifted his legs into her legs and lined up his feet with hers.

"Wow!" Hannah said. She stood up in a hunched over position. Timmy's back was sticking out behind her. His shorts had fallen off again.

She picked up the book and straightened up. Timmy adjusted to let the rest of his body line up with hers. His head moved inside her head last of all.

As Hannah stood still, holding the heavy book, Timmy completed his alignment inside her body. Even though he was larger in size than she was, three to four inches taller, he was now completely immersed inside her body. He lined up his eyes with hers, and let her vision become the same as his.

Slowly, Hannah walked over to her dresser and deposited her book there. She turned and looked back to the place they had been. Timmy's abandoned shorts still lay there.

She went over and picked them up. Timmy was being carried along with her motions, a passenger in her vehicle. She put the shorts away in the proper drawer.

Slowly, Hannah turned around in her room. Timmy was nowhere to be seen, but she could feel him inside her, like warm sunshine on her skin. She walked into the bathroom and looked into the mirror.

Timmy looked into the mirror along with Hannah. The only reflection he saw was hers.

She shifted back and forth, opened her mouth, and raised her hands. Timmy followed along, being carried and manipulated without effort.

Hannah looked at her reflection again. "Oh my!" she said softly. Timmy was completely inside her. They both existed in the same physical space.

"I feel right at home here, Hannah." Timmy said.

Her eyes, her reflection in the mirror, grew very wide.

There had been no sound at all. The voice she had heard had been entirely inside her and silent.

"I heard you, but you didn't make a sound!" Hannah responded.

"That's not all, Hannah," Timmy urged her to raise her right hand. It lifted up and pointed at their reflection in the mirror.

She had not spoken aloud either.

Timmy and Hannah explored their new relationship; their new *sharing*.

It was very intimate. They could converse silently, and quite effortlessly. Their thoughts seemed to flow back and forth in torrents, each stimulating the other and eliciting a rapid response. What would ordinarily seem to take hours to discuss could be shared in mere heartbeats.

It wasn't always polite and well edited. Such immediacy tended to curtail the normal hesitancy to reveal the first thing that pops into your mind.

Of course, each being quite young and relatively innocent, even between them, they had few dark and terrifying secrets to keep. Most of it was harmless bathroom scatology that they would never have volunteered in open discussion, but this kind of intimate conversation was of such immediacy that the dark secret would be blurted out without particular consideration or hesitancy.

None of this created any hostility or antagonism between them.

Quite the opposite: Timmy came to find that Hannah was a real, thinking and caring, *feeling* individual, and Hannah discovered that Timmy was just as nice on the inside as he had always been on the outside. Timmy was a sweet individual, loving and caring, and Hannah was a thoughtful, observant soul with a big, generous heart.

If they were enraptured by the physicality of their relationship before, they were essentially *married* together by this new sharing. They were not only kind and kindred souls; they were linked together in a way that could no longer be dissolved.

"Timmy, my man, this changes *everything!*" The thought stood clear and golden in her mind.

"I agree, Hannah. You know I love you, don't you?"

"Of course! How could you not?"

Brightly and joyously, he laughed in response. They smiled. This was just so much OMG-FUN!

Hannah inhaled a deep breath and sighed. Seated at her dresser, she knew that there was no need to go anywhere, in order to have a wonderful experience and joyous emotions, and that there was at the same time an urge to go *everywhere*, so that they could share together the fun that it would be.

8. Church

Sunday morning, Timmy was as bright and bubbly as anyone had ever seen him. He bustled around, helping in the kitchen, serving his brothers and father, helping mom.

Timmy could grab the toast out of the toaster without getting burned! It was one of his favorite jobs to do.

"Do we have to go to this church?" Oliver lamented.

Wade looked over at him. Oliver seemed to shrink back in his seat. "Yes. Your brother is going to sing, and our neighbors are looking forward to having us there."

"I don't remember seeing you going to church before, Dad." Dexter commented, "What's the big deal?"

Timmy brought his father a freshened cup of coffee. Angie watched him, with the coffee carafe still in her hand. Timmy placed the cup in the saucer without spilling it. He smiled and backed away.

"Thanks, son." Wade acknowledged. He looked at Dexter, but included Oliver in his gaze as well. "Mrs. McMasters has recruited Timmy to be in her choir, and we're all going, to lend support and encouragement to him in his first official performance. You think that's a good idea, don't you?"

"Dad, I think it's a great idea." Dexter sat forward, "Really, you would have been proud of Timmy when he sang yesterday. He was …" Dexter looked over at Timmy, standing now near the toaster again. "He was *surprisingly* good."

Wade looked back over his shoulder. Timmy was, of course, wearing a big smile on his face. Wade winked at him and turned back.

"We're all looking forward to it. It's going to be the first time we've gone out as a family in a long time." Angie said, preparing some orange juice for the boys.

"Is it okay if I ride with them, Mom? With the McMasters, that is?" Timmy spoke up. "It will be a better way for us all to go, in two cars I mean, and Hannah and I will both be going up into the choir to sing."

"Four in each car," Dexter observed, "That does make sense."

Angie looked at Wade, seeking approval. He nodded slightly.

"That's a good idea, Timmy. Did they invite you to go with them?"

"Hannah wants it that way," he said simply. "I think they'll be okay with it."

Wade looked at him, but said nothing.

"Everybody finish eating now. We won't want to be late getting started." Angie placed the two glasses of orange juice on the table.

Theo was watching the two children especially closely. Hannah was treating Timmy as though she were the momma cat and he was her kitten. She escorted him out the Miller's door, and opened the car door for him.

"Shouldn't you have your seat belt on, Timmy?" Corinne asked, peering over into the back seat.

"It's all right, Corinne. I'll drive carefully." Theo said.

Hannah and Timmy were holding hands, and did so at every opportunity. Theo had not failed to notice this, but chose not to say anything further.

The climb up to the choir loft was without incident this time. Dexter and Oliver were sitting with the congregation in a pew in front of Wade and Angie.

Corinne was saving Timmy's debut for a special song, but she did not know that Timmy and Hannah had cooked up a scheme to make it a duet. What Corinne had in mind was tricky to perform, and even more so when dividing the forces as the kids were planning, but they had come to the enterprise with single-minded purpose.

When Timmy stepped forward, as planned, Hannah stepped forward with him.

Their performance was remarkable in a number of ways. The voices soared and reverberated like lilting nightingales, and the very walls and ceilings seemed to vibrate and echo in synchrony. It was, briefly, enchanting and mesmerizing. Eyes closed, and tears flowed in joy at the beauty that was being visited in those soaring vaults of heaven.

So much so, that only eight pairs of eyes were watching when Timmy's robe fell through him as he focused so intently on the performance. For nearly eight seconds, he was delivering a lilting aria with such concentration that he was unaware of any sudden chill, which he would not have felt anyway.

Hannah noticed, and bent to retrieve the fallen garment almost as soon as Timmy had stopped for a breath. She helped him back into it in a flash, as it were.

The eleven-year old boy behind them, the one with the glasses, had seen the garment fall, and begun blinking rapidly. By the time he was confident of his vision again, things were right once more.

Dexter and Oliver were watching him. Oliver nudged Dex about two seconds into the display. They were both grinning like baboons.

Corinne saw what she could only believe was a vision, that the transcendent beauty of the music was causing her to perceive a heavenly visitation.

Eighty-four year old Myrtle Stowe observed the faux-pas, and merely assumed it was a part of the ceremony. Things had become somewhat different in these modern days, she had noticed.

Theo saw the robe fall, and grew apprehensive. He glanced around, noticing that most people were looking down, in respectful appreciation of the solemnity and loveliness of the portrayal.

The Bishop himself was the final witness. Having seen a miracle, which apparently no one else had reacted to, he simply offered up a silent prayer of thanksgiving for such a sign and portent of the Creator's Love.

In all, the transgression passed without comment. Miraculously, one might say.

It was fortuitous, considering, that no one had thought to bring a camera.

————— ✦✦✦✦ —————

Timmy and Hannah rode back home in the back of the McMasters' car, under the frequent glances of Theo McMasters, who was still trying desperately to fit what he had observed and discovered into a coherent understanding of what had hitherto been a sensible and predictable universe.

It wasn't working very well.

Corinne was delighted. She burbled and prattled on and on about what a wonderful celebration it had been and how the Bishop had thanked her personally and how even old Widow Stowe had stopped to tell her what an eye-opening performance it had been, and how she had such wonderful plans for even more creative expressions, now that she had such remarkable talent available and …

"Hannah, that was simply wonderful!" Theo said, looking once more into the rearview mirror.

"Oh, yes, sweetheart, you both were just marvelous, you little stinkers! You knew I had planned that as a solo aria. That took a bit of confidence, Hannah, to come forward like that!"

Hannah held up Timmy's hand in hers and smiled. "I have all the confidence I need for anything right here, Mom. When Timmy is with me, we can do anything!"

Corinne turned in her seat to look at them more directly. "You are a very remarkable young man, Timmy. We were very fortunate that the house we chose happened to have you living in it!"

"*Haunting* it, more like," Timmy smiled, "up until recently, I haven't been able to get out to go anywhere. This has been great fun! Thank you all very much!"

Hannah kissed his hand and smiled at him.

"Well, it seems we should try to make you a more official part of our family then, so that you can be with us more!" Corinne continued with her delighted bubbling.

"Too late, Mom! He already is." Hannah said with a shy smile.

Corinne cackled with delight, but Theo looked more thoughtful, and glanced once more into the rearview mirror.

"Hey, anyone want to go out for ice cream or something? Family outing, you might say?" Mused Theo.

"Why not a movie, Dad?" Hannah suggested quickly.

"A movie? Something you especially want to see?"

She shrugged. "Just something to get out, kinda have fun together. If Timmy can come, I know we'll enjoy it."

"That is so sweet!" Corinne said. "It will be her first date!" she said in a whisper to Theo.

He rolled his eyes. "We'll ask the Millers." He said to the rearview mirror.

Wade, of course, shrugged his shoulders. Angie seemed fretful.

"I'll take care of him, Mrs. Miller," Hannah placed a reassuring hand on Angie's arm.

She smiled. "All right. You are so good for him. You've made him happy. I can't say no to you."

"All right then," Theo said, "We'll go after dinner. Would you like to eat with us, Timmy?"

"No thanks, Mr. McMasters. I like to dine here. I have … special dietary needs. We'll be able to go whenever you say."

"Wade, do you have a minute? I'd like to talk to you while we're waiting." Theo asked.

"Would you like some coffee?" Wade suggested. They went out on the porch for a moment.

Wade sipped on his coffee and looked at Theo. "What's up?"

Theo put his mug down on the low rail. He rubbed a hand through his hair. "I wanted to ask about Timmy."

"What about him?" Wade said guardedly.

"He's a remarkable boy. Utterly charming! In the short time I've known him, I've become very fond of him. But I want to talk about Hannah, too."

"I understand." Wade said softly. "Timmy's not quite normal. It might be best to have them see less of each other."

A grimace, a sad imitation of a smile, passed across Theo's face. "Too late for that, I guess." He noticed his coffee, and took a sip, looking out toward the street.

"Not quite normal, you say? Hannah seems to think that he is very, *very* special. She showed me, for example, that Timmy can walk through walls." Theo finished softly.

Wade studied him. "She showed you what?"

"She had Timmy come through the wall of the house, after I came upon them together, and scared him away. I saw it, twice I guess. I don't need to see it again to know it's true."

"They were together?" Wade raised his eyebrows.

"Not what that sounds like. They were talking. But he was there, and he hadn't come in the front door."

"That doesn't sound good." Wade said neutrally.

"You don't have to play games, Wade. I know *you* know what Timmy can do. Probably the only person in both houses who doesn't know is Corinne, and she thinks he's an angel!"

"He is a good boy. I love him a lot." Wade said. "Maybe he's not an angel, but he's a good boy."

"I'm not worried about that. I'm worried that there's something I should be doing now. I don't even know if there *is* a right thing to do, or if it would be wrong to do nothing." Theo stared out into the yard.

"I think you've said it well." Wade commiserated. "By any chance, are you a drinking man?"

Theo stared at him in stark incomprehension for a moment, and then they both burst into laughter.

It was the first time Timmy had been to the movies since his "accident". Nothing much had changed, and Hannah helped him with everything. She had even prepared socks for him to wear, coloring them with crayons to make them look like sandals.

She opened doors for him, and held his hand as often as possible. She was very gentlemanly about the whole situation, it must be admitted.

Only two items of physicality caused him problems. The first was a turnstile that people were passing through as a means of counting them or controlling gate access. Timmy slipped under a rope barrier, eliciting a stern look from the ticket agent, until Theo reached out and rotated the turnstile in his stead.

Then in the theater, Timmy could not get the seat to respect him. It stubbornly insisted no one was present when he tried to sit on it. Finally, Hannah pushed it down and put her leg over the corner to hold it down for him. Timmy then sat with his legs over hers, which sounds uncomfortable for her except that he weighed nothing, and she got to hold and rub his legs throughout the movie.

In all, it was a rewarding experience. Theo and Corinne sat a few seats over, knowing the kids would no doubt be whispering to each other. Hannah and Timmy enjoyed the separation, for it allowed them to make the necessary adjustments without drawing attention.

Returning home was uneventful, and the children were soon sent their separate ways to bed, for tomorrow would be a school day for Hannah, and Timmy professed to be extremely tired.

And then as soon as he possibly could, Timmy slipped into Hannah's room and joined her in its darkness.

Hannah was staring into her bathroom mirror when she saw the naked boy approaching her from behind.

"Hannah, may I?" Timmy asked politely, watching her reflection in the mirror.

"I've already brushed my teeth, and I've peed." Hannah said in a tremulous whisper. "I think I'm ready."

Timmy reached out and gently fluffed her hair. Then he reached into her arms, and kissed her on the cheek.

He stepped into her feet and pushed forward into her body, bringing his head in through the back of hers until he could see through her eyes again.

They stood together, each braced on the sink counter, until the alignments were completed.

Hannah looked up and smiled. She was alone, and not-alone, once more.

She stood up straight, and Timmy moved with her. He was painted inside her.

If her father came in now, rampaging about some "little pervert", he would not be able to find him. Hannah smiled.

She turned, and took off her nightgown, placing it on the sink counter. She pulled down her panties and looked. There was nothing to see except what she had always seen, when she had chosen to look.

"I was just curious," she said internally.

"I could push it out, I think, if you want me to."

"No," thought Hannah, "I wouldn't have any more use for it than you do."

"Fine with me," responded Timmy, "that's a weird idea!"

"Just checking. Ready for bed?"

"I'm ready for anything, but I guess we should try to sleep. Tomorrow will be a big day. It's back-to-school day."

"You still want to go with me?" Hannah said.

"I want to be with you, wherever you are! But I'm interested in going to school with you too. Everything is an adventure for me!"

"Everything is an adventure for me too! I'm glad you're with me!" She pulled her panties back up, and put on her nightgown again.

"Those panties are even lighter than my shorts," Timmy said, "but I guess I couldn't wear them anywhere."

"You really are a per-vert," Hannah said, "whatever that is."

"Don't ask me, it's your father's word," Timmy giggled, "I think it has something to do with a boy being in a girl's bathroom."

"Okay, just in case, the next time I go to the bathroom, you close your eyes."

They were both laughing and giggling as Hannah climbed into bed. Soon they were asleep.

Hannah woke up when her mother opened the door and called. "Hannah, school day. Rise and shine!"

She yawned, and stretched, and threw back the covers. Hannah went in to the bathroom and looked into the mirror. She smiled.

Hannah pulled her panties down and sat on the toilet.

"Aah," she said. Cleaning up, Hannah then put her panties in the hamper. Going back out into her bedroom, she quickly made the bed and put away her nightgown. Grabbing the underwear for the day, she headed back in to take a shower.

Hannah knew he was watching, and feeling everything she did. She felt his satisfaction as she yawned, and moved, and stretched. He'd have something to say in a moment or two, but for now she was enjoying his quiet joy and pleasant company anyway.

She started the shower, and then stepped in.

"I could wait for you outside," Timmy said inside her mind with amusement, "shall I step out to do that?"

"Don't you dare!" Hannah responded, "You might try to peek."

"Yes, ma'am." Timmy said, "Would you mind if I help?"

"Go right ahead," she answered, "let's see what you've got."

Timmy began gently asserting control over her arms and hands, picking up the soap and washcloth, and moving them around. Hannah had only to watch, mesmerized, as her hands moved of their own accord to wash her body as if they were someone else's hands.

Timmy was fascinated, not only with the fun of washing a real body, and feeling its skin respond to his touch, but also the physical action of picking up things and moving them with no more effort than blowing a soap bubble out of his way. It was strange and delightful to be strong again!

Hannah had to remind him to keep an eye on the time passing. She did not want to be late for school; not today!

They rinsed off, and dried, and then Hannah got herself dressed, Timmy becoming a passenger once more.

They went downstairs.

Timmy got a thrill when he saw Mr. McMasters, before realizing of course that Theo could not see him in his masquerade. It was still exciting. Timmy and Hannah kept up a running commentary about their reactions.

Soon Hannah was heading out the door to school, and Timmy was with her, packed like an apple in her lunchbox; a bright and shiny apple, fresh and clean, and as naked inside Hannah's skin as Hannah was inside her clothes.

That is to say, they tended to forget about that.

She climbed up on the school bus with a bounce in her step. Timmy's presence inside her energized her, as if he were actually there with muscles of his own to assist her.

Hannah knew that Timmy did not eat, that his actions were powered by something neither of them understood, but she felt the results of it. She was stronger, and lighter, filled with energy from an unknown source, and she was ready to face the day, and the week, the year, and the rest of her life with inexpressible elation.

Each of them articulated the same thought, and formulated it at exactly the same instant, expressing in a silent, crystalline concept, like a neon marquee, **"This is going to be Fun!"** and their reaction to *that* was a rollicking merriment which sent them down the aisle of the school bus as if they were dancing marionettes on strings of joy!

9. School's Out!

Hannah sat precisely in the middle of the connected porches of the two families. She had her chair tilted back and her feet propped up. Her eyes were closed.

Now nine and a half, Hannah had an amazing physical presence and precocity. She also had a casual attitude toward clothing, especially in warm weather. Right now, for example, she had a simple, flower-print tube shirt with ties, on top, and red shorts on the bottom half. Her feet were bare.

She preferred the back yard, now that the fence dividing the two properties had been removed. The big back yard which had appealed to each family was now twice as appealing to both. Among other things, that's where their ball diamond was, and a lot of grass for Wade to mow.

Oh, it wasn't big enough for true baseball. But they could pitch and catch and play at it, even with choosing up teams and sides.

She heard the jangle of a bicycle coming in the gate and opened her eyes.

"Hi, Jeffy! Ready to play?" She smiled pleasantly.

The boy with glasses, who was also in Hannah's school, (or had been!) and in the choir as well, smiled. "I'm not as good as you think I am, Hannah." He parked his bike beside the porch.

She took his hand. "I just want you to be here! Let's go through the house."

Jeff hesitated, "Which side?"

"Doesn't matter. I'll show you." Hannah led him to the right, into the Miller residence, without even knocking.

Wade was sitting at the table, with a cup of coffee. "Hi Hannah! Who ya got there?"

Hannah brought Jeff over and leaned in for a kiss from Wade. He winked at her.

"This is Jeffy Conners. We need him to even up the teams."

"Welcome aboard, Jeff! I'll be out there in just a bit myself."

Angie came over and ruffled Jeff's hair, leaning down to kiss Hannah as well. "Hi, Jeffrey. We're glad to have a friend of Hannah's over. I hope you'll have fun."

"Come on, Jeff! She'll be feeding you and kissing you if you don't get a move on!" Hannah said with a laugh in her voice. She dragged him out the back door.

Oliver and Dexter were out there already, tossing the ball back and forth. "Hiya, Hammy!" Dexter called, as he threw to Oliver.

Oliver waited until he caught the ball before he turned. "Is this Jeff?"

"Yep! Jeff's going to be on my team."

"Losers you." Oliver shrugged.

"We'll see about that!"

"Really, Hannah, I'm not that good. These guys are a couple of years ahead of me."

She smiled. Jeff was at least a year ahead of her. "Don't worry about it. We're just here to have fun." Hannah squeezed his hand once more before releasing it.

They moved out to take up corners for a four-way game of tossing the ball, first in one direction, then the opposite, and then in a random direction.

Jeffy warmed up to the exercise nicely. Despite his stated misgivings, and a general lack of practice, he was pretty good.

Wade stepped out on the back porch, sipping his coffee. Angie joined him, and held his arm.

"Don't you miss him?" she said softly.

He smiled. "He's out there. You'll see. The teams are more evenly matched than you think."

"They call her Hammy." Angie observed.

He grinned. "Yeah. It's a joke to them all. Who knows? Maybe they're right to treat it that way. He gets to be a part of it again, and so does she."

"I think about her." Angie said, "I can't help it. She was lonely too, wasn't she?"

"*Was*, yeah." He finished his cup and handed it to her. "That's the operative term. She was lonely, and he was lonely. And now they're as happy as two clams in a clamshell."

"And he really isn't gone, either! It's like they're married, and living in the same house with us, and ..." she looked up, with tears in her eyes.

"And they're still kids, with all that's still ahead of them." He grinned. "Believe me, they are having fun with this like you wouldn't believe!"

"It's just so strange! She was so little, and so brave!" Angie shook her head in wonder.

"She's even braver now." Wade said, "They make something together that's more wonderful than having all their other combinations." He smiled. "Timmy can be with us, and Hannah can be her sweet self, either in this house or that one. Or they can be together, in this house or that house and we're still not missing either one. It's like having a fountain of happiness right here with us."

Angie smiled too. "A fountain of youth as well. I wonder what that's going to be like?"

Wade kissed her and moved toward the yard. "We get to find out!"

"Hey, Hammy! You throw like a girl!" Dexter called, teasing.

"Yeah? I've seen you naked, Dexxy!" she called back with a grin.

"Oh, you have not."

"Well, I have, and it's nothing to brag about!" said Oliver.

"You should know!" Hannah pointed out.

"All right, gang! Let's keep it clean. We've got company today." Wade said as he walked out to the pitcher's mound.

Angie smiled and went back into the house.

The rules for this were complicated. Wade was pitcher for both teams. The teams, Hannah and Jeff on one side, and Oliver and Dexter on the other, would have to get a base hit to get on, or perhaps walk, (that could happen), but what made it complicated was having only two batters.

The one on base, if not driven home, would have to leave a proxy invisible person, and everyone would simply have to remember. Then the one "on" would be at bat again. Well, it was complicated, but it led to boisterous good fun.

Hannah played barefoot, for some reason, but she was incredibly fast and agile. She approached baseball with a dancer's grace, and an inner fire to succeed. The inner fire was supplied by Timmy, who was as much the player as Hannah. He brought the same, almost, years of practice and experience to the game as Dexter and Oliver.

Corinne and Theo McMasters returned home from shopping, and finished putting away the groceries. They escaped to the back porch with lemonade.

"She is so athletic! I'm amazed." Corinne said, watching Hannah.

"I think something got into her." Theo said quietly.

Corinne looked over at him. "Oh, you! You're as devilish about this as Wade! Our innocent little girl is out there competing with boys almost twice her size."

"True, but she has twice the spirit."

Corinne rolled her eyes.

"Did you ever wonder what it might be like?" Theo looked over. "My mind won't let such things go. I think about what's going to happen when this, or that, and I just worry it like a dog with a bone. What if you could take my spirit inside you?"

Corinne looked a little startled. "Well, we could talk more than we usually do. I don't know. Hannah seems to like being the cup that runneth over. I'd probably like it too."

"I think you're right. I'm just thankful that they are kids, and not teenagers at the moment. I'm sure my mind will go crazy trying to figure that out."

"You won't have to." Corinne assured him. "They'll sort that out too, when the time comes. Did you know that Hannah wants to open a doorway between the houses in the upstairs hall?"

Theo almost spilled his lemonade. "Whatever for?"

"She says, they have a lot of stuff to trade back and forth, and Timmy can't carry it. She already keeps a wardrobe for him, and quite a few toys and stuff."

"I don't know. It seems like then all she would be is their plaything."

Corinne pointed out in the back yard, where Hannah was playing with the boys the way she used to play with dolls. "I think they might be hers. Who can tell what they're cooking up?"

"Hmm. As a practical measure, a door on the lower level would work pretty well. Make it a lot easier to have our group dinners and such."

Corinne brightened, "Hey! You're right! Angie and I are constantly swapping things around. That would be so much easier."

"But would you want the house to be that open to our neighbors?" Theo reminded her.

"Neighbors? Are you kidding? We're related to them in ways we can't even describe! I love Angie! You've seen how she's brightened and flourished in the last few months, and I know you've grown closer to Wade."

"Wade's a good man. Look at that." He pointed out the activity in front of them. "I never would have believed it could happen, or any of this, really." He sipped his drink.

Angie came out to join them, having gone through the house to walk out on their porch with them.

"There's another thing we'll need, too. These porches need to be connected." Corinne said, pouring lemonade from the pitcher into Angie's glass she had brought out.

"Connect the porches? Oh, that would be nice!" Angie said.

"We were also talking about opening a door between our houses. I think the best place would be to connect the dining rooms." Theo admitted for consideration.

"A door between the houses?" Angie said.

"Hannah wants it." Corinne said.

"Whatever for?"

"For all of us, Angie." Corinne smiled, "Certainly, Hannah doesn't need it."

"You mean Timmy doesn't need it," Angie reminded her.

"Yeah, well, that's why Hannah doesn't need it!" Theo said, chuckling. They all laughed.

Wade came up to sit with them. Theo got him a glass for lemonade.

"Who won?" Theo asked.

"They did!" Wade answered, breathing hard. Everyone laughed.

"We've been talking about making changes to the houses." Angie said.

"What changes?" Wade asked.

The kids were beginning to gather around.

"We thought it would be nice to have just one porch back here, like we have in front." Angie said.

"And Hannah wants a door between the houses," Corinne said. "We thought maybe between the dining rooms would be best."

Hannah looked at the twins.

"Maybe a big door?" Wade suggested. "What about double sliding doors?"

"Wow!" Theo exclaimed, "That's brilliant! Nothing in the footprint needs to really change, and we can always close the doors again for separation."

Hannah gestured to the boys to follow her. They went up on the other porch. "If they join these porches together, you know what we need? A dugout!" she whispered to them. "We can keep our equipment in it, and wait out rain for awhile, and other stuff."

Dexter and Oliver looked over the area between the porches. "We have to dig out some dirt."

"Dig out our dugout?" Oliver said.

Dexter raised his eyebrows. "Yeah, exactly."

"Good, you're with me on this, then?" Hannah asked. The boys all nodded, even Jeffy.

Hannah went over to the edge. "Mom, Dad! We want to help! We'll be your workers."

Theo looked over. "What?"

"We want to help with the project, and we want to build a dugout for our ball field, right here!"

Theo looked at Wade. "I think we need a contractor."

Wade smiled. "I know just the guy."

<hr>

Hannah and the boys went back into Timmy's house. Dexter spoke up, "All right, here's what we need. They're going to build two doors right over here, between the houses. Dad said they would be pocket doors, which means they slide inside the wall."

"They have to take the wall out?" said Oliver.

"A lot of it, yeah. Usually the problem is the stuff that's inside it, and has to be moved." Dexter had been watching home improvement shows with Wade.

"I know what's inside the wall," Hannah said. "I mean, I know how to find out."

"We know what you mean," Dexter said. "We should mark everything out in chalk. Anyone have some chalk?"

"I have some upstairs on my side." Hannah said. "I'll go get it!"

With that, Timmy separated from Hannah, and flew up through the ceiling and the wall toward her room on the other side. Soon there was the sound of a screen door softly closing, and then another.

Timmy came back in from the front door with chalk in hand.

Jeff Conners was staring in shock.

Hannah looked over at him. "Oops." She said softly.

Timmy saw Jeff's expression and stood still for a moment. Then he shrugged, reached into the wall and began tracing electrical lines and stud locations. With one hand held outward, he lined up and marked out the locations of things that Dexter told him to look for.

Dexter looked over the drawings. "Good, good. Boys, we could almost do this work ourselves, but we don't have the tools. What's wrong with you?" He said to Jeff.

"Him!" Jeff said shakily, "What is he, a ghost?"

"He's our brother, Timmy. You've been singing with him in the church choir. What's the matter with you?"

"Take it easy on him, boys. Remember we've been trying to keep this a secret. Jeffy didn't know." Hannah said softly. She approached him and gently put her hands out to him. "Take it easy, Jeff. He's not going to hurt you."

Jeff backed away from her. "You aren't going to suck me up, too, are you?"

"*What?*" Hannah stared.

"He was inside you!" Jeff said shakily. "How'd you do that?"

"Hey, I didn't do it. *Timmy* does it. Look at him! Why do you think he doesn't have any clothes on?"

Timmy looked down. "Oh, yeah. Sorry, Jeff. I tend to forget. Here." He handed Jeff the chalk.

Jeff reached out for the chalk, still shaking.

"Maybe I should just go back in …"

"No!" Jeff looked as though he might collapse.

"Alright, wait a minute. Sit down here, Jeff." Dexter took command. "Somebody get him some orange juice."

Oliver brought over a small glass of orange juice. Then he got another for Hannah and himself.

"Thanks, Oliver." Hannah said.

Jeff looked around. "You guys act like this is all normal."

They looked at each other, and then nodded. "Why are you acting weird, Jeff?"

"*I'm* acting weird!"

"You certainly are!" Dexter said. "Look, we've got a project going on here. Are you going to be helping us or not?"

"Project?"

Wordlessly, Dexter pointed at the drawings.

"Oh." Jeff drank his orange juice and attempted to stifle his shuddering.

"Feeling better?" Timmy asked.

"Yeah, a little." Jeff eyed his lack of clothing.

Oliver reached out and smacked him gently in the back of the head. "Stop that!"

"Hey!" Jeff complained.

"Leave him alone, Oliver." Hannah said. "Hey, look at that! Look how big that opening is going to be! Wow! We'll be able to go back and forth without going outside any more!"

"That will be a big help to me." Timmy admitted.

"Could you please put some clothes on?" Jeffy asked.

Amused, Oliver handed Timmy a small apron his mother used just to be decorative.

Timmy tied it around his waist. His backside was still bare. "Is that better?"

Jeff stared at him, and then giggled, and then laughed. Some orange juice came out of his nose. "Ow, ow! That hurts!" and then he laughed some more.

Angie came into the kitchen and looked over this scene. "What is going on here?"

Hannah said, "We were starting on our plans. Look here." She showed Angie the drawings.

"Someone has been drawing on my wall?"

"It's just chalk." Hannah said, while gesturing to the others to clean up the spilled orange juice. "Look how big your door is going to be!"

"Oh, my! That will be nice! We'll be able to have Thanksgiving Dinner all as one big family." Angie looked around at Jeffy. "You may come to dinner with us, too, Jeffrey, if you'll behave yourself."

"Yes, ma'am. Thank you, ma'am."

"Let's go upstairs." Hannah suggested.

Quickly, the crew of children made their way out toward the front and scurried up the stairs. A moment later, Angie's apron came fluttering back down.

Up on the second floor, they all burst into laughter once again.

"You looked good in your apron, Timmy." Oliver suggested.

"Wait! Wait! *That's* why you were calling Hannah "Hammy"! I get it now!" Jeff said excitedly. "Because he was *inside* her! H̲annah *and* Ti̲m̲my̲." He looked puzzled. "How do you do that, anyway?"

"We found out by accident," said Timmy. "I was hiding in the same place Hannah was. I didn't realize anything was unusual, but Hannah noticed it."

"The first time he put me on, like a snow-suit, I realized that it was like getting a whole new family. He became a part of me, like a brother I didn't know I had."

"Getting a brother I didn't know I had happens to me all the time." Timmy said calmly.

"Wait a minute! I'm the one who's most original." Dexter maintained.

"You're the one who's most *like* the original, you mean." Hannah said. "Timmy was disappearing, a little at a time. When the thing that was in my house decided to reward you for your "hospitality," it restored Timmy in various ways. We got three Timmys out of it."

"And *we* got *you*," Timmy said.

"Well, *you* got her, anyway." Oliver said.

"Okay, thanks for the explanation," Jeffy said, "but now I'm more confused than ever."

"Kids! Come and eat!" Angie called up the stairway.

"Food first, Newbie." Oliver said.

Everyone made a dash for the stairway. When they entered the kitchen, Timmy was already in place, standing by the rounded corner of the snack bar.

Jeffy looked back toward the stairway.

Hannah took a seat near Timmy. Jeff sat at his other side. Timmy was standing between them. Oliver and Dexter took up seats as well.

Angie brought over two small plates with peanut butter and jelly sandwiches and placed them in front of Oliver and Dexter. The sandwiches were sliced diagonally.

"Do you like peanut butter and jelly, Jeffrey?" She asked him.

"Yes, ma'am, please! I love it."

Angie brought over two more small plates for Hannah and Jeff. Hannah's sandwich was sliced into quarters, and Jeff's was sliced straight across.

"Milk, or juice?"

"Milk please!"

Timmy began carrying the glasses to each recipient. He used two hands on each glass.

Then Timmy picked up one of Hannah's sandwich squares and held it for her to bite.

Jeffy watched this for a moment. "Why are you feeding her?"

"She wants me to." Timmy answered.

"They always do that." Oliver said.

"It gives Timmy something to do when we're eating. Timmy doesn't eat." Dexter explained.

"He could put on some clothes." Jeff complained.

Hannah took a sip of milk, looked to see if Angie was looking, and then stuck out her tongue at him.

"What is it with you and clothes, anyway?" Dexter asked, "Do you have a fetish or something?"

Jeff rolled his eyes.

Timmy stuck out *his* tongue at him.

Jeff grinned and started eating.

✦✦✦✦

"What's this?" Wade said from the dining room.

Angie glanced over. "The kids have marked out our opening for us."

"Oh," Wade said, turning toward his correspondence desk, the drawer in which he kept letters and overdue bills. "That reminds me."

"Mr. Cannon? Okay, Roger then. This is Wade Miller. I have a medium-sized project or two I'd like to discuss with you. Yes, the house on Willow Run Court. You can? That's great! We'll see you then!"

"That's the contractor who did the renovations on Theo and Corinne's side. He's going to stop by later."

"If it's supposed to be a secret, why did you guys show me?" Jeff asked. The conversation had adjourned to the back porch. They were all sitting on the top step.

"That was an accident. I guess we forgot you were there." Hannah said.

Dexter examined a chocolate chip cookie, his last one. "It would probably be a bad idea to mention any of this to anyone."

"Don't worry, I won't. They might not put me in the Looney Bin, but they for sure won't let me come back here."

Hannah looked over, looking past Timmy. "You *want* to come back?"

"Well, sure! This place is fun!" Jeff smiled.

Timmy looked at each of them in turn.

Hannah saw his reaction and smiled. "What's wrong, Tim? Are you feeling jealous?"

Timmy looked at her. "Jealous? Me?"

"Well, I'm your girl, aren't I?"

"I guess. Or maybe I'm your boy. Who knows?"

"I can usually tell, I think, when you're being 'Hammy'. Something in the way you move, I think." Dexter mused.

"Something in the way she moves me …" crooned Timmy softly.

"Yeah, she moves you all right." said Oliver, "You're more like her breakfast than her boyfriend."

Hannah smiled, "You will never understand." She said very serenely.

"I wouldn't want him in me!" Oliver stated.

Timmy looked over at him. "I never thought about doing that," he paused, "but now that I consider it … I think it might be a *really bad* idea."

Oliver's eye's widened. "I don't think about us being the same once. We've been going down separate paths ever since, but … yeah. I think you're right."

"Well, that would go for me too." Dexter added. They were quiet for a moment.

"What?" Jeff said, "You want me to volunteer? I don't think so!"

"No, no. We were just thinking." Hannah said, "You can't have him anyway. He's mine."

"Fine by me." Jeff seemed relieved. Then after a moment, "What's it like?"

Oliver reached around and smacked him gently on the back of the head.

"Ow!"

Timmy tapped him on the shoulder. When Jeff looked around, Timmy stuck a finger in his eye.

Jeffy rocked back, but there had been no pain. Timmy's finger had been completely insubstantial.

Timmy smiled at him. "It's like putting on clothes, a little. But I'm putting her on and she's putting me on. Finally we get adjusted, and it's actually rather comfortable. I like letting her carry me around. It's like being a baby in its mother's arms."

"And I like having him there." Hannah said. "I feel more secure, and I'm not alone."

"We talk a lot when I'm in there. I let my 'inner girl' out."

Hannah leaned over and gave him a kiss. "And I let my 'outer boy' in!" She smiled.

"Weird!" Jeff proclaimed.

"You'd like it." Hannah said, "Maybe we should try to find a girl for you to let in."

"A ghosty-girl for me? I don't think so!" He paused. "Do you think there are any?"

"I should smack him again," Oliver said.

"Don't bother. It isn't doing any good," responded Dexter.

"There's no one else like Timmy." Hannah asserted.

"You're most likely right about that." Dexter said. Oliver nodded.

"So, we gonna play ball?" Dexter asked.

"Just a minute while I suit up," Timmy said. He slid sideways into Hannah, and put his hands into her hands, and his feet into her feet, and his head into her head.

After a moment, he was invisible again. He gave her a kiss from the inside.

Hannah kissed him back. "Hammy's up first at bat!" she called, running out into the sunlight.

10. The Opening

Roger Cannon looked at the wall in question. "There's no doubt that it's a bearing wall. It's the main backbone of the house. But that's not really a problem. We'll have to establish support for this wall the way we would a porch roof when we're rebuilding the deck. That is, we'll move the bracing out and down, so that we can cut into the wall and place our beam."

"Right. So, price, time, and what else do you need?" Wade was thinking out loud, along with Roger.

"Well, let's see. We'll need two weeks for this part, and that assumes I've got the manpower and the materials. That will give us the price. We're looking at five grand inside the house. The porch job is not a problem, just time-consuming. We'll need another twenty-five hundred for that."

"Alright, that sounds reasonable. So what else is there then?"

"With a partial payment, I can have most of the materials I'll need here tomorrow. My problem is manpower. We're full up. I only stopped here now because I'm on the way to get some material for another project."

"Look behind you." Wade said.

Standing quietly at the back of the room were Oliver, Dexter, Hannah, and Jeff.

Cannon smiled.

"I know they're not old enough to hire yet. But these are your volunteer laborers. With all the material that will have to be carried out, and carried in, you'll save a lot on your own labor by simply telling my boys to tote the barge and lift the bale. I can help a bit with the heavier items, too, depending on the time of day. But they've got all summer."

Cannon glanced back at them again. "One of them's a girl," he stage-whispered.

"Hammy can hold her own. This is as much their project as it is the rest of us. Tell you what; you start the demo, and get us to the support stage, and we'll do the clean up and prep work for each next stage. You'll only need a third of the manpower."

"My crew normally numbers only three."

Wade grinned, "Well, there you go! Simple math!"

"All right, if you're serious, and if you've got two thousand dollars for materials, I can have it delivered tomorrow. But I have one more question; who drew the pictures?"

Wade glanced behind him. Cannon looked that way too.

Dexter and Hannah were pointing at each other.

Roger grinned. "Well, whoever did it, that's good work, and it will help a lot. I could probably use you guys on some of our other problems."

"Mr. Cannon?" Dexter was following him out. "May I ask a question?"

"Call me Roger. Sure."

"Mr. Roger. How is it you know already what you're going to need? I mean, you just looked at it, and you didn't take measurements or anything, and now you're getting material delivered tomorrow. How do you know?"

"You're interested in this work, Mister Miller?"

"Call me Dexter. I like watching the programs on TV. They always have computerized drawings and stuff."

"Dexter, then. Let me guess, they start out in shirtsleeves and end up working in the snow, right? Five to six weeks to get the project done?"

Dexter nodded.

Cannon smiled. "We don't work that way. We don't have *time* to work that way. We order lots of standard materials, and make everything on site. We don't want to run out of anything, because that slows everything down. Anything that's left over, we deduct from the bill, and use on the next job. See how it works?"

"I like it! You're not slowing down to take camera shots."

Cannon pointed his finger at him and winked. "You got it! We work it different with the permits office, too. To our local guys, "as-builts" are more important than "prelims", because that shows what is actually there, instead of what somebody imagined."

He continued. "Let me give you another clue. We have two projects going on here, for example. Inside the house we'll need temporary support walls that will have to come out later. And then we'll use *that* material for the second project, as structure and decking. No waste involved, and less moving stuff around. I've already planned out what goes in when, and how it's all going to look. Any problems, we'll work around them as we go."

"I get it! That's what they call, "work smarter, not harder", right, Mr. Roger?"

"And faster too! The faster you work, the more you're getting paid! That's our motto. I'll see you tomorrow, kid!"

"Bye, Mr. Roger!" Dexter watched him climb into his truck.

"You wrote a check for two thousand dollars?" Angie looked at him in surprise.

"I've been saving it up. I thought I might need to buy a truck. Or maybe renovate the kitchen. I had a feeling something was coming along. It always does."

"I could use a dishwasher." Angie mused.

"You *have* a dishwasher; that little neighbor girl, what's-her-name."

"She does jump up and do them a lot. Such a sweet girl." She smiled.

"I thought she liked washing them because she liked seeing Timmy putting the dishes away. I guess she thinks he has a cute butt."

"He *does* have a cute butt. Oh, well, it saves me the effort. Now, while you're up, why don't you bring me an iced tea?" Angie smiled at him again.

"You just want to watch *my* cute butt!" Wade said as he went into the kitchen.

"Uh-huh, that, and it'll give you something to carry in your *other* hand."

11. Play Ball!

The building of the dugout did not begin after the opening of the wall. It began the day after the material was delivered, when an entirely different crew showed up with a bobcat and some masonry supplies. At the end of the day, the footings for the dugout were complete.

Two days later, the block walls were up. Except for having no roof, it was usable as a dugout right then.

Altogether, it took just under three weeks, which was surprisingly fast considering the magnitude of the projects.

But the really amazing part, to everyone concerned, was the quality and scope of the work that had been done.

The double pocket doors looked as though they had always been a part of the design of the house. Closed, two families lived and functioned with complete autonomy and separation.

Open, a single extended family unit oscillated around and through the new opening, with breakfasts and dinners being more than merely functional occasions, but daily celebrations.

The doors stayed open from that point on.

In the dugout, comfort was utilitarian. Wooden benches marked the seats, and rough plywood cabinets provided equipment storage. But the steps leading out also turned up to the upper level, making a rather elegant "spiral" type stair to the porch level.

Even the entrance to the dugout was framed in and closed with a second-hand patio door and fixed windows where they stowed, allowing a six-foot opening for good weather, lots of natural lighting, and protection for the space when it rained.

A large roof extension sheltered the porch addition and the dugout entrance. It was a snug and comfortable hidden place looking out on the back yard.

"A toast! My friends, a toast!" Theo raised his wineglass filled with white grape juice. "To dependents, and Independence, and dependence again. May we all enjoy the independence to depend upon our mutual friendship for many, many years!"

"Hear, hear!" Wade added, lifting his glass at the opposite end of the table. At the joined table, Angie, Dexter, and Oliver sat near him, while Corinne and Hannah sat at Theo's end. Timmy took a position near Hannah, but he was constantly moving about, fetching things from this kitchen or that, and as a result, he was the only one who could be considered dressed entirely too casually for the occasion.

It had been discussed, between Corinne and Angie, whether to try to keep Timmy "in harness" during the dinner, but they agreed that any dinner was merely make-believe for him anyway. The only way he could actually participate was by helping others.

And the only sensible way for him to do that was in his natural manner, moving quickly and directly as the need arose. Timmy was not ashamed to be seen without clothes, but he was ashamed to be required to wear clothes.

"Wade, I'll have to admit, I had my doubts. I had the feeling that we'd be getting on each other's nerves by now. But it's really working well. We don't intrude unnecessarily, and help is always convenient for whatever is going on. It struck me that this openness is a recognition of something no one else in the world has, a real, honest-to-goodness marriage of minds."

"Your mind and my mind are still very far apart on a lot of things, Theo." Wade said cautiously.

"Well, that's true," Theo agreed, "but I wasn't talking about *our* minds. I meant the mind of your son Timmy and the mind of my daughter Hannah."

"He means Hammy, Dad." Oliver observed.

"Exactly!" Theo beamed. "Well stated. Our "Hammy" is neither entirely Hannah, nor Timmy either, but a combination of the two, which brings out the delightful exuberance of both. Hammy is brash and confident, while both Hannah and Timmy are quiet and withdrawn."

"Is there anyone here who can't tell when Hammy is in the room with them, rather than only Hannah?" Theo asked.

Heads looked around, but no one took up the question.

"A marriage?" Timmy asked softly, almost inaudibly.

"Well, yes. That's rather the way I think of it, but a marriage of minds, which is a way of saying that people come to understand each other."

"I wonder what the ceremony looks like?" mused Angie.

Wade smiled. "Let's find out!" He cleared the space in front of him and stood up. "Hannah, come down here for a moment, please!"

Hannah looked at her parents for a moment. They nodded their assent. She walked down to stand in front of Wade.

He lifted her up and stood her on the table. "Who giveth this young lady for a marriage of minds on this day?"

Theo and Corinne stood up. "Her mother and I!"

"Timmy, son, up on the table with you. Don't step in the food." Wade said.

Timmy arose through the table and settled lightly down on it.

"And who giveth this young man to be mentally married on this solemn occasion?" Wade took Angie's hand and helped her to stand.

"His father and I do!" Angie said.

"Come on over here, son." Wade said.

Timmy approached, walking along the table.

Oliver pulled his drink away from Timmy's path. Dexter rolled his eyes.

"Take her hand, son." Wade said.

Timmy held Hannah's hand and stood beside her.

"Hannah, do you take Timmy to be your mind partner, to live inside you when you want to be together, and to go out from you to do other things when that is what you both want?"

Hannah looked at her mother, who mouthed the words 'I do' to her. "I do." Said Hannah.

"Timmy, do you take Hannah to be your mind-partner, for you to occupy with her permission, and to entertain and amuse, to accompany and be her companion, and to help her to be cheerful and helpful to others, or to go out from her when that is what she wants, and do other things when that is what you both want?"

"You mean, all the things we're doing already?" Timmy asked.

"Play the game, son." Wade whispered.

"I do!" Timmy smiled.

"Then, by the authority invested in me, which is none, and in the sight of God and this company, I pronounce that you may be one with her," Wade gestured, and Timmy moved into Hannah's body by simply sliding sideways. In a moment, he was invisibly inside her. "And I now pronounce you Hammy, and I may kiss the Hammy."

Wade leaned in and collected a kiss from the girl, and then set her back down on the floor.

Angie came over and kissed her now, holding her cheeks with both hands.

Hammy started down toward the other end of the table.

Although they were not really asked, both Dexter and Oliver shook their heads no as if to say no thanks.

Hannah walked on down to where her parents were, and both of them gave her a kiss as well.

"And now it's official. Hannah and Timmy are mind-married. M and M families, I present to you, Hammy!"

Hannah bowed to the assembled company.

"And that's what the ceremony looks like!" Wade said. "Boy! That's thirsty work!"

"More brandy, Wade?" Theo held up the white grape juice.

"Don't mind if I do," Wade responded, "but I must say, your brandy seems to taste a lot like grape juice."

"That's the mark of an excellent year!" Theo countered.

"I keep expecting something to happen. The other shoe to fall, if you know what I mean." Wade said. "These kids are too young to understand what this kind of thing means."

"I'm a bit young to understand it too. Do *you* understand it?"

Wade reflected. "I've had time to think about it. I know that I don't understand the science behind it, if it is science. But Timmy was withering spiritually being shut in the house all the time. Spiritually may be all he has."

Wade looked up, "What your daughter has made possible for him is miraculous. He's … I don't know … He's entirely different now. Happier, God yes! But he's more confident, more ready to take on the challenges of life. Now he can go out and see the world; look it in the eye and see who blinks first. It has been … a wonderful thing for him."

"It's been good for her, too. Do you see how she reacts around Dexter and Oliver? She's like a tiger around them, utterly fearless! Oh, I'm confident that she would have landed on her feet under any circumstances, but this truly is miraculous! She's being exposed to wonders and insights that no girl has seen since Madame Curie made her wondrous discoveries. Hannah will be looking at the world as if she's lived through it a dozen times already."

"I keep thinking that we're going to wake up and find out we've been suffering a delusion, but every day I keep falling further into the dream." Wade shook his head.

"Well, dream on, brother dreamer. Dream on!" Theo poured a bit more juice in Wade's glass. "We haven't reached the end of it quite yet!"

12. Tryouts

Hannah was sitting in the dugout with Jeff. She was on the back wall seat, with her feet resting on one of the "bucket" seats. Jeff sat on the sidewall seat, and had his feet on her bucket too. They were watching it rain as evening fell.

"One thing I can't figure out," Jeff mused. "How can he fit his feet inside yours? I mean, his feet are bigger than mine, and look at that." He moved his bare foot like a hand waving, next to her smaller and relatively dainty foot.

"He says it's like stretchy clothes," she responded, "but it's hard to say who's stretching and which one gets bigger or smaller."

"Is it true that he doesn't get any bigger? Maybe soon you'll be almost the same size, and it'll be even easier."

"I've gotten an inch taller since I met him, and he hasn't changed. His brothers have grown at least two to three inches taller, and he's still the same size. But he says it couldn't be easier or quicker than it is now anyway. We fit like an old shoe already."

She crossed her feet, letting her right foot rest against Jeff's right foot. "Hold still a minute." She looked at him. "Really. Don't move at all."

Timmy extended his foot out from hers, and entered Jeff's foot with it. After a moment of orientation, he began wriggling Jeff's toes.

"Oh. My. God! I don't believe it!"

Hannah giggled.

Jeff looked at her. "I can't believe it. Is that what it's like for you?"

"That's nothing," Hannah smiled. "When his head is inside my head, we can talk to each other without saying anything! He moves in and hugs me all over."

"Eww! I wish you hadn't said that!" Jeff shuddered.

"You're silly! Don't you realize that every time you hold my hand, you're holding his hand too?"

Jeff was watching his own foot move by itself. He tore his eyes away from it to look at her again. "Yeah, I know that … but that's … I don't know. It's different. I tend to think of you as Hannah or Hammy, and I like you both."

"Well, what about if I kissed you? You are kinda cute, you know."

"A kiss? Um, … Do you mind if I think about that for a little bit?" He studied her face. "It's not that I don't like you, and it's not even that I don't like you and him being Hammy, it's … I don't know, maybe it's the idea of kissing girls at all."

Hannah studied him. "Timmy kisses me all the time. He can even kiss me when he's inside me. We're … I don't know … maybe soul mates? I trust him, and I love him, as if he was me and I was him. You can't share anything like sharing a body if you don't love each other completely."

"That," Jeff looked a little pale, "That, I *know* I'm too young for."

Hannah stared at him for a moment, and then turned a little red and laughed. "Heh, I wasn't talking about *that*, and Timmy and I are too young for that, too."

"Oh!" Jeff looked away, "Sorry."

"It's okay. It's confusing, really." Hannah reached out to hold his hand.

As Jeff reached out, Timmy's hand came out of Hannah's arm to clasp his hand, and Timmy's body slid out sideways to sit between them, with his left hand holding Jeff's, and his right hand holding Hannah's.

Timmy's feet were still divided between the two of them.

Jeff looked down at the feet, and his eyes grew very large. Timmy wriggled Jeff's foot and Hannah's foot.

"Uh-oh!" Jeff said.

Timmy smiled. "I won't do anything to hurt you. Would you like to try it?"

Jeff looked at Timmy's hand, held in his hand, and his foot, merged with Jeff's own foot. Nothing was hurting, but his heart was pounding like the heart of a captured bird.

Jeff swallowed, and looked over at Hannah. She smiled encouragement.

Slowly, he nodded his assent.

"You're sure?"

"Go ahead," Jeff said, with his voice quavering, "let's give it a try."

Tim moved slowly and visibly around behind Jeff, merging into him from behind. He stretched into Jeff's hands and feet, and then brought his head into alignment. In a moment, Jeff was sitting there with his right hand held out, holding emptiness.

"Let's move around," suggested Timmy, silently and internally.

Jeff's eyes looked a little wild. Slowly he got to his feet.

Hannah was watching him with rapt interest.

Jeff went up the steps, and the side steps to the upper porch. He turned and looked out over the yard.

"Let's go in the house. You have to pee," A silent voice.

Jeff realized it was true. How did he know that?

He turned as if sleepwalking, and went in through the kitchen, the dining room, and entered the powder room.

Moments later, Timmy's silent voice spoke to him again. "That's the first time I've peed in over a year! Thanks! What a relief!"

Jeff could feel Timmy smiling at his little joke. They went back out on the back porch. They were looking out into the rain-drenched ball field. "Take your glasses off." Timmy's voice told him.

Jeff took his glasses off and put them in his pocket. He looked out into a blurry darkness. And then the scene before him focused into crystal sharpness, as Timmy's eyes did the seeing for them both.

Jeff stared out at the scene. Dark clouds, and wet grass, in sharp, shining focus. It was beautiful!

"Let's go back down now."

In a daze, Jeff slowly moved back down the steps into the dugout.

He kept looking out to the limits of the yard where glistening images danced for him.

"Take your clothes off, and we'll go for a walk in the rain. I want to feel the rain." Not as if in a stupor, but as if in a fantasy, Jeff slipped out of his clothes. Ignoring Hannah, he looked out in the yard as he marched up the steps and out into the splashing, cold rain.

Except that he wasn't getting wet. Timmy had extended his surface-sense just beyond Jeff's actual surface, and Timmy was feeling the raindrops, but he wasn't feeling the cold. They stood there with their arms outstretched, letting the heavens fall, and smiling into the sky.

Then they turned. Hannah was watching, from near the bottom step. Jeff walked back to the dugout, and down to the step below Hannah's. He turned and looked into her eyes. She was smiling.

He kissed her. They kissed her. With real, human lips, and the reality of actual touch, both Timmy and Jeff kissed Hannah for a long moment, and they all smiled.

Then Jeffy stepped away, and began getting dressed.

Timmy left him then, and soared up the steps and into the yard, flying around the play area and circling the bases, (in the wrong direction, but that didn't matter). He came back to them as Jeff finished dressing, and awkwardly fished out his glasses again.

Timmy came to them and held their hands. "Are we good?"

Jeff stared at him. "Oh, yeah! We're good! We're very good." He looked at Hannah. "Thank you!"

Hannah lowered her eyes. "That was wonderful! I knew you'd like it!"

Jeff put his arms around each of them. "You are the best friends I will ever have! Ever, ever, ever!"

Timmy kissed him on the forehead. Then he merged with Hannah, and they kissed Jeff again, quite properly.

Jeff had tears in his eyes, but he bravely said, "I think I need a root beer!"

He and Hannah went up to the Miller's kitchen once more.

Transcendence

Book Two – Second Timothy

Chapter

Transcendence

13. A Home To Go To

Jeffrey was standing idly in the Miller's living room, tossing a baseball into his glove. Whap, whap. Not a loud sound, but repetitive.

Wade was sitting in his favorite chair, oriented more or less toward the TV, which was not turned on at the moment.

He watched for a bit, and then spoke. "Boy, don't you have a home to go to?"

Jeff looked over. "Yes, Sir!"

"Well, why don't you go there?"

Jeff put down the ball and glove, and walked over. He crawled into Wade's lap and rested his head on the man's shoulder. "Is this better?"

Wade tousled the boy's hair, and patted his head gently. "Yeah. That'll do."

They sat quietly for a few minutes.

"How many people live in your house, Jeremy? Your *other* house, I mean."

Jeff smiled. "Jeffrey. It's just me and my mom. And it's a condo."

"Is it roomy?"

"It is for me. I have a bedroom for myself. In the other condos, my room might be an office, but I like it."

Wade nodded. "Not too many kids in your development?"

Jeff shook his head.

"I can see why you like coming over here, then."

Jeff nodded. "You have a nice big house, and a big back yard. I like it here." He paused a moment. "But the people are special too."

"Yes, that they are." Wade said lightly, "I didn't expect to have a big family. The responsibility came kinda suddenly."

"Like magic, isn't it?" Jeffrey asked.

"It wasn't so magical when it happened. It was scary as the devil!"

Jeff sat up. "You're a hero, Mr. Miller. You chased away that devil."

"*What?*"

"You ripped his arm off, and ate it, like Beowulf against the monster Grendel."

"I think there are some inaccuracies in the way you heard the story. Let me guess, Oliver?"

Jeff nodded.

"Let me up. I want to show you the letter my "monster" wrote to me."

Wade retrieved the parchment scroll from its special place, and rolled it out for Jeffrey to read.

Slowly, the boy scanned over the document repeatedly.

"Timmy's *immortal*? He can't be killed?"

"Well, he doesn't get older. I haven't wanted to try killing him." Wade responded, "Oliver, on the other hand … I mean, we have a spare and all …"

Jeff looked at him with fright, and then realized that he was only kidding. Wade was a great guy, who even played ball with them.

"So then this … whatever it was, just left? You never saw it again?"

Wade put the parchment away. "I never saw it in the first place! I don't think Timmy actually saw it either. Neither one of us knew how powerful and dangerous it was. And then it was gone."

"And that's when Timmy was changed."

"Yeah. Timmy, Oliver, and Dexter. My newly enlarged family."

"So I guess I won't be able to find a ghost girl for myself, like Hannah said."

"Ghost girl?"

"Somebody who could live inside me, the way Timmy lives inside Hannah."

"Why would you want that?" Wade asked in genuine curiosity as he resumed his seat.

Jeffrey stared at him, taking his glasses off and wiping them with his shirt to prolong the moment, before answering, "Timmy is a miracle! Having him inside you is like having a friend, not just right beside you, but sharing your thoughts as well. It's …"

He broke off, standing close and looking intently at Wade for a moment. "You haven't had him inside you yet, have you?"

Wade blinked. "Well, no." He looked thoughtful, "I don't think he would fit."

"You might be surprised," Jeff looked down, breaking the intensity of the moment. "Maybe one day, you'll see."

Wade was quiet for a moment.

"He goes to school with Hannah," he said gently. "Has he ever gone to school with you?"

"No …" Jeff said slowly. Then he smiled, "That would be so cool!"

Timmy had come down the steps a few moments before, to meet with Jeff. As usual, his approach was soundless. In this instance, he had also troubled to put on some clothes, in the limited fashion that he favored, since it was all he could accomplish.

He had stopped his approach and listened to the conversation, seeing that Jeffy was not waiting for him as expected. The point about going to school seemed a good place to intrude.

"I'll be ready to go whenever you are, Jeff." Timmy said.

Jeff looked over at him, and smiled.

Wade also turned to look at him. "You'll be taking the same courses you've already studied, you know."

Timmy smiled at them. "That's what I do when I go with Hannah, too. But it's still different now. Actually, I think I'm learning better this time. Among other things, I have to pay more attention, because I can't take notes."

"Really?" Wade asked.

"Yeah. Hannah is a good student, and she takes notes. I'm just listening, for the most part, but I'm paying attention, too. Hannah tells me I should practice memorizing things, because I won't have notebooks."

"Why would you need to, if you're not taking the exams?" Jeff asked.

Timmy shrugged. "Life has a way of bringing tests when you don't expect them. Right, Dad?"

"Exactly right, my boy!" Wade beamed. "I've been worried that you weren't able to continue with your schooling, and you'll be the one who needs it most."

"Wait, why?" Jeff asked. "Timmy isn't going to go out and get a job somewhere, is he?"

"I could work for Mr. Cannon, I'll bet." Timmy said, "But I think Dad has something different in mind. Don't you, Dad?"

Wade looked at the two boys, very near in appearance now, but with vastly different futures ahead of them. "Indeed so. You're going to be around a long time, Timmy. None of us knows how long. The more you can learn, the more you can find ways to do good things, and maybe even important things. That's going to make a difference to you, and it could even make a difference to the people around you."

Wade adjusted his position, and looked very serious. "I want you to go to school any way you can, Tim, until you learn everything they have to teach you. I don't know why you'll need it, but you'll need it."

"Okay, Dad," Timmy answered. "You heard him, Jeffy. We're good to go!"

"All right!" Jeff grinned excitedly.

"Right now though, boys, it's time to play ball," Wade reminded them. He got up to join them.

Monday through Thursday, Timmy went to school with Hannah. On Fridays, he traveled inside Jeff.

They were in different grades, and before long, they were in different schools. But this arrangement made better students of all of them.

You can imagine it would. You wouldn't want your best friend to see you make a bonehead mistake, would you? So Hannah and Jeff paid more attention.

And then Timmy found it challenging also. Too often, he was

geared up for quizzes for which he and Hannah had studied, and he ended up taking a test in Jeff's class.

Of course, Timmy's tests didn't get graded. But he didn't want to make bonehead mistakes in front of his best friends, either.

They got better, and they got through the school year eventually.

Because summer could never come quickly enough, or last long enough. In summer, Jeff practically lived at the Millers' house,

Hannah developed a brash self-confidence, and a greater interest and ability in sports.

Jeff also overcame his natural shyness, and learned to be more forthright in addressing the class.

Timmy learned a lot of things about other kids and their tendencies, and also learned a considerable amount regarding the sometimes fickle nature of the anatomical lottery.

In constantly moving back and forth between Hannah and Jeffrey, Timmy developed grace and skill in the process of aligning himself inside them. This was not something anyone else could have taught him.

When it came time for Timmy to use these skills he was honing, he could do it without effort.

14. Buttons and Buttonholes

Timmy was visiting in Hannah's room, in her absence. This didn't happen often, but it wasn't unusual. He felt more comfortable away from his brothers, even to the extent of being away from where they *might* be.

Hannah was on a shopping trip. Her mother had determined that she needed some new blouses, as the ones she had were beginning to get a little tight across the chest.

Corinne had gotten used to Timmy's presence in association with her daughter, but a shopping trip for clothes seemed to be a small step over the line. She wasn't comfortable with his being along.

Timmy knew that any short interruption between them would be quickly made up. There wasn't much they didn't share in total intimacy. He went over to Hannah's drawer for shirts. With both hands, he was able to move it just enough to be able to reach into it. Her furniture worked better than his. He got a shirt out and tried it on.

The first thing he noticed was that the buttons were on the wrong side. He played with it a while, finally getting it buttoned, and keeping it on while he bounced silently around the room.

The shirt, (or blouse), wasn't tight across *his* chest. Well, that might be because he wasn't growing …

Timmy stopped, aghast at the thought. He had trouble even thinking it to himself.

He wasn't growing *boobs*.

He stood silently in Hannah's room, wearing her shirt, (and nothing else), and thought about her recent growth. He had known Hannah for … quite a long time now. He could slip into her body as easily, more easily actually, than he could put on this shirt. Her physical growth and burgeoning maturity had caught up with his head start. He let the shirt fall through him.

He picked up the shirt, which was still buttoned. He folded it carefully, and put it back into the drawer. The drawer closed more easily than it had opened.

Timmy moved over and stood in front of Hannah's mirror, looking at himself. It wasn't something he did very often. Among other things, his image never changed. He was looking at a nearly twelve-year old boy, quite naked, and particularly hairless, other than the wavy mop of hair on his head.

Except for his height, his skinny legs and shoulders, the features of his body were almost child-like. Well, naturally it was child-like for a twelve-year old, but developmentally it seemed more like a six or seven year old.

He was tall enough, but in the middle he was like a baby. Apparently, the being responsible for taking away his substance, and leaving only his spirit, had recognized that any continuing development, or even any particular utility of his plumbing, was simply not to be.

Timmy had been ensconced in a timeless state, almost as if he had been photographed in a loop of repetitive physical activity.

That changelessness did not leave any room for Timmy's incipient maturity. Not only was it stopped; it also seemed to have receded slightly. Perhaps that was the price of letting an alien or otherworldly being implement a head-to-toe makeover for you. His, or its, standards might not be your own, and the "flyover country" along the way from the head to the toe might simply fly right by.

He could not recall whether what he was currently seeing was the way he had been before the "accident", but it was possible his memories were affected too. Would such a being "simplify" him in the course of changing him utterly? It was a credible possibility.

How he maintained what appeared to be a biological organism, he didn't understand, and would likely never know. Obviously it wasn't biological.

His shape was the same, but his *surfaces* were different. His downy hair follicles seemed to have been completely eradicated. His skin *had* been simplified, he realized, simply for the sake of eliminating hair follicles, sweat glands, and other microscopic features.

It seemed likely his maturational and biological complexities had also been simplified, for the sake of getting rid of his adolescent, growth, digestive, and immunity-response hormones. All of that complicatedness, shrugged off and discarded as unnecessary!

Ordinarily, this wouldn't bother him. It was thinking about Hannah growing more mature that was rather rocking him back on his heels. Timmy rocked back on his heels and smiled at himself.

He knew what Oliver and Dexter would be saying and thinking about it. They would think that he had a wonderful opportunity to caress and fondle Hannah's new boobs. But Timmy realized that he did not have, and *would never* have, the hormonal stimulant to make him think that way, that was making *them* think that way, and that was turning their bodies into something resembling werewolves. They were starting to grow hair on their faces, and on their arms and chests, and especially in their armpits and other pits.

Their muscles were growing too. Werewolves for sure!

Timmy looked down at his body's reflection. His quite literally *useless* appendage didn't bother him anymore. At one time he had been embarrassed about it. But his gonads had apparently never been activated or had been deactivated; he had no need to urinate, and no portion of his genitalia served any purpose at all, even decorative.

By now, having been naked most of the time in front of everyone who knew him, it was like having a nose in the middle of one's face. No one ever mentioned it, and it was simply never discussed.

Timmy pondered the matter. He was stuck in a pre-pubescent state, and would remain so. Meanwhile, his little girl was growing up.

He took a deep breath, and grinned a big smile. There might not be a pubescence for him in his future, but he would be sharing *hers!*

Timmy had confidence that Hannah would not be attracted to his brothers. That was certainly a relief! At the moment then, her only romantic partner might appear to be Jeffrey. That didn't bother him. He had already shared Jeff's body, and Jeff adored Hannah as much as he did.

He studied his hands. They too were boy-like; childlike. Dexter and Oliver had calluses on their hands, and freckles on their faces from exposure to sunlight.

Timmy's hands were soft and delicate. Even Hannah had more strength than he did! His skin was unmarked and milky, almost translucent, except where it sparkled and glittered.

He thought about the buttons and buttonholes he had just worked with. He knew that he could teach himself to switch right hand and left hand. He had even practiced writing with the opposite hand. But now he was thinking about what buttons *do*. They have a special purpose, to travel *through* things by *twisting*, and then hold their positions in that place by *not* twisting.

Timmy stared down at his weak, small, but *magical*, child's hand. He had the feeling that he might be on the verge of a discovery.

There was a small bit of loose change on Hannah's dresser. Timmy picked up a dime and began manipulating it, holding it in his hand and twirling it around his fingers. Perhaps this could be his "button". Maybe what he wanted to do was impossible, but at least it would help to start small.

When Hannah returned, Timmy was deep in contemplation. He was floating about three feet in the air, in the lotus position, in her bathroom.

Seeing him there, she was surprised, but she remained quiet, putting her purchases on the bed as she decided where to store them.

After a few minutes, Timmy came floating out of the bathroom, still maintaining his odd posture, even though he had to turn sideways to get through the door. He was still manipulating the dime.

"I borrowed a dime from you," he said.

"You may keep it, if you wish," she responded. "What are you doing?"

"Just thinking, really," Timmy smiled, "about buttons and buttonholes."

Hannah raised her eyebrows. "Okay. Hey! You want to see what I got?"

"Sure!" Timmy relaxed from his position, but still remained floating in the air, as if he were seated in a chair.

Quickly, Hannah took her clothes off, except for her panties. She opened the packages and spread the new clothes out, carefully removing all pins and fasteners.

Timmy watched her, looking closely to see if what he had suspected was true, that she was beginning to bloom somewhat in the chest region. He slid sideways for a moment to confirm his observation. Hannah smiled at him.

"Wait a moment, and we can make this more efficient," Timmy said.

"What do you mean?"

Timmy moved his body into hers. By now, this process was virtually instantaneous. Once inside her, he made sure to paint himself faithfully exactly as her exterior skin was shaped, taking note in particular of her recent growth.

Then he exited again, but instead of being himself, he was displaying the copy of Hannah that he made. He looked exactly like her twin, except that she was wearing panties, and his version was entirely nude. There was also the matter of his hairstyle, which differed from hers. Still, he looked quite feminine.

Hannah stared at him. "Oh, my god! I didn't know you could do that!"

"I wasn't sure myself," Timmy said softly, trying to bring his voice closer to her vocal range. He stood up straight and proud, and turned for her.

"Oh my goodness! I ... I never imagined!" She reached out, gently, to touch her image.

Timmy stood still, letting her fingers brush across his skin.

"You're ... I mean I'm, I guess ... very pretty ..." she paused.

"You're beautiful! Every inch of you!" Timmy smiled, "You just never get a chance to see it."

Timmy went over to the new clothes, selecting one blouse and putting it on.

Hannah watched him in curiosity.

Again, he straightened and turned for her, so she could see what she would look like when wearing the new garment.

Hannah giggled. "I think that looks very nice, but I'm pretty sure I shouldn't walk around with my butt hanging out!"

Timmy looked over his shoulder, as if that would allow him to see what she was looking at. Hannah giggled again.

Timmy shook out of the blouse, and caught it as it was falling. He placed it to the side as he reached for another. "You can try some on too, you know." He smiled at her as he put on the second blouse and began buttoning it.

Hannah sat on the bed and simply watched him.

Unperturbed, Timmy went through every new blouse, putting it on, twirling to show her what it looked like. He walked across the floor as if walking down a fashion runway. In all, he was pleased to put on quite a show for her.

Eventually, he stood naked again, waiting for her response.

Hannah stood up and walked around him, looking closely and from several viewpoints. "You make a very good me," she said.

"You're very pretty, you know." Timmy said.

"You draw a nice picture." Hannah responded. "How did you make your ... dangly bits ... stop dangling?"

Timmy looked down. Sure enough, his boyness was thoroughly suppressed. He shrugged his shoulders. "It's just like being poured into a container, I guess. I just took the shape I was in."

"Why don't you ..." Hannah bit her lip a little, "why don't you see if you can make something like clothes appear? You know, just immaterial stuff that isn't really there, but looks like it is."

"I ..." Timmy looked a little confused. "Wait a minute." He moved into her again.

This time, he extended his surface sense to the *outside* of her panties.

Then he exited her once more. When he made his surface this time, it included a thin portion of space that looked like transparent panties. In a moment, he made them pink.

Hannah's panties were a pale yellow. She got down on her knees and examined his replica very closely. It looked, and felt, exactly like an article of clothing.

Rising, Hannah swung her hand rather aggressively at his butt. Her hand passed through him entirely, but his panties stayed in place.

Gently, Hannah wrapped her arms around him and kissed him.

"Wow!" Timmy stood very still. In this condition, he was exactly the same height as Hannah. He didn't want to move, lest the magic disappear somehow.

Hannah smiled. "That may seem like a very small step, and not particularly useful, but I'm betting that you're just beginning to understand its potential." She kissed him again.

Timmy looked down. Slowly his panties turned white; a nice, bright white, representing very clean cloth.

He concentrated. His panties slowly changed into shorts, the kind he normally tried to wear, and which constantly fell off. His body changed also, back into his normal male appearance. But this time he wasn't naked.

He was wearing shorts. He looked again at them, and concentrated. Pink flowers began appearing on them, as if they were made of a floral print.

Gently, Hannah reached down and stroked his butt, her fingers tracing over the bump of the fabric's waistband and hemline.

Timmy looked up. His eyes were open very wide.

Hannah smiled at him.

Timmy stepped back a pace. In a moment, he was also wearing a white tee shirt, with pink bands around the neck and arms. He turned in place for her.

Hannah clapped her hands together, and hopped with excitement. "That's wonderful, Timmy! Now you won't have to stay hidden from the world!"

He looked up at her with astonishment. Slowly he walked over to the wall leading to his room, and passed through it.

Seconds later, he was back, still "wearing" his self-generated clothes.

Hannah clapped again. She came to him and embraced him again, kissing him with her eyes closed.

Timmy rotated around the kiss, and entered her once more. When Hannah opened her eyes again, he was no longer visible.

"You're growing up, Hannah." Timmy said inside her. "I think you've already passed me now. You're already older than I will ever be."

Hannah walked over and looked in her own mirror. Naked except for her yellow panties, she studied her reflection. "They're just starting, aren't they?"

"Yes. If you don't want them to be too big, you should continue exercising strenuously. Maybe we can dance more."

"It's never a strain when you're with me."

"It's fun for me too." Timmy admitted.

"Are you going to let me kiss Jeffy?" Hannah teased.

"Sure," Timmy answered, "I like him too, but I especially like kissing." Once more, he kissed her from the inside.

Hannah smiled. "Growing up won't be so bad, then, will it?"

"No," Timmy answered, making her lips smile, "it won't be bad at all."

15. What Is This Place?

Timmy, Hannah, and Jeffrey were sitting around a campfire, looking, when their eyes opened, into the flames. All were naked. Jeff looked around. "What is this place, and why are we naked?"

"Your glasses are gone, too," Timmy responded, "This is my memory-realm, a place in my mind where I have put things I want to keep safe and treasure."

Jeffrey put his hands up to his face, confirming that his face was naked, too.

"That's very flattering, I suppose," Hannah remarked, "but why are we naked?" Jeffrey nodded in agreement to the question.

"When I was inside each of you recently, I made a complete memory scan of every memory you had in your brain, and I recorded it here." He looked around. "This is an artificial construct of my own mind, a place I developed to be able to keep memories preserved and information available in an accessible pattern."

"I don't remember our ever being naked together all at the same time. This would seem to be a false memory." Hannah persisted, but she was smiling.

"It's all *very* false. You two are composites; your minds and your bodies don't match up. For Jeff, I fixed his eyes, but his body is the one I first encountered, although his mind has nearly three additional years of memories in it. You *appear* younger, Jeff, but you're older than you look."

"For you, I only backed up your body's age to about a year ago, before your recent teen growth spurt. The net effect is that it reduced your chest development just a little bit so it wouldn't be noticeable and embarrassing in these circumstances. In other words, I "simplified" your image the way mine was simplified."

"This image is one you still have of yourself, one you were pleased to have, and it's a stable plateau of your development."

Hannah looked down at her chest, a little confused that her memory of it was different from its current appearance. She put her hands up to confirm, as Jeffrey had done with his face, that something was indeed different. Her brow furrowed.

Timmy continued, "Our body images are always naked. It takes a special effort to put clothes on your own mental image of yourself."

"It wouldn't take much effort for me to remember my glasses!" Jeff persisted, "I've gotten pretty used to having them!"

"But you don't need them here." Timmy suggested. "They wouldn't be of any use."

"They wouldn't be of any use ..." Hannah repeated softly, her hands moving idly across her chest.

Jeffrey started looking around. The dancing fire was not a conclusive test, but the glistening leaves and stark branches spread out from their location like a well-managed park. "I can see!" Jeff exclaimed, "but it is still dark, so there isn't much to see."

"There isn't much here yet." Timmy continued, "So far, I've only brought the most important items."

Jeff and Hannah looked at each other.

"What else do you plan to bring, and what are we supposed to do here, other than not grow breasts?" inquired Hannah.

Timmy smiled ruefully. "I've been stuck for more than three years in a pre-pubescent state. Believe me, you can get used to it, just as you can get used to being naked."

He looked into the fire for a moment.

"Anyway, we can talk, of course. I wanted to be able to consult with you before I try certain things out in the real world. As to what else to bring over, I thought it would be good to have our house, and maybe the school, perhaps even the church. What would you like?"

Hannah looked thoughtful. "Did you ever think about consulting with us *before* you brought us naked into your world?"

"Are you saying naked bothers you?" Timmy asked with a smile.

"I think you already know the answer to that. Maybe we should ask Jeff."

Jeff stood up, brushing off his derriere, and walked a little distance from the fire. He looked up at the sky, meandered around a few trees, and then slowly wandered back.

"This should probably bother me more than it seems to. Among other things, I'm not used to walking barefoot, but I'm not feeling any pain from it. And I should probably be feeling embarrassed and shy about being naked in front of you two, but for some reason I'm not." He looked at Timmy. "Maybe your copy of me is off a little."

Timmy smiled. "Your observation is evidence, of a sort, that your mind is fully intact, and that your memories are faithful transcriptions. What is unlikely to come over are the chemical keys and stimulants. That's something I had to get used to, myself. Essentially, you aren't embarrassed because you aren't afraid, and you aren't afraid because those chemical messengers don't work here."

Jeff looked down at himself, and looked thoughtful. "If chemicals don't work here, I shouldn't have any problem, because as I understand it, it's chemicals that make us … us boys, that is … do the weird things we do."

"Boys … yeah. That's right." Timmy said gently.

Hannah got up, brushing herself off as Jeff had done. She went to him and hugged him. Then she gave him a kiss. Jeff smiled at her.

Hannah turned, and shrugged. "I guess you're right. No chemistry. Sorry, Jeff."

"Ah!" he said. "*That*'s what that was about. Well, you're welcome to try again when you want to, but I'll have to agree. The fact that you didn't feel "chemistry" should bother me, but because of the *lack* of chemistry, it doesn't; if that makes sense."

Hannah gave him another quick peck on the cheek, and a squeeze, before turning back to Timmy. "Okay, what's next? Is there anything else to see?"

Jeff took the opportunity to compare his height with hers. It was obvious that she was taller in comparison to him … no wait, it was that he was shorter in comparison to her. He had the body of an eleven-year old, while hers was that of a twelve-year old. It didn't bother him at all that she was closer in size to him now.

Timmy rose without standing, and then stretched his legs down to the ground. "Well, I guess we could go look at the house, if you want to. It's over that way." He gestured, and started walking along that direction. Hannah and Jeff followed.

As they walked, a general light came from above, and the fire diminished and went out. The trees thinned, and the ground slowly changed itself into Timmy's back yard.

They walked up and stood looking at the dugout, in its secluded darkness, and the beckoning lights of the Miller kitchen.

"Is anybody home?"

Timmy shook his head no. "Where would you like to go? Entertainment, reading, music?"

"I'd like to see my bedroom," Hannah said.

By some coincidence, they all seemed to blink at the same time, and they found themselves standing in Hannah's bedroom. She blinked again, and looked around. Absolutely everything was just as she had left it.

Hannah looked at Jeff. In the brighter light, his nakedness was more apparent and noticeable. "I'm used to seeing Timmy, and he's used to seeing me. You're very handsome, Jeff. You have a nice body."

Jeff glanced down, and shrugged. "I like looking at you, too. You're very pretty, Hannah."

"It's kinda weird to think that we're here like this, and our parents aren't around. Isn't it?" Hannah said. She went over and sat on the bed.

"I don't think I've ever been in your bedroom, Hannah. It's nice."

Timmy was looking around also. "I think maybe it's time we fixed this problem too." He looked meaningfully at the wall that separated

Hannah's bedroom from his own. With a gesturing finger, he directed a doorway to grow in the wall.

Much more quickly than the door that had grown on the level below, the wall accommodatingly opened up to form a doorway about three feet across. There was no door for the doorway, on either side of the wall. It was a new, permanent, opening.

Timmy walked through, and Jeff and Hannah followed him. Rather abruptly, Timmy banished the decorations and mementoes of his older brothers, and gave the room a brighter, fresher appearance. The bunk beds, for the first time in ages, were neatly made up with fresh, bright coverlets.

"I'll take the top bunk!" Timmy said, "You can have the bottom one, Jeff."

"Wait, I'm going to live here?" Jeff looked puzzled.

"Well, you're going to *be* here, anyway. If you want to lie down, you can do it here. You can also read and study here, or whatever else you may want to do."

Jeff and Hannah looked at each other.

"When will we be able to go home?" Jeff asked softly.

Timmy floated up and settled lightly on the top bunk. He looked over at them calmly. "You *are* home. This is your home now."

Hannah was staring at him. She turned to look at Jeff for a moment. "You do what you want, Jeff, but I'm going to start wearing clothes." She went back through the doorway.

Timmy rolled over on his back. He placed his hands on his face.

Jeff thought he heard a soft word. It sounded like, "Damn!" He looked around.

"I'm guessing; just guessing, you know, that these closets and drawers are holding *my* clothes for me, right?"

With a note of resignation in his voice, Timmy answered again, softly. "Well, sure. Yeah. Of course."

Jeff walked over to the closet. Taking a deep breath, he opened it.

His clothes and shoes were inside.

The next morning, without explaining why, Timmy was walking around wearing pink floral shorts, and a white tee shirt with pink arm and collar bands. Jeff put on a pair of khaki shorts and a blue and white striped polo shirt.

Hannah wore a pullover shirt and denim play shorts with a bib front. She looked darling.

"Alright then, what's on the agenda for today?" Hannah asked without prelude.

"Well, we're still in memory here. I want to get your approval to copy some more people."

"Specifically who," said Jeffrey, "and *how?*"

Timmy shrugged. "I think it takes a little bit of time. It may be noticeable. Maybe I'll get quicker with practice."

"Hmm. If it's noticeable, it might be scary." Hannah considered, "Maybe you should try someone who won't be afraid, and see how it works out."

"Who?" asked Jeffrey.

"My mother." Hannah suggested. "She thinks you're an angel. Maybe she'll think she's getting a visitation or something. At least we can find out if it's scary. She's pretty sensitive to all that supernatural crap."

Timmy blinked, and looked at her. "You're something supernatural yourself at the moment, you know."

Hannah smiled, "Maybe so, but I'm not crap." She fluffed her curls and made a short bow.

"Okay, but I'd also like to try a stealth operation, just to see if I can pull that off. I want to add to my repertoire of knowledge and skills without having to spend a hundred years studying."

Now Jeffrey stared at him. "You get scary sometimes, you know?"

Hannah looked thoughtful. "Think you could sneak up on my dad? He's pretty alert, and if he senses something weird he might start comparing notes with mom. We could get some valuable data right here at home," She looked around, "I mean, if here were here, that is."

"All right, here's how we'll work it out ..."

<hr>

Timmy materialized them back into the real world on a Saturday morning when both were present in his house. That is, he picked a day when both were present, and planted the memories they shared of their visit in his memory-realm back into their brains. Then they went hunting for victims to assault.

"Mom?" Hannah found Corinne just finishing up some chores in the kitchen. "Are you ready to take a break? I wanted to try a relaxation technique out on you."

Corinne looked around. "Well, I guess I could sit down for a moment. What did you have in mind?"

"Oh, it's nothing special. Just something I was reading about. It's not even anything like a "laying on of hands" although I guess it might look like that." Hannah looked a little flustered and embarrassed. "Anyway, all I have to do is put my hands on the sides of your head and try to focus on sending good vibrations, or "positive mental energy" into you. At the very least it should relieve a little stress."

"All right. I don't see how it could hurt anything. I'll sit over here, then. Alright?"

"Perfect. I promise not to hurt you."

Corinne smiled at that, and sat down to relax.

Hannah bent over her, rubbing her hands together. "Close your eyes, Mom. Try to relax."

She gently stroked her mother's temples, and then placed her hands on each side of Corinne's head.

Timmy moved gently into Corinne's body from Hannah's, trying to avoid as much friction as possible. Only after he was fully inside, and stretched out completely, did he begin the memory sweep. He tried to make it seem like a wave of nostalgia, as fleeting memories might trigger brief visions, sights, and even smells. Considering the wealth and volume of information gleaned, the whole process took very little actual time.

It was only possible because Timmy had expanded and opened his mind to all the latent memories available, within a contiguous space inside the resting woman's brain. No actual travel of energy or neuron activity was needed. It was like a contact print or rubber mold. It took place in microseconds of real time, but covered decades of four-dimensional data. In just a few heartbeats, it was over. Timmy moved away, leaving a lingering sense of relaxation as he departed back into Hannah's body.

As quickly as that, everything that Hannah's mother knew; everything that she had experienced and thought about afterwards, and even every tiny detail that she had forgotten, Timmy now knew. Mrs. McMasters was an exceptionally gifted, observant, and talented person, who loved life and all who shared it with her. More than anything, she doted on Hannah and adored her husband.

Hannah held the pose for a little while, and then broke contact gently herself and stepped back. She waited quietly.

Corinne opened her eyes with a look of astonishment. "That was so real! It's like you woke up my whole mind!" She looked dazed. "I don't think that's a relaxation technique, Hannah. I feel very energized and curious."

"But I didn't hurt you, right?"

"No, no. I feel fine. I feel great! You might have a future as a therapist!" She got up carefully and looked closely at Hannah. Then she shook her head and smiled. "I'd better get back to work, or I might be tempted to just sit here and bask in the glory of the moment. Thank you, Sweetheart!"

Hannah smiled and backed away, still feeling a bit tense from the subterfuge.

"Well?" she asked Timmy internally, once they were safely into a different room.

"I've got it. It's enormous. Give me some time to get it into position. One thing I can tell you now though. I thought I loved you before, but now I've got a double-dose of it. I can remember giving birth to you, and holding and cuddling you for *years!*"

Hannah stood motionless for a bit, digesting that information. Jeffrey approached.

"Yeah, yeah. I'm okay. You guys go ahead. I'll just wait here for you." Jeffrey hugged her.

During that embrace, Timmy moved into Jeff.

Jeff took another look at Hannah, who nodded, and then he went in search of Mr. Theo.

"He was out on the porch, reading the newspaper." Jeff told Timmy silently.

"I'm ready," Timmy echoed back.

16. We Can Go Swimming

"So, we're back here again?" Hannah observed, leaning against the doorway from her bedroom to Timmy's.

Jeff opened his eyes and began stretching. He swung his legs out of the bunk bed and yawned. "Morning, I guess, Hannah." He blinked. "What in the world are you wearing?"

She grinned. "My dance outfit. I've got some for you two to wear also. Timmy has danced with me before."

"Ballerina dancing?" Jeff's eyes got big. "You've got to be kidding!"

"Ballet dancing," Hannah corrected, "and I'm not kidding at all. Come on, get up!"

Jeff stood up and stretched again. He was wearing white skivvies. Hannah looked amused.

"Oops. Sorry. This is what I use for pajamas when I'm at home."

"Well, I guess you're home now. You can use my bathroom if you need to."

"That won't be needed here," Timmy answered for him. "We don't eat or drink in the realm, although that could change as I add features." He floated down from the top bunk, dressed in his now standard pink flower-print shorts. There was no tee shirt.

Jeff shrugged. "Okay, what did you want me to wear, then?"

Hannah smiled. "Here, try these on." She held up a miniscule pair of leggings. "They're for dancing in."

Jeff was shaking his head, but he reached for the leggings. "Me, a ballerina." He rolled his eyes. "I'm only doing this because I love you, you know."

"Everybody loves me," Hannah responded, "It's a rule here."

Timmy looked thoughtful, but nodded slowly.

Turning his back on Hannah, Jeff shucked out of his skivvies and pulled on the leggings, stretching them enormously to cover his lower half. Then he put one leg out in front of himself and bowed.

Hannah applauded. "That's the spirit!"

"I'll just wear this," Timmy said, "Go ahead and start your music."

Hannah just tilted her head and nodded. The music started. "Timmy and I will begin, and then I want you to do everything that Timmy has done, alright, Jeffy?"

Jeff was still looking at the apparition he presented in the tights, but he nodded.

Their hours of practice together had helped considerably, and in this memory realm, Timmy was as strong as he wanted to be. He and Hannah danced a short segment for Jeff to observe, and then Timmy backed away to let Jeff take the lead.

Intention counted for a lot in one's ability to perform in the realm, so Jeff displayed a fine form, considering that he had never actually danced a day in his life, even for practice.

After what seemed an extended session, they stopped to assess their progress.

"I don't understand it. We've been going at it for a while now, and I'm not even tired!"

"That's the way it works here, Jeff. Let me point out, though, that the things you learn and practice here won't do your real-world body any good until I upgrade your memories from here." Timmy explained.

"You mean I'll be able to dance for real?" He looked at Hannah.

"Actually, yes, if you want to." Timmy assured him.

Hannah jumped up and down, applauding. "I hope you'll want to, Jeff. Timmy is a fine partner, but he can't actually lift me up when we're dancing for real. You should be able to do it as if you had been practicing for years! Everyone will be so surprised."

"Wow! This makes coming to this place have real meaning then! I'm predicting though, that when I'm out in the real world, where the chemicals live, I'll be as embarrassed as I could ever be, to be dressed like this in public!"

"You dance with me, and I'll kiss you for real. Then we'll see if the chemicals are working!"

Timmy raised his eyebrows, but he nodded in agreement with this as well.

"Well, all right then." Jeff looked around. "What else shall we do? It still seems kinda early, if time means anything here."

"Time means nothing here, as you rightly suspect. But if you want to, we can go swimming."

"Sure!" Hannah and Jeff both assented quickly.

Timmy smiled. "A change of clothing is required." He blinked his eyes, and exactly that quickly, Hannah and Jeff were both wearing racing swimsuit bottoms, but no tops.

"Hey!" Hannah objected.

"That's the uniform here for swimming, or close to it. You'll see what I mean. Come on with me." Timmy led them out the bedroom door and down the stairs to the main floor of the house.

There they could see the pocket doors between the two houses, open as usual. Timmy took them around to what had been a closet under the stairway in the real house, but here it was another stairway.

It led to a landing, where they turned a hundred and twenty degrees, and continued down another flight of stairs to a second landing, before turning once more. In the memory realm, Timmy and Hannah's basement contained a huge indoor swimming pool.

There were people already swimming in it.

Hannah and Jeffrey looked at each other.

"Hello," Timmy called. "Corrie, Teddy, and Ange, I'd like you to meet Hannah and Jeffrey."

The three children swam over to the pool-side and climbed out. Corrie had short blonde hair, wet now of course, and she was wearing what looked like a small, silvery chain-mail bikini bottom fastened to curved metal ellipses about six inches in diameter, which were cupped snugly around her hips.

The others had similar design "swim suits" made of what looked like metal, with the squashed oval loops binding smoothly on their hips. Teddy's bikini was a bronze color. All were topless, and none appeared to be any older than ten.

"Hi!" Teddy said, "We need some new people! There are only so many games three people can play."

"We'll get more," Timmy said, "don't worry."

"Teddy …", Hannah said, looking at him closely, "is your last name McMasters?"

"Yes it is! Do I know you?"

"Not yet, but we're going to be good friends, for sure!" Hannah looked again at Corrie. "And you're Corrie?"

"Corinne, actually," Corrie answered, "Corinne Meadows. Everyone calls me Corrie. Hi!"

"And I'm Angela Somers. Call me Ange! This is a great pool!"

Jeff had a look of baffled confusion slowly being overcome by dawning comprehension. He looked over at Timmy and raised his eyebrows. Timmy nodded.

Jeff shook his head as if that might dispel the craziness.

Hannah reached out and held Corrie's hands, lifting them. "Let's look at these outfits! They look so neat!"

Teddy smiled. "They're the best! They're light as anything, they don't get in your way, and the water drains away as soon as you get out. You're dry in no time. It feels like you aren't wearing anything at all."

"I wouldn't have been surprised," Jeffrey muttered softly.

Ange raised her hands. "Up here, I'm *not* wearing anything! But I don't have anything worth hiding, so who cares, huh?" She spread her arms and smiled coyly.

Hannah nodded, "I have hopes, but at the moment, I'm afraid you're right. A top on me wouldn't make any more sense than a top on Jeffy."

"Oh, thanks! At least I'm not dressed as a ballerina." He looked at Teddy's suit. "How do you take that off? I don't see any fasteners."

Teddy looked down. "Huh? Well, I haven't had to take it off yet, so I'll worry about it later!"

Ange and Corrie were also looking at their bikinis. Corrie fumbled with the curved metal loop for a moment and then gave up with a shrug. It was pressed against her hip so snugly that she couldn't even get a finger under it.

She looked over at her companion. "Hey, we match!" She put her arm around Ange's shoulder. Angela grinned, with a bright, happy smile.

"Are we going to swim, then?" Ange looked around.

Quickly they all jumped into the pool and began playing.

Later, perhaps hours later, (and who could tell?), they climbed out again, to consider what other mischief or activity they could find.

"Anyone for badminton?" Timmy suggested.

"Lead the way, badmister!" Jeff exclaimed.

Timmy showed them a second staircase, which climbed in a spiral in one corner of the enormous room. It took them up to a strange sliding door, which admitted them into a really confined circular space. When they closed that door, another one slid open, and they found themselves in the dugout!

Timmy got the badminton equipment out of the cabinets, and led them off to the side yard, where a net was already in place. Quickly they chose teams and began playing yet another energetic activity.

The sun felt warm on their bodies as they jumped and swung the rackets. Their voices echoed around the very spacious yard, and they had a wonderful time.

More of what could have been hours passed, and they stopped with the score either tied or forgotten.

"I think some refreshment is in order," suggested Hannah. "Timmy?"

"Um, ice cream and root beer?"

A cheer went up. The troop decamped to the Miller's kitchen, where Timmy quickly passed around several frosty mugs of root beer, and small bowls of vanilla ice cream.

The children drank, and ate the ice cream, and nearly wore out their smiles beaming at each other.

"I'm thinking a bit of a nap is in order," Tim suggested, "shall we find some beds?"

Holding hands, Ange and Corrie followed Timmy up the stairs, where rooms had appeared in addition to those of Hannah and Tim.

Ange and Corrie climbed into a bed together. With Ange's arm wrapped protectively around Corrie, they were asleep in seconds.

Teddy found an adjacent room, which had another bathroom, and went to bed there.

Hannah continued through to her room, and Jeff and Timmy went back to their bunks. In minutes, the house was quiet again.

17. Blowing Bubbles

"What, more?" Jeff asked, looking into Timmy's eyes.

"Yes. I have in mind to conscript your mother, and I think we might be able to waylay Mister Cannon. There's some work going on in the area, and I think he might be there." Timmy certainly looked adequately conspiratorial, with his piratical pink and white shorts.

"My mother!"

"Why not? You said she was a nurse, right? Remember that I'm gathering knowledge, and I'll certainly want to get as much medical knowledge as possible."

"That's not the point!" Jeff said with exasperation. "How do you think I'm going to feel if I see my mother turned into a child playing in your swimming pool?"

"I don't know." Timmy said calmly, "How *are* you going to feel about that?"

"She's my <u>mother</u>!"

"Yeah? Don't you think she would enjoy being young and playing games too?"

"Aaaaagh!"

"Look, I know you're not used to thinking of things like this, but preserving her memories is a way to preserve her life, her unique qualities and the things she finds special and wonderful. Among other things, that's a process that ended up producing <u>you</u>! I doubt that you really know your mother as a person, anyway. Don't you want to interact with her on an equal footing, instead of someone who is always and only worrying about you?"

"Not really, no. On *this* side, the chemicals work, and I've found myself looking at girls. I don't want one of them to be my mother. Heck, I'm even growing hair! And maybe muscles!"

Timmy shrugged. "Have you talked with Hannah? She might be able to tell you something from the other side of this situation. She's already met her own mom and dad as equals, and been given a chance to find out what they're really like."

Jeff considered. "I like them. They're fun."

Timmy raised his eyebrows.

Jeff blew out his breath in exasperation. Drawing in a calming breath, he looked at Timmy.

"But *why?*"

"It's difficult to explain. Let's say that I'm doing research, trying to find out what I'm supposed to do in the future. I've got a chance, now, to get knowledge, experience, and wisdom from people that I know do have it, and have the right kind of wisdom for my purposes."

"Who knows more than your mom and dad, huh? For a kid, that seems to be logical." Jeff leaned back.

"Well, logical at this stage anyway. If we were teenagers, we'd have the opposite opinion."

"*How can you know that?*" Jeff stared at him.

Tim smiled. "You've been living your life. I've been living everyone's. Collective wisdom is not wiser, or more right, but it is instructive, based merely on long-term observation."

Jeff threw up his hands. "I can't argue with that!"

"We're not arguing. I'm trying to get you to help me Xerox your mom's brain."

"Xerox?"

"You know, make a copy. It's not going to hurt her."

"Oh. I know that. It's just … you're going to make her a little kid, aren't you?"

"Not little. About ten in apparent age. As I told Hannah, it's a plateau region for mental development. The brain is fully grown, but it's still plastic enough to learn a tremendous amount. It's better than what I did to Hannah, backing her up."

"You're backing all of them up!" Jeff pointed out.

"In more ways than one. But I meant, making her revert back to a stage before what she currently remembers. I think it bothered her that her growing breasts were made to disappear."

"I never saw them, darn it."

"They're a little misshapen when they first start. They have to get a little volume to them before they start getting really pretty. For her to fit in with the other girls, I had to make her look more like them."

"It's complicated, isn't it?" Jeff commiserated.

"Much more than you could imagine. That's been my whole problem. I got stuck in a stage emotionally that precedes what everyone is expecting; what *you're* feeling now. I *can't* mature emotionally, and *I don't know how to provide that for them!*"

"So you can't make all of them look like, well, really well-built?" Jeff raised his eyebrows.

"Now you're *really* talking complicated! Not the physical part. We all know what we like to look at, right?" Jeff nodded enthusiastically.

"But that's when the mental complications start. You get jealousy, competition, girls ganging up on other girls. It's hateful and I didn't want any part of it, even if it would be nicer to look at."

Jeff slumped in resignation. "Well, in that case, since I won't have to be ogling my mother's bosom, I guess I can help you make a copy of her."

Timmy smiled, "She's going to be a prize, I'm sure of it."

Jeff looked thoughtful. "Maybe we could start on Mr. Cannon. I may need more practice before I'm good at mindnapping people."

"Just keep in *mind*, I'm not stealing their minds, I'm stealing their *memories*."

Jeff nodded. "Let's go for a bike ride."

They found the construction site, but Jeff shook his head. "I can't get near him. They'd freak out to have a kid go in there and be in danger."

They watched, studying the situation. A workman or two saw Jeff and gave a casual wave, and then went immediately back to work.

"Yeah, they'd see me, but they wouldn't let me get close."

"I've got an idea." Timmy said inside Jeff. "If he gets close enough to a wall, and stays put, I can approach from inside the wall."

"But how will you get over there?"

"That's easy. I'll just go underground, like a mole."

Jeff nodded. "Once you leave me, I can't guide you. You'll be on your own."

Timmy shrugged, inside Jeff, without making the lad move in any way. Jeff rolled his eyes.

"Worst case scenario, Jeff, is that someone will report having seen a ghost."

Jeff made a funny half-grin with his face. "Well, I'll be here, waiting for you. Try not to knock me over when you come back. Good Luck!"

"Thanks!" Timmy looked around to make sure no one was looking at them, and then oozed out of Jeff into the ground.

Jeff felt the departure, but decided to maintain his position waiting for Timmy's return.

This was something Timmy had never practiced, although he would have been great at "hide-and-seek". Moving silently was not a problem for him.

Slowly he worked his way to a nearby wall, waiting for the right opportunity. When Roger Cannon picked up a power-saw and prepared to cut a plank, Timmy moved in, rising like an insubstantial wave out of the ocean.

Timing his entry, Timmy pulsed into the contractor just as he started the saw. Timmy hoped that any sensation would be masked by the vibration and noise.

Inside Mr. Cannon, Timmy held still until the cutting operation was completed. When Roger set the saw back down, Timmy adjusted himself into Roger's body. As Roger straightened up, Timmy began the mind-sweep.

By now he had perfected the technique. Copying a life's worth of memories was no more difficult than taking a high-resolution photograph, but only if someone had Timmy's ability to share physical space with the mind being copied.

Mr. Cannon appeared to sense, in some way, that something was amiss. He stood up straight to steady himself, as if feeling a bit of dizziness. Timmy took the opportunity to sink into the floor.

A moment later, he was back inside Jeff. "I've got it, Jeff. This one was well worth the effort. Mr. Cannon knows a lot!"

Jeff saddled up for the ride back to the Miller house. He looked around to see if there were anyone to wave goodbye to, but no one was watching. In the end, it seemed all too easy to do. A lifetime of memories, slipping away like a scrap of paper being blown by the wind. At least they weren't being lost, but instead were being preserved, in a way.

Jeff enjoyed riding his bike. The pleasure was made no less by having Timmy as a companion. Not only was he no burden at all, but his presence also seemed to give energy instead of taking it.

"Will you have to visit the realm to download the memories, Tim?" Jeff asked his companion silently, as he was pedaling.

"That's not the way it works, Jeff. The realm is inside me; all of it. When I visit it, I'm already there. So are you and all the others, just waiting for me to be there, so that the time can start ticking."

"How can it all fit inside you? The house, the pool, all the people and all the memories, all of it in your head?"

"Well, where's my head, Jeff? You're not carrying it, are you? My head might weigh more than yours! It's there; believe me. It's all a part of that in-between dimension that makes everything I do possible, including blowing bubbles."

"Blowing bubbles? What's tough about that?"

"Where does the breath come from, Jeff?"

"What do you mean?"

"When I want to blow on something, air comes out of me. It only stops when I want it to stop. I can blow on something for five minutes straight if I want to, or longer. So where does the air come from?"

"I don't know!" Jeff opened the gate and rolled his bike inside the Miller house yard.

"I don't know either."

"Oh."

"Yeah. That's what I said. I think my brain may be getting bigger. I've got all these people inside me now, but I still don't feel crowded."

"You're talking different now. Did you know that? For example, you said, "Xerox". Who says that these days?"

"Good point. I can't help learning from the people I copy. I can hope, though, that it will make me smarter in the long run."

"Why do you need to be smarter?"

"I don't know, and that's probably exactly why I need it."

Jeff shrugged his shoulders as they went into the house. Tim shrugged his shoulders too.

When Jeff went home at the end of the weekend, Timmy went with him. In the close circumstances, entering Mrs. Conners was very easy. She seemed entirely unaware of his presence.

Later, when Jeff was getting ready for bed. Timmy made a suggestion from inside him. "Jeff, I realize that I was scheduled to go with you to school tomorrow, but I think it will be better for my studies to go with your mother instead. She's supposed to attend a ceremony of some nature, for someone else, and it will give me a chance to collect a lot of information. When you see her again, I'll be with her, and we can connect up again."

Jeff, brushing his teeth, tried feebly to say something.

Timmy reminded him that he didn't need to form words to communicate.

"You're going to be inside my mother all *day?*"

"Except for the time that I'm harvesting other people, yeah. Don't worry about it. She won't even know I'm there."

Jeff made a kind of whimpering sound back in his throat, but he realized that what Timmy was suggesting made sense. At least it should be over soon, and his mother could be left alone again. "All right, but for gosh sakes don't scare her. She needs that job."

18. To Both Satisfy And Circumvent

The next time they visited the realm, it was much bigger. It had a school and a church, both of which were always open, although no adults were anywhere in sight.

The buildings were there for study and practice; study and basketball in the school, and singing practice in the church choir loft. The school library served as the town library, although bookshelves everywhere would yield the volume desired by responding to a blink.

The realm also had a research clinic associated with the hospital. In this facility, full-sized staff and surgeons operated on people who were injured or needed medical procedures, but who were never conscious. There was never a time pressure, and the medics would answer and explain everything they were doing, even to a ten-year old child wearing a skimpy bathing-suit bottom, and nothing else.

Lectures were conducted by knowledgeable physicians, who demonstrated and discussed state-of-the-art procedures and discoveries. Anyone who was interested could attend; they would receive excellent medical knowledge; and they could witness and even participate in surgical procedures.

It was there only as a stage set, so that Timmy, who was the only one really interested in medicine, could manipulate the instruments and procedures that a fully documented surgeon of any type could wield. Timmy intended to become proficient in medicine.

This entire town was built for dozens of children, all of about the same age and appearance. Most went about wearing the metallic swim apparel, which was so functional, and which seemed to constitute a form of chastity belt, to both satisfy and circumvent Hannah's concerns.

Even Jeff acceded to the dress custom, although he could escape it at will, simply by choosing to wear something else. If he didn't want to choose, his bottom was (almost) covered by a silkily flexible metal corset, with loops of metal gripping his hips like strong hands. He admitted that they were more comfortable than they looked.

"It doesn't feel like metal. It doesn't feel like anything; maybe fingernail material?" He said, "Heck, I forget that I'm wearing it, and I even forget what I've got inside there! It's never needed for anything." He looked around at his skinny shoulders and thin arms and grinned happily.

For an overweight person, such garb would be unsightly, and quite uncomfortable, but there were none of such types present. For gracile ten-year olds, it was a kind of uniform, and license to enjoy *everything!*

The only time the metal came off, for anyone, was when someone chose to bathe. Stepping into the shower caused the bindings to disappear, and drying off afterwards caused them to manifest once more.

There were exceptions, so to speak, to this draconian dress code. Timmy would appear as he chose, of course. And Hannah had the same privilege. She, of all of them, had the choice of being naked at will. Even if she chose that, however, no one seemed to notice.

Jeff's mother, Dolores, looked very much like all the other girls, but she was immediately distinguishable by her lively ponytail. She seemed to strike up an instant friendship with a girl named Myrtle, who always went about with flowers in her hair.

Bedrooms and dressing rooms had blossomed all over Timmy's house, in alcoves off the swimming pool, in a quiet area accessible from the dugout, and all over the upstairs. The children milled about, playing, reading, swimming, exercising, even playing dress-up, and of course napping anywhere the notion struck them. It was a haven, or heaven, for children of whatever vintage they might have attained.

Virtually everyone Timmy had come to know in his short life (so far), had been mind-swiped and collected to add to his understanding and appreciation for the world.

Roger, formerly Mr. Cannon, had an urge to build. Being also incarnated as a ten-year old, he wanted to build a tree-house.

Timmy gifted Roger with a pirate uniform. His pirate sword was magical. He could use it to cut lumber as if the wood were cheese, or use a hook on the handle to stretch a piece of lumber in any dimension or direction.

Starting with only a single board, Roger could quickly stack up a large pile of uniform rafters and joists, sheathing boards, or wooden shingle shakes.

Tapping the handle of the sword into the face of a timber would instantly set a spike or nail to fix it in place. With some fancy swordplay, he could quickly build something as easily and speedily as anyone else could sketch a drawing.

The first thing he made was a ladder, and then he began building a tree-house in Timmy's forested back yard.

Roger's smiling Jolly Roger flag was personally installed by Timmy, who donned a Peter Pan outfit to fly up for the purpose.

19. The Cocoa Is Already Sweet

Jeff's bike was leaning up against the back wall, under the roof over the dugout. It was raining, and Jeff and Hannah were sitting out the rain, or just enjoying it, in the dugout.

"It would be nice to have a swimming pool in this house too, wouldn't it? Then we could go swimming when it starts raining."

Hannah smiled. "It never rains there."

"True." Jeff smiled "I wonder if Roger's tree house would leak?"

"Probably not, unless it would really storm. Even though he doesn't have any window glass, the roof extends pretty far out."

"Pretty far out is right! The roof stretches out like a cartoon drawing!"

"Doesn't leak, though. I like it. Roger's tree house is a good place to play music."

Jeff smiled. "Roger is good on harmonica, and with you on violin and me on guitar, it's a lot of fun!"

"Maybe we should buy musical instruments and play for real."

"Do you think we can?" Jeff asked seriously, "Play for real, I mean?"

"I don't see why not. Tim said we could transfer muscle memory. I think that means if we can play there we can play here."

"We could ask him. He'd probably want to conduct an experiment. Where is he, anyway?"

"I asked him to make cocoa. He should be along any minute."

"Ah! Real cocoa! That will be nice."

"Real everything!" Hannah observed, reaching out to gently press along the fine hairs along his upper lip. "A real mustache, for instance."

"If I reached out to touch your real … you know … I'd probably get my face slapped."

Hannah looked down, at fourteen now, she had a bit more than just the beginnings of breasts. Even Timmy had said they looked very nice. "Maybe. It depends. You can't just reach for them, you know. You have to work up to it a bit. A girl needs romance."

Timmy floated down the stairs, carefully cradling a single mug of hot chocolate. "Indeed she does need romance. And it looks as though she's getting it. Try not to get too carried away, I have another mug to bring down." He set the cocoa down on a table.

"And don't spill it! It's hot!" He smiled and flitted away again.

"What do you think he would have said if he saw my hand on you just then?"

"Difficult to say, but he takes things pretty calmly. He likes you too, you know."

"He's never said anything, or acted jealous." Jeff looked up the stairs. "I like him too, but I don't feel *compelled* to hang around him."

"Hmph. You don't have to come around all the time."

Jeff looked at her. "You're the flower, and I'm the bee. If you don't want me to come around, stop making with all the chemicals, Sweetness!"

"Ooh, Sweetness, is it?"

"Yep, last stage before Honey."

"You won't need honey. The cocoa is already sweet." Timmy said, putting down the second mug.

"Are you going to keep showing up and messing up my timing? How's a guy supposed to kiss a girl around here?"

"Carefully, I think," Timmy smiled, "She's got a wicked left hook."

"That's what I told him." Hannah said, reaching for the cocoa.

Jeff sat up too. "Thanks, Tim. I've been trying to figure out what I can get away with without getting you upset."

"Why would I get upset?" Timmy asked, settling into a seated position on nothing other than air.

"Well, because she was your girl before she could be anyone else's, I think."

"Still my girl, but that doesn't mean I wouldn't want you to kiss her. I've already given her permission to let you."

"No, you said I could kiss *him*, but you didn't say he could kiss *me*."

"That's right, I did." Timmy smiled, "You have a good memory!"

Jeff looked back and forth between them, and then reached for his cocoa.

"It's gonna be a long night," Jeff muttered.

"Somebody better kiss me," Hannah complained, "I took a shower and put on perfume."

Jeff leaned over and sniffed. "Ah, and that's why I called you Sweetness."

Hannah kissed him, but only a rather short kiss.

Timmy leaned forward, placing his elbow on his knee, and his chin in his hand.

"Oh, this isn't right. Do you have to watch?" Jeff groused.

"No, I don't have to watch. I'm wondering whether I should participate."

Hannah sipped her cocoa. "On which side, then?"

"That's an interesting question," Timmy acknowledged. "I could be in him, to see what it feels like, or I could be in you, to see how you react."

"Or you could go back to the kitchen and wash some dishes." Jeff suggested.

"We're wasting time, and I'm not getting any younger. Come into me, Timmy." Hannah commanded, setting down her cocoa. "Kiss me, Jeffrey."

Timmy swept around and slid quickly into place.

Jeff set down his cocoa and placed his arm behind her neck. He leaned forward and kissed her, holding and cherishing the moment.

Timmy felt the kiss, rotated around it, and did a mind-scan on each of them.

The next instant, they were in the realm, still kissing, as Timmy looked on.

Jeff looked around. "Aw, crap! Your boobs are gone!"

Hannah was sitting in the same position, but now in the body of an undeveloped preteen; and a topless preteen, at that. On her bottom was the familiar restriction of a metal barrier. "No sex tonight, that's for sure," she said with remarkable detachment.

Jeff was also dressed, or undressed, in the same chastity belt fashion. "The hot chocolate is gone too." He turned and looked at Timmy.

Timmy smiled. "While I've got your attention, I'd like to ask a few questions. Got a minute?"

"*Why* would you <u>do</u> that?" Jeff complained. He looked over at Hannah. "Hey! You did get younger after all! You said you weren't getting any younger!"

"Possibly no sex *ever!*" Hannah looked at him darkly.

"Time is relative. And here, time is timeless." Timmy responded airily, "You're still kissing, and we'll get back to that. But I wanted to share something with you."

"We were sharing something already," Hannah reminded him.

"That you were," Timmy said, "so let's not waste time. Take a look at this." He gestured out toward the darkened ball-field.

A scene took shape, as if projected in front of them, but it was in three dimensions. They were looking at two men engaged in conversation. Over a bottle of brandy, Theo McMasters and Wade Miller were chatting amiably, and drinking companionably.

"This is from the memory of your father, Hannah. Listen up."

"Well, we conducted what tests we could. I have some ideas, but I have no definite conclusions, or evidence to support much of it." Theo said.

Wade shrugged.

"We had Timmy blow into an analyzer. We were checking for the kind of chemical traces that everyone has. As biological entities, we all produce carbon dioxide, water vapor, and so forth in our expelled breath."

Wade nodded.

"Timmy produced no such signs of biological activity. His "breath" was nothing but air. Just … air. And fresh air at that."

"Timmy could sustain this blowing action for an incredibly long time. If you went scuba-diving with him, you wouldn't need a tank."

Wade stared at him.

"Well, that's conjecture, we didn't actually go that far. But you get the point. We knew before testing that Timmy doesn't eat or drink or consume energy the way we do. But we didn't know that he can produce either energy or matter without a source."

"What do you mean, without a source?"

"An endless amount of energy, or at least an inexplicable way to move things that we can't detect. I would strongly advise that you avoid letting the government find out about this kid. They'll want him as a National Treasure. They'll <u>take</u> him as a national resource."

Wade drummed his fingers on the table.

They both took some time to sip a bit of brandy. Wade took a deep breath. "What about the … entity? Any ideas along that line?"

"I'm thinking whatever it was came here from another dimension. That doesn't really answer anything, but it explains how so much energy can be moved around without showing up as radioactivity. This thing surfs between its world and ours, and somehow controls energy and material flow between them. I think there could potentially be a physics explanation for some of this, but we aren't going to have enough information for that, either."

"Physics?"

"Consider this; the entity was influenced by Timmy, I don't know how. But instead of consuming him and just moving on, it decided to *expend* energy restoring him. Oliver and Dexter are clones, but Oliver is left-handed! This is remarkably similar to the famous split-beam optical interference experiment. You shine one single source through two openings and you get phase interference. Oliver and Dexter are like mirror images of each other, and Timmy is like the optical source for both."

Theo continued. "Timmy was taken somewhere, somewhere different. Like a fish being hauled up on a boat. Because they were intrigued by something about him, they decided to put him back, but he had been out of water too long. So they used an apparatus to replicate him, getting the split-beam double copy, *and* a permanent optical tear between dimensions!"

"I'm betting Timmy had some long-lasting effects on the other side too, but we have no way to know that. For now, Timmy has the potential to be something incredibly powerful in this world, either for its destruction, or possibly its salvation."

"So what do we do now?" Wade asked simply, holding his hands open searchingly.

"He's your son." Theo answered. "Give him endless amounts of love, and try to show him the right way to be. It's all any parent can do for any child, but this child is possibly like a living neutron bomb. He'll need to be handled properly."

Wade nodded. "Love, huh? I can do that." He looked up. "Theo, we've got a ringside seat to the most eventful happening ever. Keep the booze coming, will you?"

They clicked their glasses together and raised them up.

And that's where Timmy stopped the projection.

Hannah and Jeffrey looked at each other, and looked at Timmy.

"So what's your question, then?" asked Hannah.

"I think I may be able to tap into this energy. I'd like you to help me try to figure out how."

"Oh. That's all? Sure. Why not?" Jeff stared at Hannah.

She nodded. "My dad thinks you're going to be important to the world. I think he's right."

Timmy smiled. "Okay, thanks. I just wanted some confirmation. Thanks, guys!"

And they were back in the other dugout, still kissing. Jeff broke contact and looked around. Steam was still rising from the hot cocoa.

Jeff went back to kissing Hannah. Um, kissing Hammy, that is. He didn't care which.

20. The Pockets Of A Honeybee

Hannah saw Timmy examining something in the back yard, along the fence where the flowers grew. She walked out to join him, walking carefully because she was barefoot.

As Hannah approached, Timmy rose to greet her, still looking up at her after reaching his full height. She had six inches on him now, and when they met he had been the taller one. Just short of twelve years old, and just short of five feet tall, Timmy had not gotten one day older, or a millimeter taller, in the last six years.

He hugged her, patting her fanny affectionately, and she did the same to him.

Hannah took the opportunity to check the waistline of his garment. She could not slip her finger under the band, so that meant that Timmy was generating the image, as usual. She patted his butt again anyway.

"What are you looking at?" Hannah asked.

"Butterflies," Timmy smiled. "They toil not, neither do they spin, yet Solomon in all his glory was not arrayed like one of these."

"Why take ye thought for raiment?" Hannah smiled.

"Exactly! Thought, for raiment, is all I have available." With a glance downward, he made his shorts disappear.

He looked at the flowers again, and the insects which were in attendance to them. "If I could do what they do, I'd have the brightest colors you've ever seen."

"I don't see why you can't. You already have speckles and glints of reflection coming off your skin. That's all the butterflies do, use dusty scales that reflect the colors they need."

Timmy looked more closely at his skin. In the bright sunlight, he seemed to be coated with a kind of fairy dust.

Hannah sat on the ground in front of him. Timmy sat down too, just within reach of the flowers.

"You're like some kind of lawn ornament out here. Maybe we need a fountain, and you could stand at the edge of it."

Timmy laughed. "Yeah, I'm dressed for it. But I can't pee, into a fountain or anywhere else. I haven't peed for six years."

"Maybe we could get you a little bow and some arrows. You could fly around and be Cupid."

"Would be a good party costume, but we don't throw parties. You said I looked like Cupid before, remember?"

"Still do." She grinned, "And now I look more like *her*. It doesn't bother you at all anymore, does it?" Hannah tilted her head as she looked at him.

"What doesn't?"

"Being naked around people."

"Oh, that. No, that doesn't bother me." He chuckled, "Oh look, they can see my elbow! Oh look, they can see my knee! Oh, look, they can see my butt!" He shook his head.

"I like seeing your butt. It's cute."

"Thanks. I thought maybe you were talking about the social scene bothering me. We keep a low profile."

He reached out, and lifted his hand through a flower where a butterfly had just landed, lifting the butterfly as his hand rose. It seemed puzzled a bit, and then fluttered briefly back to its sweet meal.

"How did you do that?"

"What, pick up a butterfly? They aren't heavy."

"No, how did you arrange to pick up *only* the butterfly? If I tried to do that, I'd crush something."

Timmy looked at his hand. "It's hard to describe. I just concentrated on it. It isn't any trickier than lots of other stuff I do."

"Could you pick up only the pollen?"

"The pollen?" He looked at her.

Hannah nodded her head earnestly.

He looked back at the flowers, and selected one. Bringing his hand through the stem and upwards, he cupped his palm under the blossom, and raised it up slowly. The flower did not move at all.

He brought his hand closer to view. There was the tiniest golden dusting of powder in his hand, as if he had picked the pockets of a honeybee.

Hannah was looking enraptured. "Timmy, that's miraculous!"

Timmy pulled her hand, under his, with his other hand. Then he let the powder fall through his hand into hers.

Hannah looked at it. "Timmy, I don't know what we can do with this ability of yours, but this is incredible! *You* are incredible!"

She dusted her hand off, sat forward, and leaned into him for a kiss; a very gentle kiss, as always.

As she settled back down again, a tweetling sound came from her pocket. Hannah fished out a cell phone. "Hello?"

"Remind Timmy that we have three neighbors who can see into that part of the yard, and give him another kiss for me, Sweetie."

"Yes, em-oh-em." Hannah replied cheerily, putting away the phone. She leaned forward to kiss Timmy again, whispering, "My *other* mom; your mom! She's worried about whether you're safe with me."

Timmy leaned around Hannah and waved to the back porch. "I wish I had a phone like that."

"Hah! You can't even keep your pants on!"

"I guess that's why she worries. Someone could come to take me away."

Hugging him, Hannah continued the bantering, "Oh yes. You look so delicious, I just want to gobble you up!"

Timmy grinned. "Hah! Like *that* could happen!" He manifested his shorts again.

Hannah shrugged, "It's happened before. Shall we go in?"

They rose together and went back into Timmy's house.

Angie put out a roll and a cup of tea for Hannah. For Timmy, she had a kiss.

Timmy flew up and settled on the counter, pulling one leg up on his knee. He faced the table and smiled.

Hannah directed her voice toward the center of the house. "Mom, I'm visiting the Millers!" In the distance, there might have been an answer.

"Did you make this, Emmy?" Hannah asked.

Angie dimpled. Em-oh-em was by now a familiar endearment. "I just warmed it up and added some frosting. They taste so much better warm."

"Jeffy is missing out, for sure," Hannah commented.

"If he shows up, I've got more. I love that boy." Angie said, looking carefully at Timmy, who nodded agreeably.

"Uh-huh. I think I do too, which means we're going to have to figure something out." Hannah said around some munching.

"Figure out what?" Angie said.

"My guess is that I'm not going to be able to marry Timmy, although I'm not prepared to give him up, either. Not many guys would be understanding about that, but Jeffrey is already comfortable with the weirdness."

"Marriage?" Angie seemed taken aback, "But you're so young! You don't need to worry about that yet."

"Not yet, but soon. And we've got a really special situation here." She glanced at Timmy, who nodded again.

"Besides, I'm already spoken for, to an extent. I'm mind-married to Timmy. So whoever comes second will have to deal with that."

Timmy blew her a kiss. "She's talking about a physical marriage. Jeff's probably the only guy we know who would be willing to settle for that, because he told me he's feeling lots of "chemicals", by which he means testosterone."

Angie looked at her son, and blinked.

"The big problem, as I see it," Hannah continued, as if she were discussing honeymoon destination choices, "is where we're going to live, and what careers we may fall into."

"Oh my goodness! I can't imagine your ever living anywhere but right here!"

"But," Timmy pointed out, "this house is already two families. It's not a triplex, or quadruplex. It's just a duplex."

"Maybe we can buy one of the neighbor's houses, and then we can have more privacy in our back yard." Hannah suggested.

"Best one for that would be the house to our south. It needs some fixing up, and I think the Andersons might be considering downsizing someplace." Timmy offered.

"Whoa, whoa, whoa!" Angie said. "Just hold your horses here. This conversation is getting way too carried away. Sweetie-pie, you're only *fifteen!*"

"Damn near an old maid already," Timmy said.

"You watch your language, young man! I can still turn you over my knee for a spanking!" Angie said in pretended irritation, to which everyone laughed delightedly.

"Right! We can't afford to wait much longer to start planning! We've got careers to decide on, property to buy and renovate, a marriage and honeymoon to plan, ..." Hannah started ticking things off on her fingers.

"Some way to pay for this expensive paradise you have in mind ..." Wade said from the doorway.

Timmy flew over to give his dad a hug, and then to the refrigerator to fetch him a beer.

Hannah got up to hug him as well.

Wade sat down at the table, where Angie was placing another warm roll. "All right, let's take it from the top. I only came in after Timmy was getting spanked."

Timmy brought him his beer. "We should probably get Jeff over here too. He might want to find out he's getting married."

"And Theo and Corinne, too. It's not too late to start a drinking binge." Wade said.

Hannah called Jeff on her cell phone. Angie walked next door to see if the McMasters were available.

"Now let me explain," Hannah started out, after speaking briefly to Jeff. "I only meant to discuss this today with Timmy, because he doesn't get excited about things no matter how crazy it sounds."

"And I always agree with her precisely about anything she wants to do, no matter how crazy it sounds."

"Smart boy," said Wade, taking a sip of beer.

"Jeff will be here in a couple minutes. We all love him, right?" Hannah asked, looking around at the assembled faces.

"I know I do," Timmy said without pretense.

Wade lifted his beer toward Timmy in agreement. "He's a good lad!"

"Well, I like Jeff too. He's almost like one of the family." Angie said.

"What's this about Jeffrey?" Corinne asked, wiping her hands on a hand towel she had brought over.

"We're thinking about marrying him off. Do you have a shotgun?" Wade asked Theo.

"A shotgun? No. Why would I need a shotgun?" Theo looked confused.

"Just insurance," said Wade. "Anyway, Hannah has the floor. Carry on."

"Here's Jeff." She gave him a kiss, as he looked around dazedly. "I was just saying that Jeff is probably the only boy who would marry me considering that I come with a lot of psychological baggage."

"That would be me," Timmy raised his hand.

"What?" Jeff said.

"And obviously, we won't be able to live just anywhere. We need to be close to this house, and the people here."

"Huh? What's going on?" Jeff looked around.

"My boy, welcome to America." Wade lifted his beer again.

"Jeff, do you want to marry Hannah? Not today or even tomorrow, but maybe a couple of years from now?" Timmy asked him.

"Well, yeah! Sure! Of course I would." Jeff said without any apparent qualm at all.

"You don't have a job." Suggested Theo.

"A well-paying job." Continued Corinne.

"No. Not yet." Responded Jeff. "Actually, I haven't figured out what's going to pay the best; a music or entertainment career, or perhaps a professional service. I have so many talents, you know."

"That he does." Timmy agreed. Hannah nodded, too.

"Seriously, what's going on?" Theo said.

"A bit of fun, Theo," responded Wade, "but a bit of serious fun."

"Well, it's pretty simple, actually," Timmy began, "Hannah wants to marry Jeff, and Jeff wants to marry Hannah. I'll live with them, of course. They'll probably buy the house next door, and Jeff is going to make a small fortune as a psychologist. A *child* psychologist," he amended.

"That," mused Jeff, "sounds pretty good." Hannah nodded.

"Wait a minute!" Theo barked. "Is this all some silly prank?"

"Why no, not at all," answered Timmy, "and the first thing we'll need to do, as soon as everyone starts breathing normally again, is to have Hannah and Jeff go next door and chat with the Andersons."

"See there?" said Wade, getting up with his beer to go back to his chair, "I told you we needed a plan." He ambled away, letting the conversation rise in chaos behind him.

21. A Permanent Compromise Position

"The Andersons?" Jeff asked. They were sitting in the dugout, having retreated there as soon as possible. Jeff and Hannah each had a can of root beer in hand.

"I have a plan." Timmy said.

Jeff and Hannah exchanged glances.

"Yeah?" prompted Jeff.

"I'm going to recruit them."

Hannah looked at him. "You mean you're going to steal their memories, so you can add their personalities to your memory realm?"

Tim nodded. "Not just that. I should have done it before. Don't you see? We need to find out what they want to do with their lives, what their dearest dreams are, and what they may be planning for their future." He looked from one to the other of them. "I'm your man!"

"You want to … influence them?" Hannah said cautiously.

"No. I want to know what they want. Then I want to see if I can get it for them." He looked thoughtful. "If they want something that doesn't have anything to do with the house they live in, we might be able to do some switching around."

"Like what?" said Jeff.

"Don't know yet," answered Timmy, sitting back and relaxing.

Hannah was quiet for a bit. "So, you want us," she waggled a finger between Jeff and herself, "to go over there, and "chat" with the Andersons."

"And you'll be there, with us," said Jeff.

"And then I'll do my thing," finished Timmy. "Then we'll take them to the realm, see what they're *really* like, and what they love best about life, and we'll see if we can get it for them!"

"Ah!" Jeff sat back. "Piece of cake! In and out; over by morning. Nothing to it."

"Hmm," hummed Hannah.

"Mr. Anderson? Mrs. Anderson? We're your neighbors, sort of. I live next door, and this is my friend Jeff, who is a family friend. May we come in?"

"Oh, Hannah!" Mrs. Anderson beamed, "Come on in! We've been watching you grow up over there for so long. Henry has been so fond of seeing you and your friends. Come in, come in."

"We brought you some candy, kind of a housewarming gift, sort of. We know you've been here for quite a while, but we never got around to it before."

"Oh, thank you. That's so sweet. Candy, Henry. Come on in and have a seat."

The house was dark, not foreboding, but simply darkened by window shades that seemed to have found a permanent compromise position, instead of a constant up-and-down adjustment.

Henry had risen, but was going back to his recliner. He looked to be in his mid-fifties, and a bit tired today.

Mrs. Anderson, Alice as it turned out, was thin and regal; Late forties at the outside. She seemed genuinely pleased to have company.

Henry had been a very accomplished pianist in his youth, but his job had taken him away from that for the most part. He seldom tickled the ivories these days.

The kids and the Andersons spent the better part of an hour

chitchatting and comparing interests. It was a good visit. Hannah promised to come back again, and invited the Andersons to come to Church with them, to at least hear the choir, which was so lovely.

Mrs. Anderson said that they would try, and thanked them for a wonderful visit.

And then they left.

In the realm, Alice and Henry found each other immediately, and bonded instantly. They ran off together as soon as they heard about Roger's Tree House. They were bright smiles and handholding, skipping and joyous, as two children had never seemed before.

Hannah and Jeff watched them dancing toward the forest with considerable delight. It was such a happy scene.

"You've got a right good place here, Timmy. I'll have to admit it." Jeff said. His resigned and disapproving glance downward when they had arrived signaled that he was still a bit miffed about always losing his maturity when he came here. But he accepted it as the price of admission. This was a joyous place to be.

Hannah was holding his hand, clad also in the standard fare of a metal impediment to both hanky and panky. Their "uniforms" afforded no pockets, so handkerchiefs were not available to go into the pockets that were not available. Hannah squeezed his hand and smiled at him anyway.

Besides, no one ever sneezed here.

Teddy came up to them. "Boss, we've got a problem."

Tim looked at him. "Boss?"

Teddy grinned. "You're a guy who can get things done. You seem like the person to ask."

"Okay, ask what?"

"We need a way to communicate. This place is so big, a fella could spend all his time trying to find the person he was playing with yesterday. We need a way to send messages somehow, or know where someone is. Any ideas?"

"Hmm. What did you have in mind?"

"Cell phones?" Teddy grinned again, and looked down at his bronze potholder. "Maybe we'd need a way to not lose them."

"Tap the metal ring on your right hip twice, and speak a name." Timmy suggested.

Teddy paused a moment, and then tapped his hip. "Ange?"

A disembodied voice responded, speaking a couple of feet above Roger's hip. "Teddy?"

"Yes, this is Teddy. Where are you? I've been looking for you."

"I'm in the school library. Did you want me to come to you?"

"No, that's fine. I'll be over in a little bit. I've just found out we can communicate like this. I'll show you how it works."

"Oh, thanks!"

"Okay, then. This is Teddy, out." He said, and then grinned at Tim.

"Will that work for you?" Timmy asked.

"That's great! Thanks, Boss!"

"Before you go, make sure the word gets spread that there's a way to keep in touch, okay?"

"Sure thing! I'll take care of it!" He dashed away, running at top speed.

"He seems happy." Timmy said.

"He was trying to find your mom, you know?" Jeff said.

"Yeah, so?"

"Oh, nothing. Just an observation."

Timmy grinned at him. "Anybody you want to get in touch with?"

"No, no. I'm cool at the moment. But I'll remember about it. He glanced down at the hip ring and looked thoughtful.

"Okay, so," Hannah was looking around at the activities and joyful chaos all around them. "What's going on with Alice and Henry?"

"They're talking to Roger. They want him to build them a boat."

"A boat? What would they do with a boat? Wait! There's no place to sail a boat, is there?"

"There is now." Timmy answered. "In the other direction from Roger's Tree House, there's a big lake, with sandy beaches and enough breeze to whip up some waves. It's not quite an inland sea. You can see the distant shore. At the moment, it's all trees."

"They want to sail away?" Hannah looked toward the trees.

"They just want to sail." Timmy said. "It's always been a dream of theirs."

He looked off toward the trees, where Roger would no doubt be asking questions about how big a boat, and how many cabins and masts and such they would need.

He would build it; that was for certain.

Timmy grew quiet.

Hannah and Jeff looked at each other. They waited.

"Henry has cancer." Timmy said.

22. How Could There Be A Lake?

Timmy was sitting, lotus fashion, on Hannah's bed. His mood was, well, not somber but distant. He had been thinking, steadily, for three days. All the joy and spontaneity that had led them to the realm to bring Alice and Henry there seemed to have evaporated.

Hannah did not know what to do. She was, as a consequence, attempting to annoy him out of his funk by appearing naked in front of him as frequently as possible.

Demanding to know which positions and suggestive poses were more erotic and stimulating.

Eventually, he laughed and hurt her feelings.

She put her clothes on and sat down on the bed, depressed herself now.

"I'm sorry." Timmy said softly, the first words he had used in some time.

Hannah looked over.

"You're beautiful, Hannah. Any way you present yourself, I love you."

She looked down.

"That isn't my thing. If it was, you'd have an entirely different feeling about me, and I think our history together would have been a lot more sour."

"I didn't think about that." Hannah said, "I was just trying to get a rise out of you."

"I don't "rise" in that manner, more's the pity, because you have the talent to do it without even trying. Jeff's going to be a lucky man."

She reached over and touched his spectral surface gently. "Are you going to be with us in that … that discovery process? I'm just curious."

"We can talk about it. It's possible that I could enhance the process for you, and that might make it worth the sacrifice in privacy." He affected a deep breath as a means of pausing for a moment.

"You and Jeff will be experiencing something together that will be very precious. I'd like to think that my connection to you won't interfere with your relationship together. But I want you to know that I have absorbed about a thousand lifetimes of experience in various aspects of what you two are about to share, and I have to say, that even with that clinical knowledge, I lack the emotional connection to it."

Hannah looked at him in profound sadness. If his witnessing of all the acts of all the people he had absorbed didn't serve to bring him into an emotional bond with the concept of sex itself, then he was already some kind of creature from another dimension.

Timmy looked at her, and seemed to understand what her expression meant.

"Don't worry about it, Hannah. That's only one of several human emotional links that were severed on my behalf. The others are mostly unpleasant, and I'm probably better off without them." He patted her hand. She enfolded his hand with her own.

"I do love. I feel joy and happiness in unbelievable amounts as I witness others being happy and feeling joy themselves. I don't know what the difference might be. My feelings may be the more pure ideal emotions that some philosophers talk about. They certainly feel real, but they're likely not your kind of real. Absolutely they aren't chemical, because nothing about me is based on chemistry."

Hannah gave a quirky smile. "Dad seemed to think that you were based on Physics."

"He might be right," Timmy mused. "If he is right, my "emotions" might be a thousand or more times more powerful and speedy than your chemistry. It's an interesting notion."

"Alice and Henry can be happy in the realm. They *are* happy there. I can give them anything they want for that happiness. What I've been thinking about is what I might be able to do here in the real world. In many ways, I'm still just a twelve-year old neighbor kid. Their lives are unwinding in a bit of a snarl, but the lives *are* theirs."

"They wouldn't choose *this*, you know."

"Yes." Timmy smiled. "They wouldn't choose this. And I don't have any right to interfere with how their lives are unfolding. Their privacy, their fates, and their eventual reconnection with their creator, are all none of my business, especially because I entered this situation looking to gain from it personally."

Hannah looked at him, not knowing where his logic was leading him, but not knowing how to shape any argument to affect it.

"But I *am* going to interfere."

She tensed, perhaps gripping his hand a bit more forcefully than she should. He merged his hand with hers and wriggled her fingers.

She could feel the tears forming, tears of happiness and hope. "But what can you do?"

Timmy smiled again. "Pollen," he said.

"Huh?"

"Henry has too much pollen. I'm going to sift it out of him."

"Do you … do you think you can *do* that?"

Timmy shrugged. "Well, ethically no. What I will need to do is influence several medical practitioners in various ways to modify his treatment regimen. That alone is unethical, and it could damage them in certain ways, including possible research they might do in the future. It's no different, really, than influencing some bank president to make a deposit in our accounts to make us rich. It's something I am capable of doing, but it isn't right."

"No, no. I'm not talking about that. Of course it's right to help someone with cancer. My question was, can you sift the cancer cells out of him? *How can you do that?* That would take a miracle."

"I do miracles all the time," Timmy said. He wriggled her fingers again, and twisted slightly to let his arm merge with hers. And then he turned his body so that it would align with her body. Slowly he sank into her, disappearing from view.

"I'll be in my realm, working on ideas, and consulting with my associates." She could feel his smile. "Just take care of this side for me for a while."

"I've got it," Hannah smiled, "I've got you."

Timmy closed his eyes, and sank back inside her to rest without moving, as she carried him around in the chemical world.

Hannah sat still for a moment, and then she felt filled with energy. Now would be a good time to get some work done. Among other things, her room could use a lot of straightening. She could never tell when she might have company.

Timmy popped back into the realm in the top bunk of his room. He sailed out of it to look around and saw Jeff reading in the lower bunk.

Jeff looked up. "Treasure Island," he said. "I'm thinking maybe we could dig up some hidden pirate gold. You'll need money, won't you?"

"I thought of that too." Timmy smiled.

Hannah looked in. "Ah, you're here. Shall we go see what's been happening?"

Timmy glanced around. All of them were wearing the metal bottoms set up to be the swimming uniform. It seemed to have become the official uniform of the entire realm. Timmy raised his eyebrows.

Hannah shrugged. "I'll do my dressing up out where it counts. This saves on making explanations."

Jeff looked puzzled, as if he had already forgotten that there had ever been any other choice.

"Okay, let's go. Um, where do we start?"

"The lake," said Hannah.

Timmy reached out with his right hand to hold their hands. Quickly Hannah and Jeffrey put their hands in his.

Timmy said clearly, "The lake", and touched his left hip ring twice.

Instantly they were transported to the shore of the lake, where a large sailing vessel was taking shape.

Jeff glanced at Timmy's left hip, and said, "I'm going to remember that one."

Timmy nodded. "Just like communication, we need to be able to move about more quickly."

Hannah was looking at the boat. Roger was very busy, stretching boards here, clunking them into place with the butt of his sword, and reaching for the next one as if he were dancing.

Alice and Henry were watching with delight.

They walked over. "It's bigger than I thought it would be." Timmy said.

"We're not going to be sailing alone," said Henry. "We wanted to have room for guests."

"Where will you go?" Jeff wanted to know.

"Out there!" Henry pointed.

"What's out there?"

"We'll find out!" Alice giggled.

"Any sunken ships?" Jeff looked at Timmy.

"How could there be any sunken ships?" Timmy responded.

"How could there be a lake?" Hannah pointed out.

Timmy looked out toward the far side of the lake. It could have been twenty miles. "I believe you may be right. Out there, toward the center, there's a big ocean liner sitting on the bottom."

"Ocean liner?" Hannah stared at him.

"Uh-huh. It's the Titanic."

"*What?*" Jeff jumped.

"I have an idea," said Timmy. He looked at Jeff. "It's a kind of buried treasure."

All of the faces were watching him now.

"We'll have guided tours out to the Titanic. We'll bring in people from the real world, and charge them admission, so they can go out and walk around on the Titanic."

"Walk around on it? It's lying broken in half, and covered over with marine life." Henry reminded him.

"Oh, no," Timmy answered. "It's fully intact, lying straight and level on the lake bottom. And the lights are on."

Now everyone was looking at each other.

"When your boat is built, you can go out and look down. You'll see the lights, and if the water is still, you'll be able to see the people dancing."

"The people? They all died in 1912." Alice said.

"No, they're out there dancing, listening to the band, showing off their finery, and enjoying the fourth night of the ship's maiden voyage. You can hear the music. It's April 14th, 1912, but only on that ship."

"I think you've gone around the bend, Tim," Hannah said.

"Off the deep end, you mean," said Jeff.

"The deep end, that's right." Timmy eyed Jeff and Hannah. "We'll have to do some research out there, find the experts and harvest their knowledge, and then build the most accurate version of the ship anyone has ever seen … I mean has never seen. It will have functioning elevators, grand staircases, carpets and paneling, and the guests will all be arrayed in their finery, drinking champagne and laughing together."

"How can you do that? That's impossible." Henry said.

Timmy smiled. "I did this," he pointed around.

Hannah gulped. "Oh, boy, here we go!"

"Yep!" Timmy smiled. "This is going to be *fun!*"

Jeff shook his head. "Tim, it can't work. They'll know it's a fake."

Tim turned to him. "*Who* will know it's a fake?"

"The people! The ones who've researched it and know what it looked like."

Timmy grinned. "Those are the people who are going to show *us* what it's supposed to look like! No one who knows what to expect will be able to claim it's false, because they <u>know</u> what to expect, and *that's what we'll show them!*"

Jeff was still shaking his head. "This is impossible!" But he was saying it softly.

"That's what we do here, Jeff; the impossible." Timmy said. "It's on the other side that we have to work the miracles!" He looked at Henry and smiled.

Jeff looked puzzled, but Hannah was nodding her head slowly. "You want to make money. This part won't cost you anything. But how will you make money?"

"By charging admission!" Timmy said. "Our tourists will pay to visit the Titanic, to walk its decks, and listen to the band. They'll pay plenty!"

"But Tim, they can't come here, and then go back. No one can." Jeff pointed out.

Alice and Henry looked at each other. Henry shrugged.

"*You* do it," Timmy said softly, "you and Hannah."

"What? You'll bring them here, dressed like this?" Hannah said incredulously.

"Exactly so, Hannah. Dressed *exactly* like that. They will think that *they* are not real, but that the Titanic <u>is</u>."

"Do you have ... the *capacity* for this?" Hannah asked.

"It's growing all the time."

Hannah looked around. "Yeah. That for sure."

23. It All Sounds Like Doubletalk

Theo McMasters was presenting. Dressed to the nines, he was on stage, illuminated by footlights, and speaking into a microphone.

"Ladies and Gentlemen, welcome to our first performance of "HypNautica!" We hope to repeat this miraculous presentation in a dozen cities across the country, but *this* is the premier."

"I would have liked to charge you more. It would be worth it. But this is unproven technology. You have your doubts. It all sounds like doubletalk."

He looked around.

"It <u>is</u> doubletalk!"

Knowing they could not see his smile, he gave a short bow to acknowledge his accidental honesty.

As he was speaking, ushers in speckled white tunics reminiscent of hospital technicians were moving among the seated patrons, securing their "electrosonic head-gear" and seeing to it that each one had a numbered tag chain hung artfully around the neck.

Timmy was moving among the ushers, disguised as one of them. He had to get to every person in the theater, and there were a lot of them.

Theo continued.

"We don't want our competitors to be able to steal this proprietary technology, so the explanations are a little sparse. It combines hypnosis, electronic stimulation, *hyper*-ultrasound and perhaps even a bit of mass hysteria."

"We'll take what we can get."

"What *you* will get is the privilege of walking the decks of the Titanic, seeing its passengers as they dressed in their finest clothes. You will mingle with the famous personages of history who were said to have been lost. We have *found* them!"

"You will *see* the grandeur. You will experience the splendor! Yours will be a first-person view of the art and the majesty of the time."

"But *you* were not alive in this time. You cannot see these things with your own eyes, so we have arranged to have other eyes for you to see with. You will not recognize the person you become. Accordingly, if you are traveling with a companion, take a look now at your companion's number tag. Each of you has one. Memorize this number, for your companion will look different, and so will you! Your number tag is your only clue!"

"And now also, I want to thank you for your generous contribution to help defray our enormous costs for this venture. You have paid a price for admission, which you may think is steep. But I hasten to remind you that it is *less than half* of what the original passengers you are about to see paid for *their* cost of passage!"

"One final thing. At the end of our journey, you may wish to stay around, to kick the tires of the Titanic, and see how we managed this illusion. If you want to do that, simply keep your number tag firmly clenched in your hand as you leave the ship. Others will be surrendering theirs in order to return here."

"You who retain your numbers will be allowed to stay. But I must warn you, we are not serving refreshments! And any food you see laid out on the Titanic is for the passengers, not for all of us visitors. They paid for passage, and we only paid to look around! Do not try to eat anything there. I can guarantee that it will not agree with you. It's a little old, you know! It's "sell-by" date is long past!"

"All right, it looks as though everyone is strapped in and ready for take-off. Ushers, are we ready? Ladies and Gentlemen, are you ready? Then let us proceed! On to HypNautica!"

Theo walked majestically off the stage, to thunderous applause.

Then the house lights dimmed even further, and the curtains drew back, to reveal a laser light show on the stage, a kind of hypnotic point of concentration …

On the rising grassy embankment leading down to the lake's shore, people started popping into existence in orderly rows.

They were all children. They were all ten years old.

Each one had a copper neck chain, and a number engraved on the copper plate attached to it.

The numbered plate had a background color of green, to help make the numbers stand out. This verdigris color tone was repeated in the shorts that each individual was wearing, a kind of interwoven-ring metal cloth, securely fastened at the hips by hoops of metal.

These costumes of metal were the only decorations or garments that the children wore. Each child looked like the next one. Each had a tapered, rather tousled hairstyle of a soft brown color. The abundantly visible skin was the mild tone of a healthy tan. The occasional smile flashed a brilliant white out of the relative darkness of the evening.

And every one of them had strikingly beautiful green eyes.

They may have all been boys. They may have all been girls.

They may have been boys and girls. At this distance they were entirely indistinguishable.

But each one had a different number.

They assembled in silence, except for the imagined pop of air as another body would appear. The change in everything that they were experiencing was too different for them to do anything other than sit still in completely stunned silence.

And then the arrivals were complete.

Corrie was there to greet them. She stood on a small wooden stage in front of them, and spoke with assurance and authority.

"Welcome, travelers!"

Her blond hair, and shiny corseted bottom marked her as different from them, and perhaps an authority figure. She had the confidence.

"Soon we will get on to our transportation, to be taken to the purpose of your trip, the majestic Titanic! But we have to start somewhere, and we're starting here, on the shore of this calm sea. The Titanic is out there, and we will be taken to her."

"Before we start, I remind you again to look for your companion's number. Find your companion! Remember, "Your companion will look different, and so will you! Your number tag is your only clue!"

She paused for a moment, to let the expected confusion sort itself out.

"While we're getting ready to leave, let's take a look at our transport vessel, the wonderful "Locker Room Belle", a genuine river-bottom side-wheeler!" She gestured over her shoulder, where an enormous ferry was crawling up out of the water, its side-wheels turning, not to move water, but to grip the muddy bottom of the lake, and drive the boat up toward the shore.

A second set of side-wheels came into view. This vessel was a four-wheel drive ferry cruiser, designed to walk along the bottom of a river or lake. It was a river-bottom side-wheeler, and the only one anyone present had ever seen.

A transparent canopy covered the top, shedding water from its rising out of the lake. Beneath that, other children, presumably crew, were moving about, setting out deck chairs and such, checking the lines securing cargo, and doing the things one would expect a river-bottom ferry crew-child to do.

The majestic vessel stopped, and projected forward a gangway, which then lowered itself to the shore. Several crew-children scurried down the gangway and positioned themselves to assist people coming aboard.

The gangway also had a transparent cover that telescoped as the device extended.

"Let's go aboard, shall we? Titanic awaits!" Corrie walked to the gangway and began climbing aboard. She looked over her shoulder from time to time and smiled.

The new arrivals stood up, looking around themselves and at themselves in astonished disbelief. But they had no time to get accustomed to something they would not be able to comprehend, for they had to get aboard the transport.

Heads moved in odd ways as the children looked at everything around them, and at every aspect of their own bodies.

Overweight men and women, accustomed to waddling and wheezing, suddenly found that they were filled with boundless energy, and a desire to dance and skip.

The crowd slowly laughed and merrily proceeded on to the ferry. In minutes they were all loaded, and the gangway began rising back to its former location. The open end of it sealed over with a covering.

The boat lurched into action, moving further out, and farther down, along the lake bottom.

Several hundred feet out from shore, it disappeared under the waves.

The transparent canopy seemed ridiculously incapable of holding back tons of water. And yet their course drew them deeper and deeper under the water.

Green eyes looked upward at sixty feet of water held up by something little more substantial than a soap bubble. But it held the water back as if it were no more than fog.

They could hear the ship. They could hear its generators; see its lights.

They could hear the music! And then they were there. The mighty ship loomed before them, sitting calmly on the bottom of the sea, (or lakebed, people spoke interchangeably of the two), about thirty feet deep in the mud.

It wasn't going anywhere.

But it didn't need to go anywhere; it was the where that everyone came to see.

This was Titanic, April 14th, 1912, an evening forever; an evening to remember.

The ferry stopped, and reached up with its nuzzling gangway to find an opening for the passengers to disembark. It stopped against the railing, which had its own transparent material to hold out a hundred foot depth of water, as if it were a mild drizzle.

Far above, the surface of the lake waters scattered rippled light down like an overcast evening sky.

The partitions opened, and a way aboard was made ready. Green-eyed children scampered eagerly up the way, and on to the giant ship. Quickly they scurried in every direction, fascinated to finally be aboard the object of their long obsession.

It was so big! It was so gorgeous!

It was so *real!*

The children dodged around passengers in elegant upper-class finery, like peasant children seeking a loose crumb or fallen coin. The passengers paid them no mind, as if they didn't even see them. Chances are, had the children been actual impoverished ragamuffins in some port city, this group of people would have ignored them as utterly.

Children thundered into the radio room, the bridge, the majestic prow of the ship. They were the king of the world, for that fleeting moment they had the primary position.

All over the vessel, children scrambled, delighted as no picnickers could ever be. Not for food, but for memories, for a chance to touch, and see, and to be able to say, "I was there! I was really there! I can *never* forget it!"

This was the Titanic! The *real* Titanic! There was no question of its authenticity. Every test they could imagine proved it to be true. The proper number of funnels, the ship markings, the people, the Captain!

It was glorious!

And soon, all too soon, it was over too soon. The great ship's horn blew, and children who were not green-eyed and green bottomed called to the others that it was time to depart.

One last look! One last glance! One last being dragged by someone for not listening.

Slowly they returned to the ferry, looking wistfully back up to the ship.

They watched as the gangway sealed itself and withdrew. They watched as the ferry began moving away.

They watched as children belatedly arrived at the rail and looked down, and then popped out of existence on the Titanic, and back into presence on the Locker Room Belle.

They watched the magnificent, majestic ship slowly disappear a final time again.

They were quiet.

Actually, they were quiet for a long time, considering. Kids, you know.

And then their excitement reasserted itself and there was whooping and yelling, and rather brash activity aboard the Locker Room Belle.

They continued exploring what it meant to be children again. Energy, vitality, …

Joy.

Belatedly they remembered that they had a choice. Upon departure from the ferry, they could surrender the number tags and return to their lives, or desperately cling to them and then, what? They didn't know!

For some, there was no question. They had lives to go back to. They had jobs to do, and families to care for.

Responsibility.

As the Locker Room Belle propelled itself laboriously up the slope, like a sea turtle seeking a place to lay her eggs, the children made their decisions.

Most dropped the tags into the buckets, where crew-children showed them they were waiting. Most were going home. The majority; by far the largest majority …

But there were a few who had found something new and different; wonderful, in this short visit.

They had rediscovered childhood. A place and time too precious to surrender back again, no matter for what purpose.

They clenched the number tags desperately, and went down the gangway to an unknown fate in an unknown land, where the rules of science and of life itself did not seem to apply anymore.

No one seemed to notice that children were disappearing, the numbers diminishing. With every glance around there were fewer and fewer.

And then they were all gone. Every child who had dropped his number tag in the bucket, was gone. The only ones remaining were still desperately clenching their tags, as if for life itself.

Timmy was looking at the returning children, with their number tags. "It looks like forty-seven. Anyone surprised by that?"

Hannah and Jeff shook their heads. They had calculated that there would be a number, but no one had placed bets on what it would be.

"It seems a cruel choice, this life or the other one." Hannah said sadly.

"That wasn't the choice they had. But we couldn't tell them that." Timmy looked thoughtful. "Everybody in the theater came back to his life. They didn't get a choice to stay here and not go back."

"The choice was whether to do both." He looked over the new conscripts. "I wanted to find some people who wanted to be here, in spite of everything. That's the group I wanted. I thought they would be the most fun. Did you know that we have six sets of newlyweds?"

"Look at these two, father and son. Thomas and Tommy. What a delight! Thomas is thirty-six, and Tommy is only eleven! Isn't that wonderful?"

Hannah smiled. "They do sound as though they will be fun people. But this recruitment isn't your whole purpose, is it?"

"Oh, no. This is just icing on the cake. We're getting the money we need, for our real estate purchases and college tuitions, and we're filling out our ranks here with fun people. It's a win/win." He smiled.

Thomas and Tommy were making their way up from the lake, through the woods. It was dark, but not so dark as to be frightening.

"How are you doing, son? You aren't tired, are you?"

"No, dad. I'm doing fine. I feel great."

"You hungry?"

His companion shook his head, looking up through his forelocks, "Not even a little bit." He glanced at his father. "We look like twins now; just alike. Isn't that weird?"

"I like it! We may also look like everybody else, but if I look like you, that's a pretty good deal. You're a really good looking kid!"

"So are you!" Tommy put his arm around his father, and realized that from now on, they would be brothers.

Thomas felt the new companionship, and smiled.

Just ahead of them, they saw a girl standing, as if waiting for them. They exchanged a glance, and a shrug.

"Hi," she said.

"Hi. I'm Thomas, and this is my son Tommy."

"I can see the family resemblance. I'm Hannah," the girl said, smiling, "I know who you are. I just wanted to ask you some questions, if you don't mind. What are you looking for?" She smiled.

Thomas paused. "I actually don't know. I just seemed to reason that an adventure that started with being able to visit the Titanic shouldn't have to end so soon. I don't even know what else may be available, but the potential seemed worth investigating."

"And the lives you left behind?"

"I think I can answer that," Tommy said. "Dad was getting frustrated with his job, with where we live, and with what the future seemed to have in store for us. I think one reason we wanted to see the Titanic was just for the adventure and escape it represented."

"A journey to another world, in more ways than one," Hannah observed.

"That, and more." Thomas added.

"Okay, that works. But what *kind* of adventure are you looking for?"

"That depends on what there is. I'm getting the notion, no offense of course, that romance is not particularly stressed here." Tommy looked at him in puzzlement.

Hannah glanced down, and smiled ironically again. "No offense taken. I think you're right. I've been associated with this enterprise for six years now, and it hasn't "blossomed" to any noticeable degree." She pulled her chin up and stood straighter for a moment, but then shrugged the posture away. It was meaningless without punctuation.

"Too bad. Have you any idea why? It would seem like a logical extension."

"Would you like to walk? I didn't mean to hold you back."

They began moving uphill again. "We don't know where we're going anyway."

"Roger's Tree House is not far from here, but you can go back to that later if you want to."

"Is that like a social club or something? Tommy's a bit young for that."

Hannah looked over. "It's a tree house," she said.

"Oh." They continued walking.

"I wouldn't worry about Tommy's age anyway. It's pretty hard to get into mischief here, as I suppose you'll figure out eventually."

"Mischief?" Thomas said lightly.

"You know what I mean," Hannah replied. "He may be a little young to understand it, but I know you do. By the way, I'm actually fifteen, and I'm trying to corner a certain person into making a commitment."

"A commitment?"

"Marriage," Hannah smiled.

"I'm trying to picture you in a wedding dress," Tommy said. "I can't."

"We probably won't get married here, otherwise I would invite you to attend. I might anyway, but this is only what I used to look like."

"Wow! You were pretty!" Tommy said.

"You _are_ pretty," Thomas restated.

Hannah smiled. "Thanks! At the moment, you boys look scrumptious yourselves. I know who selected that appearance. He has good taste."

Thomas looked down at himself, and at his companion. "It took a little getting used to. Is there a reason that you can tell us?"

"It was probably just a whim," she shrugged. "I suspect though, that it represents a way to track a special group of new arrivals. You folks have come in with all your current memories from the real world intact, unlike most of the residents. You'll meet enough of them soon. They've been brought back to a more basic way of getting along with each other. I think you'll find them to be more like Tommy. No offense, Tommy."

He furrowed his brow. "You mean, they're more like kids, like me? They not only look like kids but act like kids too?"

Hannah stopped. "I wouldn't call it that, precisely. They like to have fun, and they spend an incredible amount of time and energy doing just that. They seem able to draw on some of their lifetime experiences, but only as if in a dream, as if they were playing a role then, and are simply being themselves now."

She looked up in front of them. "There's my house. Would you like to go in? It's open."

They started walking again. "You leave it open?" Thomas inquired, "Where just anyone can go in? Aren't you worried …"

"No." Hannah said abruptly, with such assurance that it was rather chilling.

"Woah" said Thomas, taking a step slightly sideways.

Hannah laughed. "You're still thinking about that romance thing? Okay, fine. What do you think your first step on that process might be?"

"You mean," Thomas looked down, "this is something permanent?"

"Close enough to," Hannah said cheerily. "Don't forget to have fun!"

"What are you talking about?" Tommy said.

"These … whatever they are!" Thomas said, trying to get a finger under his garment, to no avail. "They seem to be welded on!"

"Don't exaggerate." Hannah scolded. "They're just bathing suits. Everybody wears them."

"Everybody wears them, *all the time?*" Tommy looked puzzled. "How do you go to the bathroom?"

"You don't. Still glad you jumped ship?" Hannah inquired.

"I'm not so sure," Thomas admitted.

Hannah laughed. "I'll come and talk with you some more, but you need to look around and meet more people first. You're going to provide me with information eventually, and I'll be able to provide advice to other people. For now, you should go swimming; that water around the Titanic was *very* cold. The ball field is out there, badminton over there. This is the dugout, and back here," she opened the special door at the back of the dugout, "is the pool. Come on. Last one in has green eyes!"

24. He Had A Million Fingers

"How was the gate?" Theo asked, loosening his tie.

"Unbelievable!" Angie's eyes sparkled. "Our two families together don't make this kind of money in a year!"

"Don't forget that we have expenses; the theater rental, costumes, paramedics on standby, and all that other stuff."

"Piffle! We're in the Big Time, Baby!"

"Your baby. This would all be a big disappointment without him."

"It is astonishing, isn't it? I still cannot believe it." Angie glanced around. "How are the audience members? Any problems?"

"Only getting them to leave the theater. They keep chatting with total strangers and comparing experiences. I think we have a hit!"

"Timmy only wants to do a dozen performances. I hope this isn't too much of a strain on him. He looks so delicate."

"Ethereal is the word I would choose, Angie. This is almost like a religious experience, not only for the audience, but for Timmy as well. I looked closely at him afterwards. He was … vibrant with energy. I don't know how else to describe it."

"I wonder how it's going on the other side?" Corinne mused. "We had reports of folks being surprised to be back in their own bodies. They had made up their minds to stay! Imagine!"

"We gave them the standard response, "How do you know you didn't?" Dexter chuckled. "They went away thinking about it."

"Thanks for your help, boys." Wade was looking serious and studious. Like Oliver and Dexter, he had no experience for what Timmy's realm was like. Timmy had talked with him about it. They were both reluctant to take a chance on what was, between father and remarkable son, a delicate relationship.

"Do you want to become the Lucifer in my Heaven, Dad, or take a chance that I would turn into that for you?"

Timmy's explanations sometimes left a little something to be desired, but Wade sensed that it was Timmy's respect for him that kept them apart in this regard. In Timmy's Realm, Wade would be just another visitor, and one subject to the rules and leadership of Timmy, a role-reversal neither of them thought would be healthy.

They kept a mutually respectful distance, psychologically. Wade was impressed with Timmy's abilities, but he retained a stoic impartiality and staunch attitude of parental authority. Timmy still respected and responded to that, likely for his own comfort and confidence. He had something to fall back on, even if the strength of that support was papier-mâché.

For Oliver and Dexter, it was even more stark. They were the Kryptonite to Timmy's superman capabilities. A meeting of synthesis between them and Timmy could lead to unknown consequences. None of them had any guidance in the matter, but they all sensed that it would not work out well.

The brothers wanted to help, of course. Timmy had told them he expected to be able to help them in return. Surely it wasn't the thought of monetary gain that motivated them.

Wade looked around. His beer would have to wait.

Out in the theater, Timmy was looking over his field of battle. He still wore the sparkly tunic that presented him as an "usher". He had ushered each member of the audience into a complicated reverie, collecting each one's total life experiences in an instant, and building an alternate reality for each one to experience.

He had had to bring them out of it too. Their experiences existed only in his mind; and their interactions and conversations remained merely virtual until he brought them back from their reverie with new memories from the trip.

Hundreds of them, and he proposed to do this over and over again, a dozen times. What possible hubris impelled him to think that he had this kind of capability?

With a rueful smile, Timmy realized that the fact he had not encountered any limitations so far was strong encouragement for him to think so. To date, he had absorbed the minds of all of his friends, his school acquaintances, neighbors, church members, workmen, lecturers, scientists, doctors, surgeons, traveling lecturers, and every dabbler and tinker in arcane lore about the Titanic.

He had not just looked in their windows; he had rummaged through all their drawers and hidden memento boxes, investigated all their secrets and dark intrigues, thrown open the closets that concealed their shameful passions, and memorized every scrap of college notes and family letters they had ever written.

All of these minds were inside him, not just for the one-time viewing, but permanently. He had a million fingers, with strings tied around each one to remind him of special things which would be needed.

His mind spread all over this town, these cities, and this region. He was the housewife changing diapers in this house, and the sleeping night watchman resting on his couch over there. He was an elderly patient in a convalescent bed, and the attending physician reluctant to bear sad news to an acquaintance.

And he grew with every day that passed. His separate avatars, stored in little nests of cogitation and interactivity, built more memories each day. For every active avatar in his realm, he had two minds' worth of thinking in his brain. He had asked Jeffrey how big and heavy his brain was, but the truth was that no boy or man or team of men could lift it or move it or even comprehend its size and scope. But fortunately, his mind occupied that space between dimensions, which required no support, no shielding, no sustenance or protection.

He was a blob of thinkingness, engulfing the town and cities around him. The thing that ate …

"Are you tired?" Hannah asked.

Timmy smiled. "No. I'm fine. We had a lot of interesting people here today. Some of them came quite a distance! Or maybe they were just in town. Anyway, I have a lot of special projects to work on; I have some new friends in mind."

Hannah smiled back. "Will the Realm get bigger? With all those people roaming around, they'll be looking for things to get into."

"Sure! Why not? We'll need some Castles and playgrounds and parks and wave machines and all kinds of things."

"Movie theaters, bowling alleys, shopping malls, …"

"Shopping malls?" Timmy looked at her.

"Girls, Timmy. Girls!" Hannah shifted her hips and rolled her eyes. "Honestly!"

"But none of them wear any clothes!"

"Because they haven't *been* to the mall yet. My goodness, Timmy! What *ever* would you do without me?"

"I would dwindle. I would shrivel. I would mope in a closet until the termites ate my house. You have *saved* me, Hannah! I owe it all to you!"

"Well, maybe not all of it. But at least enough for a shopping trip!" Hannah smiled.

"Of course!" He grinned in response. "Are you ready to go home now?"

"Sure. Want me to carry your costume?"

"Would you? Maybe I'll nap on the way home."

"Climb aboard! Just wipe your feet first."

Timmy stepped into an embrace with Hannah, and she ended up with a handful of garments. He spun in place and settled into her protuberances and niches, like a baby snuggling down for a nap.

Hannah found the rest of her family, piled the clothes into a box for transport, and gave them a smug smile.

"Okay, she's happy. She's got that well-fed cat look." Angie observed.

"Is one canary sufficient?" Theo asked.

Hannah nodded. "It was a nice, fat canary."

They all piled into the limousines they had rented for the occasion, and headed back home.

"Are you ready?" Timmy asked her.

Hannah squeezed his hand. "Of course! I'll go anywhere with you."

They stood at the base of the trees supporting Roger's Tree House. A circular set of stairs wound around up to the walk-around deck level, but the stairs were animated like an escalator, going up on the left, and down on the right.

"I guess I was asking myself," he grinned as they stepped on. "These guys are real doctors. I'm only getting ready to play one out in the real world."

They entered the compact interior of the tree house and turned to a hallway disclosing a dozen closely-spaced doors.

"Pretend," Hannah said as they stopped at the third door on the right, "that they're all just sitting there in their underwear. That should ease the tension."

They opened the door. Eleven doctors were sitting around a table in their underwear.

Well, technically, these were bathing suits. They happened to comprise the green, like the Statue of Liberty, along with the more recent varieties of metallic blue and a kind of amber. Perhaps more disconcerting was that the serious expressions they wore were on the faces of ten-year old children.

Two of them appeared to be girls, but they were topless too. Being two years away from puberty, it was not yet even a distraction. Another thing that reduced the attempted seriousness of the procedure was the number of legs swinging back and forth under the table.

"Thank you for coming. I'd like to present my most trusted associate, Hannah McMasters. Hannah, this is the distinguished board of senior medical researchers that we have assembled for the Anderson Project."

Hannah went around the table shaking hands with everyone. Timmy moved to the head of the table and sat down. Several pages of paper were stacked there. The top page was a list of names and numbers. The numbers corresponded to the brass tag number still being worn around the necks of the panel. The names were the former real life names of the people they had been before being conscripted into Timmy's Realm.

Timmy showed Hannah the list. These were physicians who had chosen to linger, after visiting the Titanic presentation. She looked it over and sat down.

"You've had a chance to review the project data. Anyone want to lead off the discussion?" Timmy looked around. "Doctor Able?"

Doctor Able -- "Thanks, Tim. Initially, I was convinced that this was a lost cause. But reviewing recent events, I see that we should consider advances in procedures that may have been unknown to science mere days ago."

Doctor Chin – "The patient's prognosis indeed appears bleak. I'd like to know what the proposed treatment might be before we try to assess its effectiveness."

Doctor Walker – "Timmy is going to put his hands into the patient and sift out the cancer cells."

Doctor Able – "That sounds excellent, but how will you distinguish the cancer cells from the normal cells? That has always been our primary difficulty. Excision and destruction in situ have always been available to us. The difficulty is always identification and targeting."

And so it went for several hours. It may seem that this was an exercise in frustration and idleness, for Timmy had all this information in his head anyway. But Timmy had also set up a way for the personalities of the mind-images to control their analytical portions, in the same way that the visual cortex processes disparate information sources into a cohesive whole. Essentially, he was harnessing not only their knowledge, but their experience and wisdom as well.

The next opportunity for Timmy to act on Mr. Anderson's behalf, would take place on a Thursday, when Mr. Anderson would be undergoing an MRI scan. Timmy planned to be there, of necessity by concealing himself inside Mr. Anderson. But he wanted to have a plan of action, and not just be a hapless witness.

Timmy's general problem was a lack of experience. Although he contained lifetimes of surgical activity, his particular type of surgery was a new factor. He had tried to simulate the necessary actions, but at the moment he was still literally in the dark with it. His hands could go anywhere, *but he couldn't see!*

After the meeting, and thanking his team, of course, Timmy and Hannah were leaving the meeting room when Teddy hailed them from the adjacent doorway.

They looked inside the room he was in, which fanned out from the doorway as all of the meeting rooms did. The space inside Roger's Tree House was folded over several times.

They went in. Teddy grinned at them. He was sitting in the next meeting room with his feet propped up. He appeared to be watching a sports program. Hannah put her hands on her hips in a petulant posture.

"This is a library annex, and I'm just reviewing a documentary." Teddy explained.

"A library annex? I thought the library was housed in the school?" Hannah looked puzzled.

"It is. The rest of the school is available through *that* door, instead of the one behind you, if you want to go to the school."

"What! You've got a permanent link set up between the library and the *Tree House?*" exclaimed Hannah.

"Well, yeah. But that's not why I wanted to see you. I've got a question for the Boss." He reached into a box and handed Timmy and Hannah each a can of root beer. It was cold.

"Okay, what?" Timmy said, opening the root beer and waiting to absorb whatever weirdness Theo's avatar had come across this time.

"Wait," said Hannah. "Where did you get root beer?"

"The Miller's refrigerator, of course. Take as many as you want, then close the door, and more appear." Teddy said, implying that such a source should have been obvious.

"Anyway," he continued, "I've got a friend named Carla who wants to be able to modify the swim suit."

"Which swim suit?"

"*Anybody's* swim suit. They're all the same!"

"Into what?"

"Something more varied, a little more demure, and with a bit of flair, she said."

"Hmm. I take it she realizes the kit has to retain its utility?"

"Obviously. And she'll expect to require your personal approval for each, before that utility gets implemented."

"Okay, that seems prudent. Why does she want to do it, and what will she get out of it?"

"She said she likes to be busy, and to make things for others. She also wants to build up some good will so she can ask you for a special favor later on."

"Okay, that seems innocuous. We'll provisionally implement it immediately, and see what comes of it. You can tell her I said it would be okay." He reached into the same box that had held the root beer, and pulled out a magnifying/looking glass. "Give her this. She'll know how to use it."

Teddy grinned.

Hannah looked between them. "I think I'll look her up."

Timmy threw his hands up in the air.

25. Unimagined Unreality

Timmy stayed out of the public eye for the most part. Typically either Hannah or Jeff was transporting him. They had completed two more shows of the HypNautica project, and they were enjoying the attentions of press agents and tax specialists.

Timmy did not like, and could not withstand, rigorous scrutiny by the curious public or their nosy agents.

So far, they had managed to avoid litigation. A problem for potential legal difficulties was that there was no physical evidence of anything, either of chicanery or factuality. They merely claimed that they were taking people on a journey, and the people ended up believing it.

For any actual eyewitnesses to the procedure, the "travelers" had sat in their seats watching a light show.

Additionally, there were no complaints. Not a single one. There were even known ringers brought in to try to instigate suit for failure to perform, but that fell flat as well after the testimony of the witnesses, and corroborating testimony of other journeyers.

So the money was still coming in.

The new immigrants to the Realm were also arriving. They got exactly the same treatment as the previous guests, except for a color change, and the percentage of dropouts remained close to the same.

Apparently, even with fantastic stories, people just preferred to go back to their humdrum lives.

Of course, for those who could afford to drop a thousand dollars for an evening's entertainment, life was seldom really humdrum, but the net result was that there were no complaints, or any other impediments to the plan's continuing.

Timmy felt differently about it.

He liked that it was working, and that all of his enterprises were continuing to grow, but he was still annoyed about the lack of progress on the medical front.

He knew what he wanted to do, but he still didn't know how to do it!

Timmy's access to Mr. Anderson proved far easier than anticipated. One rather foolproof method was to simply burgle his way in, if necessary in the middle of the night. But without a plan for action, that would be premature.

For today's MRI procedure, Timmy arrived with Hannah, on a morning good luck visit. Then he remained with Mr. Anderson for the boring riding, waiting, rolling, and waiting tedious journey into the big magnetic machine.

Hannah had expressed concern, but Timmy was confident. Nothing physical had ever been able to harm him, and he had had occasion to test such things. A worker's welding equipment, and even the arc itself, had been nothing but a marvel to Timmy.

One should not look at a welder's arc, but bright lights did not harm Timmy either.

Heat or cold did not affect him, because he did not even register their existence. One could no more harm Timmy than one could cause a man pain by torturing his shadow.

Timmy hoped to find something in the diagnostic and observational procedure that would help him with his intended actions. This was an experiment, nothing more.

There was a brief moment prior to the procedure when Timmy took a chance. Henry was alone with the technician for a bit, and Timmy slipped unseen from one to the other. By now, Timmy had learned how to make a contact exposure without being noticed, and the technician should have valuable knowledge about the science of the machine.

Otherwise, it was a tediously drawn-out all day affair.

The time actually spent *in* the machine, however, was different.

Timmy could feel the tension, not only from patient and attendant, but also from the intense magnetic and electrical fields involved. It was like being at the focal point of a magnifying glass. Carefully, Timmy positioned himself so that he could see, and not be seen, and then he opened his vision to the wider spectrum that was available only in this strange cauldron of energies.

Timmy had learned, in occupying people of varying sizes, that he could adjust his own physical form. Now he tried doing the same thing with his ability to see. He didn't need to make his *eyes* bigger or smaller; he needed to make his receptive pigments appropriate in dimension to the illuminating frequency.

Unbelievably, things started swimming into focus. Tiny, tiny, microscopic details and so much complexity! It was like hovering over a city and looking down at pedestrians to focus on finding one particular pattern of fingerprint! Had Timmy not been expanding his ability to dwell on multiple levels of complexity, on literally mind-blowing multitudes of perspectives, observations, and relationships for many months and years, he would not now be able to comprehend that to which he was being witness.

Fortunately, the MRI was a tediously long procedure. Timmy had time to learn how to look, and then to learn how to see, and finally, to learn how to distinguish what was right and proper from what was misshapen and vile.

Not only did he learn to see it and recognize it, he learned to despise it. This, now that it had come into focus, was focused evil.

Timmy reached out, gently to separate the invasive tissue. Like peeling a sticky label off a new purchase, it resisted. Over a small area, Timmy removed a minuscule amount of diseased tissue, and began pushing it toward a safe means of disposal.

It was too far! At this scale, millimeters were miles! He had sifted it, but he could not find a way to discard it.

Angry, for the first time in years, Timmy clenched his hypothetical microscopic grip into a miniature fist, and shook the offending material as if trying to kill a rodent.

There was a flash of some sort, and Timmy lost track of the offending material. He realized that he had no more time to attempt any more of his cleaning technique. This space was so vast! And the tiny grime plague had spread and covered so much of it. There just wasn't enough time!

Timmy relaxed away from his focus, and resumed his quiet place as passenger in the patient. A sense of defeat pervaded him as he lay back and connected himself with the form at rest. And then he rested, and considered.

After Mr. Anderson had returned home, Timmy took the simple expedient of falling out of him, through the floor, and traveled underground back to his own home next door.

Timmy needed time to think, and absorb the new information. Fortunately, he wouldn't have to perform again until Saturday, with another HypNautical extravaganza. He would be absorbing another couple of hundred minds, juggling them all delicately as he entertained them, and then carefully settling them back into their appropriate receptacles once more, with happy new memories.

So Timmy contemplated.

The venue for the next Hypnautica was a large hotel in a nearby city. But it had been designed for things like conventions.

Of course a building full of Titanic fans was anything but conventional!

The drive was longer, but the details remained pretty much the same.

By now, Hannah's father was very much the experienced host and master of ceremonies. He enjoyed the role. Timmy had a split view of him as Theo, and as Teddy, romping through the Realm; the same character, but different levels of brash delight.

As the children began popping into existence on the grassy bank above the lake shore, Corinne noticed that this batch seemed darker in skin tone than previous batches. Looking more closely, she saw that their eyes were brown, and the brilliant smiles were even more radiant.

The metal suits were a muted brown, not quite rust-colored, but a deep, almost wood-tone color, as of weathered steel. Their hair was straight, with a deep, honey color.

Again, they all looked alike. The new guests were noticing the same thing.

As before, they were quiet, daunted by the sheer scope of unimagined unreality. It always took some time for the bubbling exuberance to reach the surface.

Hannah noticed one characteristic that seemed slightly different with this group; they seemed musically inclined. On the ride out to the great ship, groups were singing together. Who knew that visiting a shipwreck was a reason for a songfest?

On the Titanic, the ignoring of the bustling children by the well-to-do paying passengers seemed even more stark, but that was mere perception. The well-dressed were actually no more than animated mannequins, made to look like their historical forebears. Their interaction with modern interrogators was strictly scripted.

Something perhaps equally anomalous was that fewer dropouts were found on the shore after the Locker Room Belle returned from the center of the lake.

It appeared that this group in particular, had more interest in returning to their lives, or perhaps more hope of finding that elusive happiness they had originally been seeking, in a place where their training and dedication had a chance to be rewarded.

Only thirty-two of the brown-eyed made their way up the hill afterward, and out into the Realm.

It was not until Sunday evening that Timmy made a furtive foray back to the original technician who had attended Mr. Anderson. Having copied his memories, Timmy knew where he lived, so it was easy to go there on the follow-up mission.

Information was available, and Timmy knew where.

And so it was that in the very early morning hours, after a young but conscientious technician had put off his partying and gone to his needed rest, that Timmy slipped into his apartment like a rising shadow, and occupied his mind again.

"Okay, what was it then?" Mark challenged.

"Look, you know it couldn't have been radioactivity. The guy's received rad therapy, sure, but they didn't inject him with anything. The cyber-knife, remember? It's just rays, not isotopes. There's no way he could have accumulated anything from his treatment."

"All right, let's say you're right. His imaging turned out fine, by the way. I mean, he still has cancer, but we were able to take the pictures we wanted. The question remains, *something* spiked, or spooked, the super-conducting coils. If we can't figure out what it is, it could happen again. You know what happens when that much energy breaks critical temp?"

"That's not going to happen." Lewis insisted.

"Sure. Okay. Why not? What was it then?"

"Maybe it was like an echo. You know; we pump up the ions, then we let them relax and emit, but maybe we were slightly off frequency and we got a bigger kick than we anticipated. You know how that works."

Mark stared at him. "No, I don't know how it works. What are you talking about?"

"The science of it! You know you can cool a system by giving it just under the necessary frequency, and it steals ambient to finish it up?"

"In an *MRI?*" Mark was incredulous.

"Well, we're not going to stop! We'll have to have at least one more incident before we even dare report it."

"Yeah, I know. We start yammering now, and they'll just replace us. No sense losing our jobs over one hiccup. But I think we ought to at least double the record rate on the multi-channel electrical current comparison track. We'd use more paper, but it's just paper."

Lewis nodded. "All right, I can go along with that. Paper, we can afford to lose. Our jobs, we can't."

Mark raised his eyebrows and gave a wry smile. "Okay, I'm in. If it isn't repeatable, it isn't science."

Timmy reviewed the memories in quiet contemplation again. Something had happened, and it had happened when he was trying to get rid of ... that little bit of crushed nastiness. Had he crushed it into nothingness?

It was matter, but it couldn't have evaporated into energy. That would have blown up the whole lab, and Mr. Anderson too. Maybe he had … sent it away? But where? Perhaps … to that place where fresh breezes are always blowing? Had he "blown" it away?

In the meantime, Timmy practiced "seeing" in the new frequencies he had discovered. It was like tuning a radio to get the right station, but his own senses were the instruments that had to be tuned.

He discovered that he didn't need the power of an MRI, or its pulsing, cryogenic electrical circuits. That might be needed if you had to see things with your eyes closed, but it was easier to simply open your eyes.

He could go back to his neighbor's now, and use his own resources to find and isolate the cancer cells again. But that wouldn't be enough. He had already seen that doing it that way was like trying to clean up the litter of a city with a BB gun. It would just make matters worse.

He relaxed on Hannah's bed with the back of his head resting on his hands. His eyes were closed, but his mind, ever active in the Realm, supporting thousands of other minds in their endless interests and wild activities, could never truly rest.

Hannah came up from downstairs to find him like that. She sat down on her bed beside him, bringing one leg up for stability.

She looked at him, studying his appearance closely for the first time in quite a long time. His feet were crossed, and he looked very comfortable. In this situation, he was naked, as there was no reason not to be.

He was lovely. His form, like a delicate china doll, was beautiful in the way that painters and portrait artists always tried to capture, and never could. Hannah reached out and lightly touched his cheek, tracing her fingers down his chin and neck.

Ever so gently, she moved her hand down over his chest, and slid it down his ribs and along his hip.

This should have been ticklish, but Timmy wasn't ticklish. Anything excessive would have simply passed through him. He felt it, and it was pleasant. It was a caress, and a caress is a delight to enjoy while it is available, like an ice cream treat on a hot day.

Timmy opened his eyes and looked at her.

Hannah stopped moving her hand. She let it rest on his hip and smiled furtively at him. "I …" her voice was uncertain.

"You don't have to stop." Timmy said.

"Yes I do." Hannah took a breath. She still hadn't moved her hand.

"You're feeling chemicals, aren't you?"

"I think I am." Hannah swallowed awkwardly. She thought she had made a sound just swallowing.

"What's it like?" Timmy asked, "Feeling the chemicals, I mean?"

"I can't describe it …" she paused. "It's like looking at a soap bubble, with its flowing, iridescent colors. It's so beautiful! You want to grab onto it. But your touch is destructive. You reach out," she looked at her hand, resting innocently on his hip, "and you destroy it."

"Your touch is not destructive." Timmy said, still not moving at all. "You can't hurt me, remember?"

"I can hurt *us*," she smiled at him, and tears were forming in her eyes. "You're so beautiful, Timmy. Why does love have to be painful?"

"I don't think it does." He smiled. "You're probably confused because your love is triggering some primitive passions similar to hunger. You can't have your cake, and eat it too. Hunger destroys the thing you hunger for. Sometimes love seems to do the same thing, but it doesn't have to. You can have me, and not lose me. We won't have sex, but we can't hurt each other by loving each other."

Hannah just stared at him.

"It's lucky you have Jeff, you know?" Timmy smiled. "You can love him any way you want to, and you won't hurt him *or* me. Have you decided whether you want me to be there with you, when you try to find out what it's like?"

Hannah smiled. "I think I have. You ought to be there. Maybe it will make a difference. Maybe we can learn to love without hurting."

Timmy nodded slightly. "It's probably worth the experiment."

Hannah laughed, putting her hand over her mouth. "Yes, I should have guessed you'd say that. It's probably what Jeff will say too."

Timmy smiled. "Maybe you shouldn't ask him right away. A thing like that tends to prey on a boy's mind. You still have a bit of waiting before you're ready to tie the knot."

Hannah leaned down, and kissed him gently on the lips. "Oh, I do love you so!"

"Yes, I know you do. I love you too, Hannah. I love you very, very dearly. Thank you for being so you."

26. You Might Be The One

Timmy wandered the Realm, trying to put things into perspective. He had learned recently how to change the scale of his vision, his manner of examining materials and substances. But in learning this, he also realized that looking at things on a microscopic level automatically meant that the overall information load grew enormously in size.

This version of his former back yard now had people wandering through it. Leftovers from the Titanic sightseeing excursions, the avatars of his guests who had been reluctant to leave the "tour" were still touring. He saw what appeared to be ten-year old children with strangely colored hair, and matching brightly-colored eyes, walking sedately through a dark forest, both singly and in small groups.

Here they would not tire or grow hungry, and would eventually find something of interest, or someone to lead them to something of interest. It was perhaps a moment of discovery and reflection, to have lived a life of work and responsibility, and then to find all of that cast aside and yourself returned to a care-free childhood, that led them to go wandering.

Similarly, Timmy was in a mood to wander and ponder, after recent events. He might be able to change his focus of perception, to find and recognize cancer cells, but getting rid of them would take forever if he had to do it one cell at a time.

Timmy was in the position of someone who had discovered an important industrial process, only to be faced with having to build the entire industry before it could be implemented. Leonardo's flying machine faced a similar challenge, as did Charles Babbage with his difference engine.

Babbage, however, came closer to the solution, because his work, though revolutionary, could at least be implemented by the craftsmen of his day. He was able to see parts of his design come to fruition.

Mowing a lawn, for example, was not a significant challenge to be fretting about. Mowing every lawn in the nation, in a single afternoon, seemed to call for a different kind of effort. Timmy's difficulty was one of scale.

Timmy conjured up a stone bench in the middle of the forest, and sat down looking toward the lake.

"I suspected you might be the one."

Timmy turned to see who had spoken. A boy with light green eyes, and rather surprisingly green hair was watching him. "May I talk to you?" The boy said.

"Sure! Pull up a seat." Timmy moved over a bit.

The boy sat down. Timmy noticed that his number was not displayed as a badge around his neck, but was showing on what would be his belt buckle, if he were wearing a belt. He did have bright green metal encasing his bottom, a design loosely based on Timmy's original bit of psychological warfare, the tension between himself and Hannah about nudity in his realm. Timmy wanted nudity to not be a factor, but Hannah was insistent that it could not be ignored.

The bargain that he arranged was fully satisfactory to neither, but served a purpose to keep the disagreement at a stalemate. Accordingly, all arrivals were "clothed" in a garment akin to a chain mail bikini, with loops of metal secured on the hips holding the "fabric" quite taut. It looked quite confining, but had been described as feeling like nothing at all.

This metal "uniform" indicated that the boy was a very recent arrival.

Timmy remembered that Carla had a program to modify the design, and this appeared to be her handiwork.

"You were looking for me?"

"Teddy sent me in your general direction. He said to look around."

Timmy nodded. "So you have a question?"

"A few, I suppose, but mainly I wanted to meet you and talk to you."

"Okay."

"I wanted to find out how you were doing it."

"Doing what?"

"Doing the impossible." The boy replied. "I interviewed other voyagers to Titanic, and got some interesting stories."

Timmy turned a bit, to get more comfortable.

"My name is Stavros," the boy began.

"But your friends call you Rusty." Timmy said.

"Yes." He paused. "The green hair doesn't quite go with the nickname. I'm forty-nine years old, and I'm a logic circuits electronic engineer, and game designer. I never dreamed anything like this would be possible."

"So that's where it is then, somewhere in your dreams?" Timmy asked.

"No. It's in *your* dreams."

"How do you figure?"

"Nothing in *my* dreaming would account for this. I don't have the capacity for it. It had to be something outside *my* self."

"Go on." Timmy suggested.

"I thought that you perhaps had something with that headgear; maybe sending either electrical or acoustic signals to read and stimulate the brain. I now figure that's just a cover for what you're actually doing, but I have no idea what that is."

"Impressive," Timmy said. "What do you think it all means?"

Rusty looked around. "You're tapped into the brain somehow. At this level of detail, I don't see how anything in current development would offer the bandwidth or the storage capacity, not to mention the cycle rate, and I have no idea how you're creating the interface. Band width and cycle rate I could duplicate with some effort, but the interface is beyond my understanding of technology."

Timmy smiled. "It's a little beyond my understanding as well. The truth is, *I'm* the interface. Out in the real world, I'm limited in capabilities, because I am for all intents and purposes immaterial. That is to say, non-material. Out there, I have no mass. I'm like a hologram, or even a ghost. I can pass through walls, or floors, or anything at all."

"How can that be? How can you even be alive? Or how did you get that way?"

"Our explanation is that a being from some other dimension came to our neighborhood, seeking, according to the being itself, a place of shelter or rest, because it was injured in some way. In finding what it sought, it rewarded me by changing me into something more like itself, a creature between dimensions."

Timmy looked out through the forest. "That doesn't explain things very well, but it does explain me. I can walk through walls, and reach through solid things. After a few years being frustrated that I couldn't even keep clothes on myself, I discovered that I could put my head inside someone else' head, and listen to what they were thinking. Eventually, I learned how to download their entire brain processes into my own."

Timmy looked over at the boy. "And that's how you came to be here. I put my head inside yours, in that theater with the headgear and laser show, and made a copy of your mind. Then I wound it up and set it free in my own private playground, which I've been calling the Realm."

"I'm a copy?" Rusty said. He looked around. "But what is this place we're in?"

"This is all taking place in my mind. It's no more real than an imaginary flower, or this bench we're sitting on."

Rusty tapped the bench with his knuckles. "It seems real."

"What else would it seem like?" Timmy smiled. "Did the Titanic seem real? That's what I was selling, the reality of an artificial construction. After I built up the false memories of a trip to the Titanic, I downloaded those memories back into the brains of my waiting audience, and they all came away convinced they had been on board the real ship."

"Wait, I'm still out in the real world too? I thought I chose to stay here?"

"It was a false choice. I couldn't keep you from being out there. I just wanted to find people who also wanted to be here. The choice you made was to be both here and there."

"So that's why I got a new body then." Rusty looked at his hand.

"No, I could have given you the same body. The body you're in is because that's what I wanted you to look like here. This is a new place, with new people. They should look young, because they're going to be young for a long time."

"A long time? I hadn't thought about that. How long will I be here?"

"As long as I live, I guess. That's what I got presented with. My other-dimensional benefactor said it was easier to make me immortal, rather than building up a body without substance, that ages somehow."

Rusty stood up, and looked down at himself. "I'm going to be a child, forever? Why?"

"Because that's what I am. I was just under twelve when I got changed. The world of testosterone and the relationships between men and women are unknown to me, and *I can't get any more mature*. Rather than create some fake fantasy of what sex is supposed to be, I simply ignored it as thoroughly as I could."

Rusty stared out through the forest. "No sex, forever." He looked back at Timmy.

"What is this place supposed to be? Punishment for our sins?"

"It's supposed to be fun."

"Without sex?"

"Was sex fun?" Timmy asked him.

"You're kidding, right?"

"No, I'm serious. Was it fun?"

"Well, after the posturing, the pretending, and the placating, it had its moments, I'd say."

"Ah, yes; the brain's *pleasure* center. I could have you drooling and thrashing around on the ground, in a frenzy of ecstasy if you wish. Would that be a reward or a punishment, and for what?"

"Well … hmm." Rusty thought about it. "Dispassionately considered, it does seem a bit pointless, at least from this perspective." He looked down at his child's body again.

"Dispassionate is what I've got, and what we've got. The people who are here enjoy swimming, and games, and all kinds of play activities, just as you'd expect kids to do. Somehow that kind of passion and excitement I understand, and can relate to. I'm not trying to justify removing sex from your utopia, or afterlife, or whatever you want to think this is; I just couldn't deliver a quality product."

Rusty sighed. "Oh, well. That kind of explains what *we're* doing here. But what are *you* doing?"

"I guess you could say that I picked your brains so that I could pick your brains. By absorbing so many minds I'm finding new ideas and new ways to do things. Out in the real world, I could spend a thousand years going to university lectures, and I wouldn't get near the information and understanding that I get from a single session of guiding people around on the Titanic, and you guys paid for the privilege."

"Good point. We walked into that one, that's for sure. I guess there's no such thing as a free lunch."

"There is here, but there's no point to eating anything here, except as some form of celebration."

"No food, no sex, no booze either, I'm guessing. Just why did you bring us here again?"

"To pick your brains." Timmy smiled.

"Wait, you did say that! So I guess the good old work ethic can still be employed here then. What kind of problem are you working on, since you can just wave your hand and create miracles?"

"It takes a bit more than just a wave of the hand, but you're pretty much on target with that assessment. What I've been pondering, as a problem to be worked on in the real world, is how to cure cancer."

"Cure cancer? That's a little out of my field. How is that you put the memories in people's brains? I don't suppose you could just erase the cancer."

"Putting memories in their brains is a lot like reading the memories out in the first place. Just align my brain with theirs, and push instead of pull. They come out of it remembering things that never happened."

"Sounds like a CPU operation. That kind of thing I understand. So you're physically influencing the world, but at a smaller scale?"

"Funny you should put it that way. I don't know about CPUs. My Central Processing Unit is organic, or it is based on one that used to be organic. When I'm back in the real world, it's about all I can do to carry a can of soda or something. When I tried to wear shoes, my feet came out of them, not because they didn't fit, but because I couldn't make my foot materially solid enough to stay in them."

"Well, yeah, but moving a shoe or a can of soda around is a big deal when what you're used to doing is sending packets of electrons skittering here and there. A pound of force, electrically, is enormous!" Rusty seemed impressed by Timmy's ability, although Timmy had always thought of himself as weak.

"But is it electrons I'm moving? I always thought thoughts and memories used a different system."

"In the brain, memory is chemical, but thought is just a way that chemicals do signaling. If you can change a person's memories, you could probably change information inside a computer."

"I don't know that that helps me. I need to physically remove cancer cells, and computers can't do that."

Rusty rubbed his chin, as if stroking a beard that wasn't there. "As I said, this isn't my field, but isn't a cancer cell just an ordinary cell that has forgotten what it is supposed to do, or somehow got bad information in its wiring, so that it goes out to do something else?"

"The doctors say that the cancer cell has to accumulate about five different mutations, before it becomes dangerous. But I guess a mutation is a form of memory change. I've never considered it that way."

"Maybe you could "read" a normal cell's mind, and then put that information into the cancer cell, giving it the memory of what it was like to be normal, and changing it from a cancer cell to a normal cell." Rusty seemed genuinely interested in Timmy's dilemma.

"That's an interesting idea, but when I do a presentation of the Titanic, I scan a couple of hundred minds, and then "reprogram" them. I have to deal with millions of cancer cells, and by the time I've done a few hundred, another thousand have been taken over. It's like battling a forest fire with a water pistol."

"Hmm. Damn!" Rusty looked apprehensive, "Oops! I guess I shouldn't be cussing here."

Timmy laughed. "I've encountered people who've done a lot worse!"

"Yeah, I guess you have. Wow! You've absorbed thousands of minds! Your brain capacity must be enormous!"

Timmy spread his hands. "What you see is what you get. That's why I made this place; so that I would have room to spread the information around."

"Well, then you must have an unlimited ability to expand your mind somehow. One brain couldn't contain dozens, much less thousands."

"It's flexible, I guess. How does that help?"

Rusty grinned. "Bigger is better. Now if we could make it faster ..."

"I think I know what you mean." Timmy said, looking up. "Let's take a walk."

27. A Very Sensible Rule

They headed downhill, toward the lake. At the shoreline, there was no sign of the sunken ship, or its attending ferry, the Locker Room Belle. The only indication they were in the appropriate area was the small wooden stage where the greeter would speak to the arriving tourists.

Rusty gave a small grin of recognition. This was where he had started out a few days ago. He had covered a considerable distance since then, and most of it barefoot.

Henry and Alice were docked at a small pier. No other boats were in attendance. Timmy and Rusty strolled out along the pier. Alice looked up from her deck chair. It had come from the Titanic.

"Nice chairs." Timmy said.

"Two people with orange and yellow hair, with eyes of golden fire brought them to us," Alice said, as if reciting from Coleridge. "They wore number tags 131 and 132." She looked at Rusty, with his number 114.

"Not in my group, I'm afraid," He said.

"Very pleasant people," Alice continued. "They were smiling and laughing the whole time."

"Frank and Elizabeth Morris, from the History Department at the University. They were married two weeks ago." Timmy said.

"Married? They seemed so young!" Henry said, from his own deck chair.

"Well, Henry! I'm sure they must have been in love," suggested Alice.

"Frank was seventy-two and Elizabeth was sixty-eight," Timmy added. "They loved History, but they liked each other a lot too."

"They certainly seemed to," Alice said, "They made a lovely couple."

"As do you," Timmy said, "Henry, I thought your boat was bigger."

Henry grinned. "I stretch it out sometimes, when we have company. It's a Roger-built boat, of course."

"Of course." Timmy looked out at the lake. "Will you be taking it out today?"

"We take it out every evening, when the breeze picks up. The wind circles around the lake, like a minute hand making its circuit. We go out, circle the lake, and come back around. Easiest sailing you ever did." Henry reached over for Alice's hand, and gave it a squeeze.

"Sounds like the good life," Timmy offered.

"It'll do for a while," smiled Henry.

Timmy and Rusty moved on.

"They didn't have numbers," Rusty observed.

"My former neighbors," Timmy replied. "Henry has cancer."

"What, here?"

"No, out in the real world. He's the reason I'm working on the problem."

"Ah, I get you." Rusty glanced back. "What happens if you don't find an answer?"

"It messes things up," Timmy said. "We want to get Henry retired and comfortable, out in the real world, so we can acquire his property. If he's out sailing, he won't need a bungalow."

"That's what all this is about? You want his house?"

"I want everyone to be happy. The process can be like a jigsaw puzzle sometimes."

"Oh yeah, I forgot. We all gotta be happy little industrious, sexless bees."

"You want a stinger?" Timmy asked. "Tell me something. Are you single, out there in your game world?" He looked at Rusty. "You don't have to answer. I already know the answer. Maybe you're not working hard enough to make yourself happy."

"Happy through sex, you mean." Rusty said. He took a deep breath. "Hmm. You make a good point."

"I call it chemicals." They were walking up through the woods again. "Bees and ants do it that way. They get a chemical, and it tells them what to do."

"People aren't insects!" Rusty said with vehemence, "Maybe with your big brain we all seem like insects."

"We were talking about making it faster, not bigger." Timmy smiled. "My point about the bugs is that you don't have to be a slave to chemicals anymore. You can do what your mind wants to do, instead of what happens to be coursing through your blood stream."

They had arrived at the Millers' and McMasters'. "Come on up," Timmy said. They went into the Millers' kitchen. Timmy opened the refrigerator and got out two root beers. He continued on through the house, walking up the stairs and entering his bedroom.

He continued on into Hannah's room. She appeared to be in the shower. "We have company!" He called out to her.

"Is he decent?" She called back.

"Hang on a minute," Timmy looked over his guest. He changed the number to the word "Rusty" on his diminutive garment, and then said. "He is now!"

"Good," Hannah said, "in that case I can come out." She stepped out of the shower. Other than the towel with which she was drying herself, she was naked.

"This is Hannah," Timmy said.

"Hi, Rusty!" Hannah said, reading his name. "I love your hair!" She gave him a hug.

"Smart girl, isn't she?" Timmy asked.

"She's … I thought …" He closed his eyes, "I mean … why did you bring me here?"

"I wanted you to meet Hannah. Rusty is a game maker out in the world," he explained to Hannah.

"Ah," Hannah replied. She began toweling her hair, seemingly unmindful that she was baring all yet again. "I guess that's why he's curious about this place."

"Yes, I am." Rusty responded. "Among other things, it's always interesting to chat with someone who likes to break the rules, and who knows how to break the rules."

Hannah went to Timmy and kissed him. "One of the rules here is that everyone loves me. We established that early."

"That's a very sensible rule," Rusty said.

"Okay, I like him. So what's going on?" Hannah asked Timmy.

"Rusty seems to have some insight on what I'll need to do to deal with Henry's cancer."

"I keep forgetting that's what we're working on," Rusty said, looking at his root beer and taking a sip.

Hannah smiled. "Let's adjourn to the Library Annex," she said, reaching out to touch the left hip of both Timmy and Rusty.

In a blink, they were in the library annex, connecting Roger's Tree House, and the school. Hannah was wearing a silver metal bikini, and Teddy was there.

"'bout time," he said.

"You were expecting us?" Hannah said.

"I sent old number 114 out looking for Tim a long time ago. I figured they'd be back here sooner or later."

"His name's Rusty," Hannah said.

"By George, so it is! Did you have to pay for that?" He asked Rusty.

"Didn't know it happened," Rusty said. "Things happen fast around here."

"Not fast enough. So how do I deal with the problem of not having enough time to clean out Henry's trash accumulation?" Timmy briefly brought them back to his current quest.

"Describe how you managed to recognize cancer cells from normal cells. We have to start somewhere." Rusty inquired.

"Okay, I was tracking Henry through his MRI, and I used the scale of illumination there to teach myself how to focus down onto individual cells. At that level, it's easy to see what's wrong from what's right. I even collected a few to discard, but at that scale, it would take hours to move to a place where destruction or evacuation can take place."

"You ran out of time?" Hannah asked.

"Henry's running out of time. At a few cells at a time, it would take about a century to clear them all away, even if they didn't keep growing faster than I could remove them."

"Maybe you need to clone yourself," Teddy suggested.

"Out of everyone here, I'm the only one who can't be cloned." Timmy said.

"No, what he needs to do is change his thinking and acting into a programming language, and program his wishes the way he programs everything else about the realm." Rusty said.

"But this is something that has to take place in the real world, not here in the Realm," Hannah reminded everyone.

"That's what I mean! Timmy needs to learn how to make his "push" an autonomous action, and send out little scouts to recognize and act against the cancer cells, like an army of more than microscopic Timmies cleaning up a vast territory."

"But he doesn't know how to do that, or he'd be doing it already!" Hannah pointed out.

"Wait a minute. I think Rusty's on the right track here. It's a matter of programming, which is his specialty." Timmy looked at Rusty. "You said maybe I could read the "mind" of each cell, and then "remember" for it to make it healthy again." Timmy drummed his fingers on the table.

Out on the lake, Henry and Alice noticed as a vibration spread across the water, tiny little ripples as if all the fish were harmonizing at the same time.

"I have a kind of "surface sense" that I use to determine where the outside of a body or item is. Maybe I could use that surface sense to scan through a tissue, and make changes as it goes. I could be the forest fire, going through and destroying only the cancer cells … but not destroying them, just resetting them back to upright. Henry's cells are teetering on the brink." He looked around at the youthful, and in this case hopeful, faces, "Maybe I can engineer a reset!"

His eyes grew very wide, and bright. "Teddy! Root beers all around! I'm going to make a house call!"

He disappeared.

Teddy passed out root beers from a box at his feet. They were still cold.

"Does he do that a lot?" Rusty asked.

"Pretty much." Hannah observed, "He's always been flighty."

"Ordinarily I'd take that at face value. Under the circumstances, I'm assuming you mean he can fly."

Hannah nodded, sipping her root beer.

Rusty looked around. "This is the library annex?"

"Nerve center for the Realm," Teddy said, propping his feet up again. "It takes nerve to hang out here."

"Let's look around," Hannah said. "Try that door."

They went out into the short corridor of Roger's Tree House, turning left back to the main room. As usual, a chaotic throng was milling about; some new arrivals, some old-timers in their unnumbered outfits.

Carla was doing a brisk business at a table in the corner, employing her looking glass to image the garment of one Titanic visitor after another. She would use the controls around the rim of the glass to change the appearance of the metal guardian of decency, show the image for approval from the wearer, and then request authorization for the change. That permission came automatically, and another happy customer was born. People with chains around their necks were growing scarce.

Hannah was startled to see that a few girls had opted for some minimal frontal coverage by having bibs of a sort extended up from the bikini line, usually open around the navel, and then looped around the neck and back. They had exchanged one neck chain for another.

Oddly, though presumably intended to add modesty to the outfit, the skimpy coverings actually enhanced the salubrity of bare skin in confining garments. By covering more, it evoked femininity in a way that exposure had not.

Hannah excused herself from Rusty, placed a hand on her hip, and disappeared.

He shrugged, and stepped over to a window to look outside. By some coincidence of placement, one window looked out upon the distant lake, while another on the opposite side had a clear view of the Millers' house, overlooking the back yard.

In a moment, Hannah was back, having modified her own outfit so that a kind of harness of chain mail extended up and around her rib cage and neck, barely covering what would have been needed for modesty, but leaving a lot of bare skin as well. Her name, emblazoned in a florid script, was glowing in a ruby red color on a band just below her collarbone. Like the bikini portion, it seemed to have been crafted with her inside it. There were no joinings of any kind.

"From one extreme to another," Rusty said. "You and Timmy are kind of a matched set, aren't you?"

"Me and Timmy? Hmm. I can see why you'd think that. Let's just say I'm one of his first enchantments. I'm already spoken for by someone else. We'll be married soon, out in the real world. He's around here somewhere, probably swimming."

"Lucky guy."

"He's adorably sweet. You'll meet him eventually. It may not seem like it at the moment, but the population here is relatively small."

Before they left, it was apparent that names were replacing numbers on the modified outfits, although not even all the girls were choosing to cover more. A small number actually chose to cover less, having their outfits modified to display more open loops of metal, and less of the fabric of chain mail. For those who had been tourists on the Titanic, this was one way of diminishing the colored-metal badge of their arrival, but their bright hair color and strikingly hypnotic eyes remained the same.

Rusty rolled his eyes, and looked around as if to escape.

"Something quieter?" Hannah suggested.

"Please!"

Hannah reached out and touched his left hip. "The Hospital Annex Lecture Hall."

In a blink, it was quieter. They were standing in an auditorium, empty of patrons. On the stage, a fully-grown man in a lab coat, pajama bottoms, and bunny slippers, was reviewing some notes at a table. Nearby, an empty lectern awaited any request for information. He looked up at them for a moment, and then went back to his notes.

"It will be quiet here, unless you ask him a question." Hannah said.

"Thanks. I like your outfit, by the way."

"Oh, this old thing? It's just something I threw on."

Rusty grinned. "I appreciate the effort, anyway. Can we sit down?"

"Sure." The auditorium seats were spacious and comfortable, considering that their bodies were about three-fourths-normal size.

"I think I was making some progress, understanding what's going on around here, but when Timmy disappeared, I felt kinda lost again."

"We'd all be lost without him, and that's the honest truth. All of this is happening inside his mind. Most of it seems to be running on automatic, which is why it doesn't always seem to follow any particular logic. Timmy's mind is extremely logical, but it flits from one thing to another too rapidly to make sense to us mortals."

"Us mortals?" Rusty raised his green eyebrows.

"You and me. Everyone else. Timmy doesn't get older, so he made us young too."

"He was telling me about that. Is that where he gets his power?"

"Power? Timmy doesn't have any power! He can walk through walls, but that just means his clothes fall off. He can't lift any real weight, and he can barely keep anything on that's heavier than underwear."

"Underwear?"

"I think that's why he thinks naked is okay. He ends up that way himself so often, he thinks the rest of us should like it too."

"I get the impression you have a different assessment of him than I do. I think he's remarkably powerful, and if I'm not mistaken, he's out there right now, in the real world, curing a man who has cancer."

Hannah stared at him, and looked thoughtful.

"I forgot about that." Hannah said. "Timmy wants to fix up Mr. Anderson, so Jeff and I will have a house to live in after we get married." She looked thoughtful, and touched her right hip. "Jeff, I'd like to talk to you, if you have a moment."

Seconds later, Jeff appeared. His hair was dripping. He glanced at Rusty, and then said, "Hi!"

"Do you have any idea how Timmy is getting along with his project?" Hannah said directly.

"I'd guess he's getting it done. Otherwise we'd be talking to him about it."

"I'd like a little more certainty than that," Hannah said with mild exasperation.

Jeff grinned. He tapped his hip and said, "Timmy, Hannah would like a report."

Hannah blinked. "I didn't think of that."

⋅⋅✦✦✦⋅⋅

Henry was having a rough evening. He was sitting up in his recliner, just to ease the breathing, but the accumulating phlegm kept causing him to have to cough. It was difficult to rest this way.

Alice tried to comfort him. She could not stay with him all night, and it worried her that she was so far away if he had a bad spell. But she needed to rest, too. They were both losing weight.

He felt it first as a kind of tingling in his feet. He grew apprehensive, but it was just a warm feeling, as it spread upwards. He relaxed. Whatever would come, would come.

Through the next hour or so, he quieted, still coughing, but not as badly. Hearing him settling down, Alice relaxed also, and fell into a deep, restful sleep. She would feel guilty about it in the morning, but she definitely needed it now. She slept.

Henry relaxed further as well. His breathing eased, and deepened. He shifted lightly, without coughing or gagging. At last, late in the morning, he slept soundly for the first time in weeks.

In the morning, Alice slept late, rising in some alarm at the lengthy quiet. Had the worst happened? She scurried out to check on him, and found him … resting peacefully, with a healthy bit of snoring to reassure her of his continuance.

She brought him some orange juice and left it where he could reach it. Then she went in to take a shower. This would be a good day to wash away troubles and worries.

Over the next two days, Timmy came late at night, methodically moving his sense through Henry's body, carefully sifting the unhealthy cells and replacing them with fresh, invigorated ones, stitching up the stressed membranes and making Henry stronger.

He strengthened his muscles, converting useless fat cells into healthy tissues, and strengthening his bones and sinews.

Henry was, if not a new man, at least a newly healthy man.

Just for good measure, Timmy provided Alice with a tune-up too.

Then he took a few days off to rest up before the final "HypNautica!" presentation.

Timmy appeared in the Hospital Annex Lecture Hall. He looked around at the softly-lit auditorium. "Sorry, folks. I didn't mean to leave you in the dark."

"How's Henry?" Hannah asked.

"I think he's cured. As far as I can tell, there's no more cancer inside him. He'll be going for follow-up tomorrow. I guess the doctors will be triple-checking everything."

"Do you need new batteries?" Rusty asked him.

"Batteries?" Timmy looked puzzled.

"Hannah said you don't have any power."

"Oh. Well, it didn't take a lot of power. You were right. The push that was needed was very slight, but it had to be focused in just the right place."

"Timmy, Mr. Anderson is cured of cancer?" Hannah said in astonishment.

"Yeah, I think so. Mrs. Anderson is feeling better too. I figured, while I was in the neighborhood, you know."

"You make a good neighbor, Tim." Jeff said.

"Working on it, future … um … mind-mate."

"Oh, this is the fellow you're going to marry?" Rusty said.

"Oh, yes. Sorry about the sloppy introductions. Jeff has been a family friend for several years now. He knows what it's like to have Timmy inside him, so he was a good candidate for me. Naturally I'll never let Timmy get away from me, so any future husband has to want him too."

"Timmy seems handy to have around." Rusty admitted.

"A bit of trouble on rare occasions." Jeff suggested.

Timmy shrugged.

"Man! I'd like to see the expressions on the doctors' faces when they find out he's cured!" Jeff said with excitement.

"Well, I think you could probably ride along with them, you and Hannah. You're supposed to be his neighbor friends."

"No, I mean I'd like to have *this me* be a witness." Jeff explained. "Having that me see it won't do any good until you download his memories to me."

"Oh yeah." Timmy admitted.

"I wouldn't mind catching up with what the other me is doing, either." Rusty mused. "I bet he doesn't realize he's on the wrong track to happiness."

Timmy looked at him. "That's a pretty strong admission, from someone who thought his ticket brought him to the wrong destination."

Rusty raised his open hands. "Call it the voice of maturity."

Timmy looked more closely at Hannah's modified costume. He raised his eyebrows.

Hannah smiled. "You'll like what some of the others have done too. Maybe you should stick around here more."

He smiled. "Well, *somebody* has to go out and make a living, you know."

"I *used* to know how to do that." Rusty claimed. "Now, I have even more ideas."

Timmy looked at him. "Anything you'd want to do here?"

"Oh, wow! That's an opportunity! But I was talking about what I could do out in the world, actually."

"Everybody seems to want that. As I see it, the problem is, none of you are mind-readers, and I can only read minds when I'm actually touching brains with you."

"Eww." Jeff observed. "Put it away, put it away!"

"Oh, stop it, Jeff! Timmy has a perfectly lovely brain, and an even more beautiful mind. We're privileged to see what it looks like, and it is a wonderful garden." Hannah said, leaning on Timmy's arm consolingly.

"From a communications standpoint, what you would need then is a kind of repeater circuit, that you could set up in selected brains. That would keep you in touch with them, even when you're at a distance." Rusty was stroking his chin again.

"I don't know how to do that," Timmy said mildly; then after a pause, "Telepathy? *Nobody* knows how to do that."

"Nobody knows how to cure cancer, either." Hannah observed.

"How tough can it be?" Rusty wondered, "Animals communicate all the time using signals of some kind, light, chemical, ultrasonic. You just have to pick something that will give you the range you need, and figure out how to make the connections."

"You make it sound easy. No one has ever tried to design biological tissue as if it were an electronic circuit." Hannah observed.

"They probably have, but we may not know of it. In any case, their efforts may not be what we would need as a starting point."

"We?" Timmy said.

"It's your next project, isn't it? And we're your brain trust, as I understand it." Jeff said.

"It's not something I can do on this side. On this side, I'm already reading your minds, or you are simply a figment, fragment, or a functional subsidiary of mine. But out there, I'm more limited. I don't see it working unless I could put a little mind-reading me inside each separate brain I wanted to link up with. Wouldn't that just make all of them some kind of robot? Or maybe it would make someone to argue with me instead of report to me."

"You're over-complicating it. Think of it as an extended body part, like a finger. You're keeping a finger on the pulse of their thinking." Rusty suggested.

"How fast could this mini-brain send information? If it could compress the data, and make it like a tiny dream sequence, how effective would the band-width be?" Jeff said.

Timmy studied him. "I have no idea. It would probably take some experimentation."

"You need a guinea pig?"

"Are you volunteering?" Timmy asked him.

Jeff looked down at his body. "Hah! I'm volunteering the *other* me! I'd like to look down and see something different."

Timmy raised a finger, moving it slightly. On Jeff's metal bikini, the word "Jeff" appeared.

"Ah, thanks, Tim." He stared at his belly.

"No problem." Timmy looked around. "This will probably be our last tour presentation. Maybe I'll luck out and get some brain researchers. In any case, I'll have to think about this."

"I'll try to come up with some more suggestions, too." Rusty offered.

Timmy nodded, "I think I'll go sailing with Henry." He disappeared once more.

28. I Have Work To Do

In the real world, Timmy took shelter for a quiet moment in the dugout, looking out over a twilit and very quiet back yard. Images from his own imagination washed over the darkening scene and gave it an artificial liveliness. In his mind, then, he was relaxing on the deck of the "Henry Jay". Henry and Alice were moving about, as if trying to capture every last gasp of wind in their circuit. In reality, or what passed for it, they had made this run so often they could go through the motions blindfolded.

"You made it bigger again, Henry." Timmy observed.

Henry squatted next to him, still holding a line. He was grinning like a schoolboy. Well, he looked like a schoolboy, so …

Alice came over, too. "He had to make it bigger to accommodate the stateroom we fixed up below."

"Stateroom?"

She nodded. "Henry made some salvage dives to the Titanic. He brought up all kinds of nice furnishings, and he set them up for me!"

Henry blew her a kiss.

"Salvage dives, Henry?" Timmy looked at him.

"It's not so deep. Once you get on board, you've got all the time in the world. I got place settings, tablecloths and napkins, heck I even took out some light fixtures and a whole bathroom."

"And you brought it here?"

"Yep. Set it up down below. Hung up the light fixtures, and they started working. Put in the plumbing, and it started working too. I went down to the same place on the Titanic the next day, and it was all back in place there as well."

"Why would you want that stuff on your boat?"

Henry smiled a big smile again. "Showers, Timmy, showers! Alice and I like to get the salt spray washed off once in a while." He winked at Timmy, who squinted his eyes and shook his head.

Curious, Timmy got up and went below. As he descended, the jostling of the boat from the waves it encountered grew less, and its orientation, instead of leaning from the push of the wind, became upright. Walking down the corridor, one felt as though he were on land.

The stateroom opened up into a huge expanse, with beautiful fixtures and appointments, all "borrowed" from the research into historical accuracy that gave them the Titanic.

Timmy realized that a lot of things were happening in his subconscious that he wasn't even tracking. Nothing that he found disagreeable, but odd things that had their own inscrutable logic.

It occurred to him that if he could figure out a way to have a communication channel to keep open after he had copied a mind into his own, that process might just end up as something automatic, as well.

He thought about the brain and its physical function. A brain was actually two linked hemispheres, with some specialization between them, but nothing very drastic in the way of difference. Two hemispheres, one mind. The two hemispheres had a way of sending thoughts, images, sounds, and ideas back and forth, so if he could duplicate what the Corpus Callosum did, he could tap into brain functions from a distance.

There were essentially four barriers to realizing this potential; first, he would have to introduce a new body material, derived from each individual's genetic material, which would intercept and divert a copied brain signal into an alternate path. Then that path of information would have to find its way out to the exterior world, from the presumed safety and private security of the middle of the skull. Then once outside, the information would have to be translated into some form of non-physical data transmission, which could then be sent out like a cell phone signal.

And then finally, he, the insubstantial Timmy, would have to find a way to intercept the signal in order to read it and understand it.

Maybe he should just start carrying a cell phone.

Of course, as Hannah had rightly pointed out, he couldn't hang onto pockets, much less anything someone would *put* in a pocket.

Timmy realized that this last step was the impossible one. He could change people. He *had* changed Mr. Anderson. He could even design new tissues and functions in their biology.

But he couldn't change *himself.* Even if signals were being sent out from those selected clients of his, he would not be able to intercept them, and there was a danger that someone else could. That would be bad.

His public exposure with the Titanic venture had drawn more than enough speculation and interest from agency-type people. He didn't want to leave permanent evidence of his presence and manipulations running at idle, to be noticed and monitored.

The quiet, spectral boy in the dugout drew a deep breath and blew it upward. His hair moved slightly from the passing pulse of air.

He froze, thinking. Hannah's father had been intrigued and mystified by this phenomenon, his drawing air from all around him, or from some unknown place.

He thought about this. His reach was greater than he knew, but he did not know how to control it.

Timmy brought his hands up to his mouth. Concentrating, he blew into his hands, as someone might do to warm his hands on a cold day.

He opened his hands, and a dollop of water fell from his hands onto the floor of the dugout.

Timmy stared at it. He had produced water, and not just air.

Should this have been so surprising, then? In ordinary air there is a mixture of things, including water vapor. Even when he was blowing out "just air", there was moisture in it.

Timmy realized that he could consciously control what his nebulous, ethereal body did in its inexplicable way of being similar to a real boy.

It required concentration, but he had certainly been learning how to multitask and use his mind for something other than a cobweb-keeper.

Timmy knew that he had two ways of reaching out beyond his own touch and grasp. His "surface sense", which he had used to sift cancer cells from healthy ones, probably did not have the limitations he had always surmised that it did. And his ability to draw from around himself seemed to include being able to choose what he wanted to draw in.

Further experimentation was definitely required.

In his mind's image, he went back up on deck. "Henry! Thanks for the ride, but I have work to do!" Timmy waved to him, and disappeared from the boat.

⸱✦✦✦⸱

Timmy walked through the wall into Hannah's room. She was brushing her hair, dressed in her brassiere and panties. She stopped her motion and looked at him.

"Well, boy. Don't be shy. Why don't you come out and play with me?"

"Huh?"

"You seem to be distracted, Timmy. What's going on?"

Timmy realized that he had shown up naked once again. Hannah seemed not disturbed by this at all, but simply recognized that he might have something on his mind.

"I'm sorry. I get a little presumptuous when I'm in a hurry, don't I?"

"It's okay. I don't mind. Come closer."

Timmy moved up to stand beside her. "You get more beautiful every day."

"Thank you, Timmy. I don't mind also saying that you are a very lovely boy."

They stood motionless for a moment. "Want me to brush your hair?" Timmy suggested.

"If you wish," Hannah responded, "I'd like that."

Timmy took the brush from her and stood behind her. He began to gently, of course, brush her hair.

"I could do this for a long time," he said.

"I could let you do it for a long time," she answered, "but I think you have something else on your mind too."

"Yes," Timmy said, "I need to conduct some experiments."

"What are you trying to do?"

"I think I might be able to make a connection between the people on this side of the Realm, and the avatars on the other side. I'll need to do a lot of stretching."

"When did you want to start?" Hannah asked calmly.

"What, on you? I hadn't thought about that. Jeff's avatar gave me permission to experiment on him."

"Jeff's avatar has nothing to say about it. You'll need *Jeff's* permission to do any experimentation." Hannah looked in her mirror at him. "I think Jeff's avatar is acting childish."

Timmy stopped for a moment and looked at her. Then they laughed.

"Why not me?" Hannah asked.

"I don't know if you would really want that. I'm not even sure what it might mean completely."

"Try to explain it to me." Hannah said, "Please."

"If you can reach her, through me, automatically, then you can keep each other up to date on what's happening on either side."

"What have I missed?" Hannah inquired.

"Henry is robbing things from the Titanic. He says he's doing salvage dives."

"What!?" she exclaimed.

"They get replicated the next day, so it doesn't do any harm, but it just goes to show you that things are a little different there."

"I guess!" Hannah looked thoughtful. "If I could talk to her, and she could go anywhere in the Realm, then she could find out things for me, and report them right into my head. Do I have that right?"

"That should work. I hadn't considered that." Timmy stopped brushing again for a moment. "You could be taking a test, and she could look up answers for you. That might be ... I don't know."

"What about talking to other people in the Realm? Would I be able to do that?"

"Oh, sure! Especially me. But other people outside wouldn't be able to do it unless I can do the same thing for them."

"You mean like Jeff." She tilted her head. "If we could talk to each other out here in the real world, by taking a shortcut through the Realm, that might be pretty useful. That would be like telepathy!"

"It could be confusing, but it could also mean having some abilities that other people don't have. That could be … interesting."

"Yeah," Hannah said, "I think it could be." She looked into the reflection of his eyes. "What do I have to do?"

Timmy put down the hairbrush. He moved inside her, and looked out through her eyes. She was again alone in her room. There was no evidence of Timmy being there at all.

He closed his eyes, and shrank down his perception scale, until he could image her central brain, with its incredibly complicated central switching and communication hub, the Corpus Callosum. Along that corridor, Timmy extended his surface sense, and wrapped it along and through the busy nerve fibers.

Backing away from it, without detaching from it, Timmy grew in perception again. Everything was back to normal again, if such a situation could ever have a normal, but he was maintaining a "touch", a sense of connection, even though he was slowly disconnecting from her body.

Timmy appeared behind her again. Then he took two more steps back. He was no longer touching Hannah, but he could hear her thoughts.

"I still feel you, not the way it usually is, and I can see that you have moved away. But I still feel you." Those were Hannah's thoughts, not words. Timmy said nothing.

Hannah closed her eyes, and visualized the Realm. She could see her bedroom in the Realm, almost exactly as it was in the real world, but she could not see herself in it.

Hannah's avatar walked through the imaginary door between the bedrooms. "Did someone call me?" her ten-year-old voice inquired tremulously.

"Yes, Hannah! This is Hannah, from the real world. Can we join up? I'd like to talk to you."

The little girl with the metal harness moved closer. The two entities merged into a single mind, with images and voice records aligning into a collected whole. They became one mind in two places.

Hannah of the Realm looked into the mirror of her dresser. Hannah of reality saw the reflection of a child, wearing a metallic harness as if she were preparing to be a sled dog in Alaska.

Hannah of the Realm saw a reflection of a grown woman, dressed in her underclothes. She stood straighter, and smiled.

"Can we visit Jeffrey?" Hannah asked. Hanna smiled and touched her left hip.

In a blink, they were now in the lowest room of the imaginary house, where Jeffrey and others were swimming. He saw Hanna and came out.

"Hey!" Jeff said, "What's going on?"

"What do I look like?" Hanna asked him.

"The same as usual," Jeff answered, "You're beautiful, of course, but you're only ten or eleven. I do like your what-ever-you-call-it garment. It's very stylish."

"Thanks." Hanna smiled.

"I remember when he was that old," Hannah said silently. "He was cute then."

"Oh, I'm gonna ogle your boyfriend, girlfriend! Don't you worry about that!" Hanna replied, also silently.

"What's going on?" Jeff asked.

Hanna looked at him calmly. "It's a science experiment." Then she giggled. She smiled at him. "You're going to be next!"

29. Of Course I'm In

Hannah and Jeff were seated in the dugout.

"Okay, we're all here then. What's the big deal?"

"Your avatar in the Realm wants to merge with you. To make a permanent connection so that you will know what's going on there, and he will know what's going on out here." Hannah said.

"That sounds like trouble." Jeff said. "What does that little pipsqueak have to contribute to me?"

"Don't get smart-alecky! He could help you with tests, if you don't make him angry." Hannah suggested.

"Help with tests? I'm older than he is, and he doesn't even *go* to school."

"He's smarter than he looks. I'm not sure he'd say the same thing about you. You're talking about yourself, anyway." Hannah smiled, "Besides, it might give us a way to chat from mind to mind. If it works out, I won't even need a cell phone to call you."

"Really? You should have said so sooner. That's worth … wait, what do I have to do?"

"Timmy has to turn your switches on. Then you'll be connected to Jeffy, and he'll be able to talk to me."

"You've already done this, haven't you? What's it like?"

"I honestly cannot describe it." Hannah said, shaking her head. "Are you in or not?"

"I'm in. Of course I'm in." Jeff looked puzzled. "What next?"

"Well, Timmy's at bat, of course." Hannah said. "Are you ready, and shall we go ahead?"

"Do it." Jeff said, "I'm ready."

Timmy came out of her and entered Jeff. Again he began by looking out of Jeffrey's eyes. "I'll come back one day and we'll fix these eyes, Jeff. Right now I need to …." He shrank down his perception again, and focused on Jeff's central brain.

Again Timmy wrapped his surface sense around Jeffrey's communication corridor, the connecting path between his hemispheres, where images, voices, and memories traveled. Timmy made a connection between this colossal information corridor, and the isolated functionality of Jeff's avatar.

Timmy slipped out then, stretching his sense into a distant touch, but a secure one. He stood to one side of the dugout as Jeff sat very still.

Jeff looked around. He saw Hannah and his eyes opened wide. "Wow! What a babe!"

"Oh, yeah! You're connected, all right." Hannah observed.

Jeff looked down at himself. "Hey! I'm grown up! And I'm not locked up! Glory Hallelujah!"

"You'd better behave yourself, Jeff! Out here you can get spanked and it'll hurt!" Hannah reminded him.

"This is great! I'll be good."

"All right. For now, we should go our separate ways, and practice being able to access our avatars, maybe without walking into traffic and such. This can be disorienting. But before you go, I want a kiss!"

"Only too happy to oblige, ma'am." Jeffrey leaned over for a lengthy kiss.

"You're developing a good technique, Jeff. That wasn't bad at all." Timmy said.

Jeff looked over at him in confusion.

Timmy blew him a kiss.

"You're in my head now, aren't you?"

"It's a fair trade. You've been in mine for years."

Jeff turned to Hannah. "No privacy any more, then?"

Hannah smiled, "Welcome to the club, buddy."

"Okay," Jeff grinned, and kissed her again. "No problem at all."

Later that night, when Jeff happened to spot himself in a mirror, he almost fainted dead away. He jerked back to look once again, and stared in disbelief.

"Oh, no! How in hell am I going to be able to shave now?"

"You think that's bad?" Jeffy responded silently, "Think about the ugly mug I have to look at!"

After they left, Timmy settled down in the dugout again. It was quiet. It was secluded and comfortable, for him at least, and it was close enough to everything he considered important to be convenient as well.

Timmy was turning his dime over and over in his fingers. He had laboriously brought it down to this location; well, he had carried it out of Hannah's room, down the stairs, and out the back door, anyway. It was only a dime, and she had given it to him.

He liked keeping it as a talisman and reminder of his limitations. He knew that he could rise through the ceiling of the dugout and enter any room of the house above, but the dime would have to stay put. The window on the left had a ledge up top where he could keep it. His own secret stash and fortune!

It was humbling to be constrained by so insignificant a trophy.

Timmy held it steady in his left hand, and extended his "surface sense" through it, varying his focus in scale as he did so. It was an interesting artifact. A simple bit of metal, intricately carved, with mill marks around the edge, and the interplay of metal domain structure, cladding, and even oxidation and a bit of surface corrosion.

At a microscopic scale, this simple coin was as distinct and unique as an entire city. Timmy would be able to recognize it now in a stack of hundreds.

He considered trying to make an image of it, perhaps to fool Jeff or someone. Maybe fake some kind of magic trick.

Such a trick would be easy. He could, for example, show Jeff how a dime could be used to buy a soda from a vending machine. He would display the image of the coin, pretend to put it into the coin slot, and then reach inside the machine to activate its coin-receiver mechanism.

That might be a fun trick, but it would be dishonest. It had already occurred to him that he could rip off a gambling casino. That might be possible, but it would be neither ethical nor smart. Even if he were willing to discard his ethics, he wasn't ready to throw away his intelligence in a bonehead maneuver, especially since he had already discovered a method of bringing in wealth in an arguably honest fashion, giving value for value to an appreciative audience.

Timmy set the coin down and sat back. He put his hands up to his mouth and concentrated, blowing gently into his hands as a gambler might blow on dice for luck. After a few seconds, he opened his hands. Resting on his palm was another coin; identical to the one he had been given by Hannah.

He placed it beside the first. It looked exactly the same. Timmy knew that if it were examined under a microscope, it would show exactly the same scratches and other individualizing marks.

He brought his hands to his mouth, and made three more coins in exactly the same fashion.

Timmy looked at the row of coins. Five dimes lay before him. If someone jumbled them together, even he would not be able to distinguish the original from the newest ones, or any from the one next to it.

In comparison to his recent stage production and public demonstrations, which had netted his organization close to a million dollars, this foray into "making money" was not a big deal.

But Timmy felt very enthusiastic. This was big in a way that the Titanic was merely artful pretense. This was real-world significant, and he was bursting with excitement, not just at the accomplishment, but also at the potential it represented. An elephant is as much a miracle of biology as is a mouse, but there is a difference, nonetheless.

Timmy sat calmly. This required analysis; deep thinking. Was it ethical? Was it lawful? Was it dangerous?

Where did the material come from? Was he furtively leaching atoms from his neighborhood, diminishing the worth of other coins, or the strength of other materials, or was he producing something completely new from between dimensions of existence?

How would he know? Did it make a difference?

How big a thing could he make, and how big a thing would he need to make to conduct the experiment that would answer his questions?

36. Childhood Dreams And Wonder

Hannah and Jeff showed up early at the Anderson home. "Good Morning, Mrs. Anderson, Mr. Anderson! It's your pesky neighbors once more. How are you folks doing?"

"Oh, my! It's so good to see you! Henry, our neighbors again! I'm glad you came. Henry is feeling much better."

Henry showed up at the door, behind Alice. "Come on in, kids. Good to see you!"

"You seem perky, Mr. Anderson." Hannah observed, as they entered the door and looked around.

"I'm feeling great! Maybe it's that candy you brought. It might have been magic or something." He chuckled.

"Magic happens around here all the time, I've noticed." Jeff suggested.

"You know, I think you're right about that." Alice said, pondering, "It's all been different over the last few years. I remember a long time ago, this neighborhood was rather dreary. But … well, ever since you showed up, sweetie, it's like a new place!" She was looking at Hannah.

"I'm afraid I can't take the credit for it. I only do magic in little doses." Hannah smiled.

"Well, whatever's going on, I certainly feel like a new man!" Henry said.

"That's funny, Mr. Anderson, I was thinking the same thing myself. I think I'm just about old enough now to make the claim." Jeff smiled.

"I'd say you're right, lad. It's probably about time to trade in that bike of yours for a car, isn't it?"

"I wouldn't mind, but it will be a while yet. I've only just gotten my license."

"Well, you can have my share of it. I hate driving." Alice announced.

"I can drive us to my medical appointment. I feel fine."

"No, Henry, you haven't driven for months. You shouldn't take the chance."

"You know, Mrs. Anderson, I wouldn't mind being your driver today," Jeff said cautiously, "It would give me practice, and it would give you a break."

"Oh, no, lad! We couldn't impose. We'll get along okay anyway."

"It's really not an imposition, Mr. Anderson. You'd actually be doing me a favor. I have to get a certain number of daylight hours driving time, to get my full license, and I have to have a licensed driver monitoring me while I'm driving. My mom is always too busy to have time for it."

"And, you know something?" Hannah jumped in, "We would both like to go with you to see what the doctors say. Jeff and I are thinking that they are going to be very pleased with your state of health. You seem perfectly fine to us."

"I don't know. Henry, what do you think?" Alice turned to her husband.

"Well, why not? We can just sit there and give navigation instructions!" Henry seemed to be warming to the notion of an outing.

"I usually leave early, because I like to drive slowly," Alice said, "Are we ready then?"

"Just let me run next door and let my mom know we're with you. This is cool! It will be Jeff's and my first trip together! It's so romantic!" Hannah was effervescent, locking in the commitment.

Timmy, inside Hannah, took advantage of the situation to install a connection, but did not activate it in either direction. The Henry and

Alice of real life, and the Henry and Alice of the realm, would have a potentially life-saving link, but they would lead separate lives for the present.

Timmy realized that not every mind he had copied should be linked up in the way Hannah and Jeff were. It wasn't the complexity of the operation that concerned him; it was the resulting dynamics of aggressive life attitudes versus child-like wonder. The utility of a connection was inarguable, but the function of it would have to be proved.

In essence, he was building a database of minds, which could provide him with a momentum of modest ambitions, and an inertia of innocent delight. His would be a realm of the confidence and hope of childhood dreams and wonder. This was his base.

Like rocking softly in a canoe on a peaceful lake, Timmy was sleeping in a comfortable, warm, and safe place. He was inside Hannah, who was herself asleep in her bed.

Not quite a womb, not entirely an embrace, it was also not dissimilar from being cocooned in a spider's web. That is to say, the restraints were not particularly strong or confining.

It was restful. Timmy exhibited, perhaps a poor choice of words, some characteristics of his formerly human nature, such as a tendency to yawn if someone else did, and to become sleepy each day like any other young person.

It is obvious that his makeup did not require sleep, nor did his energy source need recharging. But he was a remarkably faithful copy of a normal boy, and normal boys sleep.

And so he slept. Until …

"Oh, my god!" Hannah sat bolt upright. "Jeff's been hurt!"

Timmy dropped out of her, falling rapidly through the bed, the floor, the ceiling of the living room below, and into the earth beneath the house. Like a porpoise leaping from the sea, Timmy leaped downward into the ground, where he could travel without being seen.

He was following an insubstantial, but unbreakable link to Jeff's brain, and therefore his location, only a mile or so away. In just seconds, Timmy arrived where Jeffrey was, lying on the street in front of his house, and bleeding.

Jeff's mother was already there. She had seen the accident as it was occurring, but was powerless to prevent it. A car moving much too fast for the neighborhood, and on the wrong side of the street had struck Jeff as he entered the road from his driveway.

Dolores Conners was a nurse, and she could tell immediately that this was a very serious injury. The distorted positions of the arms and legs, and of course the copious blood, told volumes even to an untrained eye. The first thing she did was to make sure the body was not moved, which might exacerbate her son's injuries.

Then Timmy arrived, erupting from beneath the ground precisely beside Jeff. He manifested a simple tee shirt and white shorts, and ignored all other considerations as he swept his awareness through Jeff's broken body.

These bones, here, were broken. Timmy reached with imaginary hands to grasp the broken ends and align them, carefully positioning the ends together in the precise way that they had been forced apart with shattering force. He held them together and made the osteocytes whole again, not glue, but real bone tissue, the way it had been before the injury. The osteons were put back together, a mineral solidity to hold the former break as if it had never been.

Timmy checked other injuries and breaks, quickly gathering up the pooling blood and repurposing it back into newly-repaired blood vessels. Minutes passed, while he worked at hyper-speed and in excruciating detail. The broken body twitched and trembled, as a miraculous infestation of healing passed through it from every orientation through to the opposite side.

Timmy carefully went over the brain again and again, checking for damaged nerve tissue or inadequate blood supply, searching for incipient clots and blood vessel weaknesses.

For ten whole minutes, Timmy moved over the stricken boy, doing what the gathering witnesses could only acknowledge was miraculous healing, and bringing a shattered body back from the brink of death.

Timmy, on his knees beside Jeff, finally stopped moving his hands over, and as some witnesses insisted later, *through* the patient, sat back on his heels and became still.

Jeff's eyelids fluttered, and he opened his eyes and looked around.

"Hey," he said. "What's going on?"

"Bad boy, Jeff." Timmy answered calmly. "You made your mother worry and get upset."

Jeff looked at his mother, who was standing in a pose of extreme anxiousness, with copious tears flowing down her cheeks.

"Mom, I'm okay!" Jeff gathered his hands under himself and stood up. He stepped over and wrapped his arms around his mother, who began sobbing and wailing softly.

As Jeff held his mother, Timmy stood. He walked over to the driver of the car, a young woman with incredible anxiety written all over her face, and a strong odor of alcohol around her.

Timmy reached a hand in through the open window of the vehicle, and placed it on the woman's neck. In a few seconds, he spoke softly to her. "You will never do that again."

He released her, and her face fell softly into her open hands as she began crying and shaking.

Timmy looked around. The bicycle was ruined, but it had seen many years of service already. Timmy walked over to a hedge, and around it, and then went away.

Timmy came back into Hannah's room in his customary naked condition, where she was fully dressed and on the verge of flight to … well, she hadn't quite decided yet, but she felt the need to go somewhere.

Timmy held her. "Jeff's fine. You can talk with him yourself. Just calm down and take a breath. And tell him to do the same thing."

He held her hands and smiled at her. Then he let go and walked over to the wall and into his own room.

Timmy looked down at his hands, briefly positioning them in the way he had held Jeff's bones together as he knitted them back into wholeness and strength. Then he turned them palms up again, and stared at them for a moment.

He got dressed, and went downstairs. The door between their

houses was of course open. This being a Saturday, Mr. McMasters was at home, and reading the paper. Evidently, he had not noticed Hannah's earlier fright.

"Mr. Theo?" Timmy approached. "I'm afraid your morning is going to be interrupted a bit."

Mr. McMasters folded his paper and looked up. "What's going on?"

"Jeff was hit by a car, and was taken to the hospital. He's all right, but his bike is ruined. I think Hannah would probably like to see him, and Jeff and his mom will likely need a ride home from the hospital, as soon as they release him."

Hannah was just coming into the room. "Can we go?"

"Sure," Theo climbed out of his chair. "Hang on a minute." He went into the kitchen. Voices were heard as he updated Corinne.

"Your mother will stay behind so there'll be room for everyone. You're coming, Tim?"

"Thanks! I'd like that."

Hannah opened doors for Timmy, as usual, but then she sat up front with her dad for the ride. She fastened her seat belt.

Timmy sat forward on the back seat, so he could be part of the conversation.

Mr. McMasters looked at him for a moment. "Don't make me get a ticket, Tim."

"I'm pretty good at hiding, Mr. Theo. Besides, I wanted to explain how we knew what was happening."

Hannah looked at him. "Tim, you're going to scare my dad."

"Don't worry, Hannah. Everything will be fine." Timmy turned toward the driver. "Mr. Theo, I can make a connection with everyone I care about, or who is important to me. I've done it with Hannah and Jeff. That's how we knew that Jeff was in trouble. We didn't get a phone call about it."

He paused for a moment. "I'd like to make that kind of connection with you also. I just think I should ask you before I do it."

Mr. McMasters glanced at his companions. They both seemed quite serious.

"Let me think about this." Theo drove quietly for a bit.

"Tim, you weren't going for the full-channel connection, were you?" Hannah asked.

"No, just tracking. So in case something happens … Hopefully not something as drastic as what happened with Jeff, we can be ready to help sooner."

The ride was quiet for a while longer. They were getting close to their destination when Mr. McMasters asked, "What's a full-channel connection?"

Hannah looked alarmed.

Timmy smiled. "I've got a character in my imagination who is a lot like you, or maybe the way you used to be. I tend to make up people who act like kids, I guess basically because I understand kids better. Anyway, I use these imaginary characters to help give me different points of view. They tell me what I think you might tell me in certain situations, like an advisor or something."

Timmy looked at Theo's face. "I call him Teddy. I think you'd like him."

Mr. McMasters selected a parking space, and they parked the car. "So this … boy character named Teddy would be able to … what? Talk to me?"

"Dad, I don't think …" Hannah began.

"No, wait. I'm curious." Theo turned to look at Timmy. "I could communicate with … an imaginary character?"

"Teddy operates what he calls 'the nerve center' which is connected between the school and the tree house. He could probably keep you up to date on everything that's going on." Timmy grinned.

"Tree house?" Theo raised his eyebrows.

"Everything's imaginary, Dad," Hannah explained.

"Sounds interesting. What would I have to do?"

"Dad, wait!"

"I don't think you should get the full connection yet, Mr. Theo. It could be a little distracting, and we have some important business ahead of us. Instead, if it's all right with you, I'll just make the connection that lets me keep an eye on you. And then later, if you want to talk to your avatar, I can just ... flip the switches that make it possible." Timmy watched his face.

"All right, let's do it your way then." Theo said. "Later on, I might want to talk to this Teddy, and maybe see if he's anything like what I used to be when I was younger. That could be fun."

Timmy reached with his left hand, through the seat back, and into Mr. McMasters' brain. He identified the massive nerve bundle that he had been using with his other companions, and wrapped a monitoring focus around and through it. Then he withdrew his hand.

"There. It's done." Timmy said.

Theo looked back at him. "I didn't feel a thing!"

Hannah's eyes got big. "You are getting scarily good at that, you know?"

Timmy nodded. "Let's go talk to Jeff and his mom. They're waiting just inside."

Theo looked thoughtful. He was realizing that Timmy knew where Jeff was, because he was "monitoring" him. The implication was that he had just given permission to be watched the same way.

Jeff and his mother were standing inside, still talking with the medical personnel. Several well-trained emergency-room doctors had given Jeff a thorough examination.

"He's in perfect health, Mrs. Conners. We cleaned the blood off, and there's not even a sign of abrasion. Your son is not injured, but he is very fortunate."

"Jeff, Mrs. Conners! How are you Jeff? I was so worried!" Hannah rushed to them.

Mrs. Conners looked surprised, and then she saw that Timmy was with them. She turned to him with tears forming in her eyes. "Oh, Timmy! Thank you so much!" She looked as though she wanted to squeeze him like ... well, it probably would not have been a pleasant sight.

Timmy backed away, holding up a hand to slow Mrs. Conners' advance. She stopped.

The intern was looking at Timmy as well. Evidently he did not feel comfortable with bare feet in his emergency waiting area.

Timmy looked steadily back at him, through eyelids that were about half-closed. After a moment, he broke the stare.

They collected prescriptions, and the few personal items they had brought. Theo led the group back out to the car, sensing that Mrs. Conners was more upset than Jeffrey was.

At the car, Jeff opened the front passenger door for his mother, and Hannah opened the back door for Timmy. He got in the center of the back seat. Jeff and Hannah got in and looked at each other, across the wide gulf of the small boy who separated them.

Timmy laughed. Then Hannah laughed too. Mrs. Conners turned. "Timmy, I wanted to thank you for coming and saving my boy's life. I don't know what you did, or how you did it, but thank you!" She was crying again.

Timmy reached out and patted her arm. "You are welcome, Mrs. Conners. Jeff is my best friend. I'm glad I could help."

Theo was looking puzzled. "When was this? I thought Jeff got hurt this morning. The first time I knew anything about it was when Timmy came and told me you were at the hospital. You're saying that Timmy was there too?"

Dolores looked over at him. "Mr. Theo, Jeff got hit by a car this morning. He was broken and bleeding, on the street. I couldn't help him! I'm a nurse, and I couldn't help him!" Her tears were flowing again. "Timmy came to us and saved my boy's life! He fixed the broken bones and made the bleeding stop. My Jeffrey was minutes away from *dying*, and Timmy healed him! It was a miracle!"

Jeff was staring at Timmy again. Timmy smiled and blew him a kiss. Jeff grinned.

Hannah was staring at him too. "You didn't tell me that."

Timmy shrugged. "I did what I had to do. It wasn't a big deal. I forgot to fix his eyes again. Maybe I was in too much of a hurry."

Theo was looking back at the kids in his back seat. Not for the first time, he realized that some very monumental things were going on in his life, and he was only marginally aware of most of it.

Focusing on driving again, he made up his mind that he would go ahead with that "full connection". Maybe his avatar Teddy could bring him up to date.

"So you were 'monitoring' Jeff this morning?" Theo asked.

"Hannah noticed first. She alerted me." Timmy said.

"Hannah?" Theo looked at her.

She rolled her eyes. "Jeff and I are kinda engaged, you know! Besides, I'm keeping an eye on him, to make sure no other girls get their hooks on him!" She smiled, at her father, and at Jeff.

Theo shook his head. "I'm beginning to think I'll need to have "Teddy" explain everything to me."

"Wait! You *told* him?" Jeff stared. Theo looked back again.

"Yeah. I think he'll go for the full connection, just like you and Hannah. Think of it as an insurance policy; you guys are growing up, shouldn't your parents get a chance to be a little younger while we're about it?"

"What's this?" Jeff's mother said.

"You might want to do it, too, Mrs. Conners." Timmy answered. "I was telling Mr. Theo that I have an imaginary person living inside my head, who resembles him, and one who resembles you, and one for Hannah and Jeff too. I can chat with them and ask them about things before I get into trouble out here in reality."

"Not that he does, or that it actually helps," Jeff said sardonically.

"Well, he certainly helped *you* today!" Mrs. Conners said.

Jeff rolled his eyes.

"I don't understand," She said. "I would be doing what?"

"You'd be connected to me," said Timmy, "which means you'd be connected to Jeff, and to Hannah, and to that imaginary girl you used to be, before you started worrying about who was healthy and who wasn't."

"Connected?"

"Yes." Hannah said. "When Jeff got hurt this morning, I was sleeping. I woke up instantly, because I knew something terrible had happened. I felt him fall."

"I'm already connected, I think."

"This is different," Hannah said, looking at Jeff, "This is *closer*."

"I think I might want this." Dolores said slowly. "Most of the time, I'm very lonely." Her eyes looked moistly reflective. "I could use a friend, I think."

"Would you want it now?" Timmy asked.

"What!" Jeff sat forward. "Mom, no!"

"Do it!" Hannah laughed, "Jeff is afraid of little girls!"

"No!" Jeff put his hands over his face and sat back.

"Such a drama queen," Hannah said. "Do it, Dolores! We love who you are. You will love her too!"

"All right then," Mrs. Conners said, "Timmy, I do want it, as soon as possible."

Timmy smiled. "Okay. Close your eyes …"

Mrs. Conners turned to face forward again and closed her eyes.

Suddenly she was swimming. She looked around and saw a number of other children swimming and playing also. She swam over to the side and climbed out of the pool.

"Dolly, what's wrong?" Her friend Myrtle swam over and climbed out too.

Dolores looked around through Dolly's eyes. She saw that all of the other children were very young, just ten or so. And Myrtle was dressed in, shockingly, a very tiny bikini that could have been fashioned from soda can pull-tops.

And speaking of tops, Myrtle wasn't wearing one.

Then Dolores realized that *she* was dressed in exactly the same fashion, and that she wasn't wearing a top either.

All the children were dressed, or undressed, in this same manner, and it was somewhat strange trying to determine which were boys, and which were girls, and why it made a difference anyway.

"Myrtle," Dolores said, "I just got connected to my grown-up self, and … this is a lot to take in." She looked around. "Where *are* we?"

"We're in the swimming pool under the Millers' house. There's always root beer in the 'fridge upstairs." Myrtle said, placing her hands on her hips, (but not triggering any automatic responses). "What do you mean, your grown-up self?"

Dolores looked at her. Myrtle. Wait a minute! "You're Myrtle Stowe?"

"No, I'm Myrtle McCubbin. Who's Myrtle Stowe? I don't even know anyone named Stowe."

Dolores remembered that the widow had of course had a maiden name. She dimly recalled having heard it a time or two. It may have been McCubbin.

"Never mind." She looked more closely. "What are you doing?"

"I'm putting flowers in my hair." Myrtle answered, as if it were the most natural thing in the world. "Would you like to see my garden?"

Dolores opened her eyes. She was riding in a car with Theo McMasters, and her son and his friends were in the back seat. "Do you know where we live?"

"We can direct him, Mrs. Conners." Hannah suggested.

"Good!" She closed her eyes again.

"Let's go see your garden!" She told Myrtle.

Myrtle smiled and took her hand. Then she reached for her own left hip.

"What's she doing?" Theo asked.

"Her friend is showing her a garden." Timmy answered. "It's a really big garden, too."

"A garden, a tree house, a school, your house … what else is there?" Theo asked.

"There's a church, a medical center and lecture hall, a lake, Sherwood Forest, Camelot, several towns along the Mississippi, and of course, the Titanic. You should know about that." Timmy said.

"Turn here, Mr. Theo." Jeff said.

Theo turned. "Yes, I should know about that," he said slowly. "How could I have forgotten about that?"

"Well, you never actually took the tour. You can, you know." Timmy said.

"If you go there, Dad, I want to go with you," Hannah said.

"It's a date!" Theo smiled.

"And we'll dress for the occasion, you can be sure!" Hannah smiled again, rather wickedly.

"All right, I'm going to do it, but not right now. It seems to be a little distracting." They pulled up in front of Jeff's condo. His mangled bike was lying on the front lawn. Several flowers had been placed around it.

"Jeff, I think it's time you got yourself a car." Theo said.

Timmy nodded. "We should use some money we made on our HypNautica! Tour. Jeff was helping too."

"I'll take care of that." He looked back at Jeff. "Looks like I have a date with you, too."

"You have to blow him a kiss now, Mr. Theo." Timmy said.

"I'm getting out of here!" Jeff opened the car door. "Mom? We're home."

Dolores opened her eyes. "Oh, my! Timmy, I don't think I'll even need that medicine. This is wonderfully relaxing. You are a marvelous doctor, Timmy! Thank you so much, again!"

"You're welcome, Mrs. Conners. Remember to take tomorrow off too. Doctor's orders."

"Oh yes! That's right! Thank you for reminding me." She turned to go into the house.

"If you feel up to it, Mrs. Conners, try to come to church with us tomorrow. I'm sure you'll find it restful and rewarding also." Hannah called out.

"Oh, thank you. Yes, that would be nice." Somewhat dazed, she let her son guide her into the house.

"You *are* going to sing for us tomorrow, aren't you, Timmy?"

"Sing?" Timmy looked at her. "Oh yeah. I hadn't forgotten." He smiled. "Yes, I think I will sing tomorrow." He sat back and relaxed.

"I worry about him when he looks happy like that, Dad."

Theo looked in the rear view mirror again. "Yes, I think I know what you mean, Sweetheart." He began backing up the car. "I think I know *exactly* what you mean."

Timmy smiled.

31. Most Of Every Sunday

"Brothers and Sisters, I come to you with good tidings of great joy, for the Hand of God is acting among us." The Priest's smile was beatific, but he wasn't through yet.

"In our small community, in our very medical center, a miracle has occurred!"

Jeffrey was seated in his customary pew, next to Hannah. He looked back, where his mother, today, was sitting with the oldest member of the congregation. She was not looking at him.

"One of our parishioners has found healing and grace in the Lord's presence, and is healthy today by an admitted miracle!"

Jeffrey slumped down in his seat, and concentrated very intently on the hymnal in front of him.

"I have received word from the doctors involved, that they had a patient whose chances were looking dismally slim. It was clear to everyone that he was dying of cancer, and had only months more to live, if even that long."

Jeff turned his head and looked at Hannah. She was watching him with some impatience, for she had never before seen him fidget like a four-year-old.

"Now, this is not speculation or guesswork. Our friend had been diagnosed, over a period of some time, with increasing and even more deadly cancer of a most serious kind. While he had been treated, both chemically and with radiation treatments, his latest appointments had frankly been for the purpose of monitoring the progress of his illness, and trying to mitigate its painful side effects."

"In his most recent medical appointment, no anti-cancer treatment was scheduled, merely an analysis of what his current state might be, and whether he was needing even more pain medication. But you know what they found?" The priest paused with his face shining with excitement, and perhaps a little perspiration.

"They found *no sign of cancer at all!* It was *gone!* It was a miracle! Entirely and undoubtedly a miracle!"

He smiled. "And those are not my words, either, although I agree with them. They are the words of our friend's attending physicians. Not amateurs, or mere clinicians, but researchers and treatment specialists, who were honestly grasping at their last straws of hope for his survival"

"It was they who said that his turnaround was miraculous. That he wasn't merely healing, or just feeling better. He was entirely and completely cured of cancer! Healthier even, than he had been a mere month before! And that, my friends, is what should give you hope in your own lives."

"No matter how hopeless and dismal your situation may appear, always put your faith in God to lead you toward His purpose for you. Put your hand in God's hand, and let Him put His hand in yours."

He stepped back for a moment from the pulpit, as organ music rose. The choir sprang into voice, and a haunting voice rose up from the first rank of the choir, where Timmy was standing, not in choir robes, but in a brilliant white suit.

He stepped forward, increasing the volume of his voice,
"When I was but a single cell,
My form had no design.
A shapeless mass without a plan,
God put His hand in mine."
With the last line, Timmy held out his left hand, and placed his

right hand along it, as if slipping on a long glove. Then he lowered his hands, and raised his voice again.

"I had no eyes or limbs,
How could I walk a line?
I did not know my fur from fin,
God put His hand in mine."

Again, with the last line, he repeated the gesture. It was intended to convey the motion of putting one's hand into something. Not the ordinary way of holding hands, but to actually slip one's hand into someone else's arm and hand; to direct and control their hand from the inside.

"A guide to how my bones should grow,
A function quite divine,
A way to do the will of God,
God put His hand in mine."

With this repetition, Hannah joined him in making the gesture.

"So as I grew, I thought I should,
My soul to Him consign,
Where else was I to go but there?
God put His hand in mine."

On this time around, half-a-dozen people copied Hannah's gesture too, listening and understanding the meaning of it, many with tears in their eyes.

"At last my muscles and my bones,
Some purpose did define,
To do His work, with His own strength!
God put His hand in mine."

At this time, most of the people in the church were participating in the gesture as the words came around. Timmy was watching, as well as singing. He could feel the people supporting him, hearing him, weeping with him.

"Some day, when I no longer may,
Work fruitfully as Thine,
Please guide me Home, my dearest Lord,
And put Thy hand in mine!"

Timmy spread his hands after the last gesture, reaching out with his inner understanding, to embrace those with whom he already shared a connection, and to establish such a connection with those who had not yet been reached.

In less than a second, every person in the entire church, both those in front of him, and those behind him, were now connected in that inexplicable manner that had proven so valuable to Jeffrey. Timmy had gathered in his flock, to number them and to embrace them.

No one felt anything, and it was done in an instant. Thoughts and feelings cascaded over and through him, thoughts of joy and inexpressible delight.

Timmy smiled, and stepped back into the line to stand quietly again.

The organ music faded, as well as the chorus of angelic voices.

The priest stepped forward again. "Brothers and Sisters, let us pray now, to be welcomed into God's healing graces and Heavenly membership, to be embraced as members of God's loving family, and to let Him guide us with a merciful and tender hand."

These were the highlights of the program, and the most memorable event of the day.

At his mother's suggestion, Jeff asked to ride back with the McMasters to their house after church, while she went visiting, she said.

"Not a problem, Jeffrey. You are welcome anytime, of course." Corinne said with delight.

"Don't you spend most of every Sunday with us anyway?" Theo inquired with a raised eyebrow.

Jeff grinned without replying.

"Don't give him a hard time, Daddy. He's still recuperating from his injuries." Hannah said protectively.

Theo looked at Timmy, as if for support.

"I can't say anything, Mr. Theo. I'm hitching a ride with you myself."

"Yeah, well, you don't cost me any gas." Theo smiled.

"He doesn't eat much, either," Jeff said, "I, on the other hand, am so hungry that I might even help with washing dishes."

"We have to feed him too?" Theo complained. Corinne smacked playfully at his arm.

"If I were smart, I'd try to change the subject." Jeff said, "Hey, Timmy! Where'd you get the suit?"

"Oh, this old thing? I made it this morning." Timmy said casually.

"You what?" Theo said.

"I made my suit." Timmy responded. "I figured, since I need really light fabrics, so they won't fall off, and fall apart, I would make something out of silk. The shoes are really light, too."

Hannah began feeling the fabric of his suit. "Hey! It _is_ real! I thought you were just "manifesting" it."

"I did manifest it! I just manifested it with a little more solidity to it."

"So you didn't "sew" it, you "made" it?" Theo asked.

"Yes. You were helpful to me in figuring out how to do it, by the way."

"I was? How is that?"

"You pointed out that when I would breathe out, that _what_ I was breathing out was just ordinary air. When I figured out that air has other stuff in it, like water vapor, I realized that all I had to do was concentrate, and I could make water appear." Timmy looked down at his bright, clean suit. "Then it was a small step from that to making anything I could think of, and I've had a lot of practice thinking of things lately."

He spread his hands. "So I made my suit."

"You just concentrated, and it appeared?" Theo had a very wrinkled brow.

"Well, it took a _lot_ of concentration, if that makes a difference."

"It's another miracle, Dad." Hannah said softly.

"It's a special kind of silk, and it's _woven_." Timmy said. "I wanted it to be strong."

"Like a bullet-proof vest?" Theo said.

"I don't think it's bulletproof." Timmy said, "It's a little thin for that. I'm sorta manifesting it as I go, to make sure I don't spill out of it or something."

He looked up. "That's why I made it white. Other colors you can almost see through." He smiled. "We all know how shy I am about such things."

"Oh, yes indeed. At least once a week I am reminded about it." Jeff said softly.

"It's beautiful, Timmy! You were so striking up there in the choir, singing. The whole presentation was beautiful." Hannah said. She put her hands out, and made the gesture he had used.

Timmy reached out and held her hand in the normal fashion.

"Ah, let's get started then, on our trip home." Theo suggested. "I'd like to begin that while my brain still works." He opened the door for his wife.

The kids got into the back seat again, with Timmy in the middle, as usual. Hannah was feeling the suit fabric again. "This is so soft and wonderful! I think this would make a good material for a bridal gown!"

Timmy looked thoughtful. "Yeah, I think I could do that."

Hannah smiled. "And we know it would fit, too!"

Theo started coughing, and Jeff got a curious look on his face as well.

Hannah looked at them. "You guys! Just for that I'm making Timmy my fashion consultant for the wedding. The rest of you can look like bums, but Timmy and I are going to be elegant!" She held his hand again.

Timmy smiled. Apparently all it took to be accepted around here was an occasional miracle or two.

32. Butterflies Aren't Heavy

Back at home, the parties separated. Corinne headed for Angie's kitchen, to see how she could help with Sunday dinner for the group. Theo found Wade, and suggested that they talk.

"I'll get the glasses," Wade said, after seeing the look in Theo's eyes.

The kids, Jeff, Hannah, and Timmy, went upstairs to Hannah's bedroom. Jeff looked around approvingly.

"Hannah, can I leave my suit with you? I don't really have closet space on my side." Timmy requested.

"Of course! It will look nice hanging in my closet. I just wish that it would fit me!"

"You'd wear a guy's suit?" Jeff asked.

Hannah looked at him darkly. "It's a *pretty* suit."

"Thank you," Timmy said, stepping out of the suit and catching it to lay it on Hannah's bed.

Hannah selected some play clothes and went into her bathroom, closing the door.

Timmy carefully arranged the silk suit on a hanger, and placed the slacks on another. His shoes, and the socks for them, he put in the bottom of the closet.

Jeff was watching the boy, so casually naked, and moving around with complete familiarity in the bedroom of his presumptive fiancé. "Have you ever heard the expression, "ménage a trois", my friend?"

Timmy paused, "I have a rather extensive vocabulary, thanks to some reading I've done recently."

He looked up. "I'm pretty sure we should not talk about it, or try to anticipate it, but instead simply let it come about in its own way, with innocence and delight. It is my intention to make Hannah's experiences all memorably wonderful."

Jeff smiled. "You are a friend unlike any other that I shall ever have."

"You need to change too." Timmy said.

Jeff looked puzzled.

"Your clothes, Jeff." Timmy smiled, "You need to change your clothes."

"Ah, yes, of course." Jeff nodded. "Unfortunately I didn't bring any other clothes with me."

"It has been an interesting morning." Timmy said. He glanced down, as play shorts and a polo shirt materialized on him. Lifting one foot, a tennis shoe and sock appeared on it. Then when he lifted the other foot, it became similarly covered.

Timmy looked over at Jeff. He held out his hands, and a pile of clothing appeared in them, as if he had made a coin swing out from between his fingers. "I made your shirt with red stripes, if that's okay?"

After a long pause, Jeff jolted himself forward to accept the pile of garments. In astonishment, he realized that they were real, and if his eyes had not deceived him, Timmy had made them on the spot, with no more difficulty than remembering today's date!

Hannah came out, having changed clothes.

Belatedly, Jeff put the articles of clothing on Hannah's bed and began taking his dress clothes off.

Hannah watched, rather bemusedly. She seemed more transfixed at the moment that Jeffrey was losing himself in the process, than that there was a minor mystery about where his clothes had come from.

In just a few seconds, Jeff too was ready to play in the back yard. He carefully folded his Sunday clothes and left them where they were.

Timmy said, "Wait!"

Jeff looked around.

Timmy approached him, looking upward at him. He reached up and gently removed Jeff's glasses, placing them unfolded on the pile of clothes.

He beckoned Jeff to lean down, and then he kissed him on the outside corner of each eye. He smiled and stood back.

Jeff stood up straight and looked around. He blinked, and then stared at one image after another.

Incredibly, his vision was now perfect, except for the sudden appearance of tears of joy as he witnessed *with his own eyes* yet another miracle.

Hannah was staring.

Timmy said, "Are we ready then?"

They went down the stairs and into the back yard. As usual, Hannah opened the doors and held them for Timmy. With a smile, he let her do so.

Oliver and Dexter were already tossing a baseball back and forth. They looked toward the house with puzzled expressions.

"Oh, my! This is going to be fun!" Jeff said softly as they made their way out to join the other boys.

"Timmy, what's up?" Dexter said.

"Let's play ball. Want me to pitch?"

"Sure, go ahead." Dexter tossed Timmy the ball.

Timmy caught it and walked over to the mound.

Dexter shrugged and went to the plate, where the bat was.

As soon as everyone was scattered around, ready for play, Dexter hit the plate a couple of times with the bat and raised it up into position.

Timmy had a relatively slow windup and delivery, but the ball left his hand with surprising velocity. Dexter smacked it into left field.

Then it was Oliver's turn. Timmy smoked one past him, and then just caught the corner, still with his deceptively slow-looking pitch.

Finally, Oliver connected also, and put the ball far enough that Dexter could come in.

They played for several innings, with Timmy doing pitching duties for both sides, just as his father usually did.

The adults were watching from the porch when Timmy suggested they let him try his turn at bat.

Dexter took the mound, and threw a good pitch.

Timmy leaned into it, and swung the bat with quick speed. The ball reversed course with a satisfying smack and sailed out almost to the ditch line.

Timmy leaped toward first base, not running but floating speedily through the air like a pouncing cheetah in its stride. He touched down at first base, spun in the air and sailed onward toward second.

Again it was a leap from base to base, almost as if he were jumping in Mars gravity. After second, he bounced on toward third, and rebounded from that corner as if from a rubber wall.

Timmy landed on home plate with both feet at the same time, having never touched any of the dirt between the bases, all the way around them. He raised his arms in triumph, and stood there with his face upturned.

Slowly a patter of applause made its way out to the players. Wade was standing, and slowly smacking his hands together in a slow-cadence handclap meant to draw attention.

Timmy smiled and walked slowly back to the porch where the Millers and McMasters were standing in stunned silence.

His father picked him up and hugged him like a normal child. His arms did not pass through him, they didn't crush him, and they didn't let go.

"I love you, son. You make me proud just to see you smile." Wade said softly.

"I know, Dad. I love you too."

After a long and tender moment, Wade turned and handed the boy off to Angie. She held him as Wade had done, as if to never let him go.

"You still don't weigh anything." She said, "I could carry you with one hand." Her eyes were full of tears.

"But I'm pushier than I used to be!" Timmy smiled. Getting down again, he turned back to the ball field, flew out to where the ball had gone, and flew back with it.

He slowed near Dexter, and tossed him the ball. "You're on your own now, brother, it's time for me to go help Mom with dinner."

Timmy touched down in front of Hannah. "My little butterfly, may I pick you up?"

Hannah, not understanding how any of this had been possible, merely nodded.

Timmy rose into an embrace and a kiss with her, and then both of them began rising in the air. They moved gently up to the top of the porch steps and settled down smoothly. Holding Hannah's hand, Timmy turned to the ball field and waved.

Dexter, Jeff, and Oliver all shrugged and began making their way back in. Jeff was talking to Dexter as they walked, showing him his new clothes.

"I'd guess," Wade said casually, "that if I asked you to bring me a beer, you'd have no problem fetching the whole refrigerator. Am I right?"

Timmy looked over and smiled. "Do you want the refrigerator, Dad?"

"No, it's all right. I'm heading that direction anyway." He looked Timmy over. "I always knew fresh air and sunshine would be good for you." He and Angie began moving toward the door.

Hannah turned to face him. "Timmy! You lifted me. You carried me!"

He shrugged and smiled. "Butterflies aren't heavy."

She stared at him. "I'm going to have to stop being amazed at the things you do."

He was looking at her. "No, don't. I'm still learning. I'll need to have a reason."

Hannah nodded and kissed him once more. Then she turned toward the Millers' kitchen, saying, "Can I help with anything, Mrs. Miller?"

33. Back To The Humdrum World

"Mr. Stavros Leonides?" the young visitor asked. He was dressed in a white silk suit and white shoes.

"Yes, come in. How can I help you?"

"I am Timmy Miller. Do you mind if I call you Rusty?"

Leonides was surprised. He certainly did not remember this lad. "Do I know you?"

"No, you don't. But I know you, rather excessively well."

"That … does not sound very good at all. What's this about, if I may ask?"

"You were one of the people who came to our presentation of the rather garishly named 'HypNautica!' event."

"Yes." Leonides replied cautiously.

"And you were one of those who chose, or thought he did, to remain with the tour rather than come back to the humdrum world."

Leonides paused. "How would you know that?"

"I am the instrument that made your journey possible. I know that, and I know everything that you knew, up to that moment. The entire contents of your brain has been mine since that day." The visitor paused, "And not only you, of course. Everyone who came to that showing became a part of my rather comprehensive knowledge base."

"That is a very astonishing claim."

The young man nodded gravely.

"I could try to prove it to you, but that would likely be merely a waste of time. Instead I would choose to simply tell you why I am here."

Leonides looked carefully at the boy. His initial impression was growing more incredible by the moment. "I see no harm in that."

The boy smiled. "I have assigned a selected portion of whatever it is I control as a repository for your information and its self-directed processing. In essence, I have an avatar of you and what you were like on a certain day a few months ago. You may be interested to know that this portion of mind, this avatar, has changed in ways that might be useful to you."

Leonides merely stayed quite still, but his eyes were very active.

"Your avatar wants to meet with you." Timmy said, "Again."

"Again?" Leonides raised his eyebrows. "When was the first time?"

"At the end of the demonstration, or tour, of the Titanic. He had green hair and eyes, an immodestly modest costume, and he wore the number one fourteen. And he wanted to stay with us."

"But he didn't," Leonides said, sitting back. "He ended up back in the real world, or should I say, I ended up back here. It was rather a disappointment."

"But he *did!*" Timmy said, smiling. "Perhaps you recognize that was a necessary deception. Even for those who wished to stay, their former lives had to continue in some manner. It would have been bad for business to have half the audience die in the theater."

"He has been with us," Timmy continued, "and may I say that he has been very helpful to me personally. You have a bright and perceptive mind, Mr. Leonides. Your avatar mirrors your personality."

"You make this sound very convincing."

"I feel that I owe you a favor, or that I owe Rusty a favor. He's the one who wants to meet you again. I'd like to grant his wish."

"What would I have to gain from this … occurrence?"

"Sometimes a different way of looking at a problem, or the world, can be of benefit. That is essentially the purpose I have in all this deception.

I am gaining a remarkable wealth of knowledge and experience in many fields of endeavor, including of course, yours."

Leonides nodded. "And what would I have to lose?"

Timmy leaned forward. "Rusty wants to make the link permanent."

"I can honestly say," the man paused, "I don't know what that means."

"It means," Timmy said casually, "that your mind would be linked to your avatar, through my mind. You would be able to see what he perceives, and hear what he hears, and you and he would be able to talk together, without anyone else knowing it, and," Timmy paused, "he would be able to talk to other avatars, and find out information which is by one means or another known to me."

"You're saying that my mind would be linked to yours, not to his."

Timmy shrugged. "It's semantics. I have a lot going on. Typically I let these things happen automatically, without taking personal interest or action." He looked directly into Leonides' eyes. "But it's true. You would have no privacy of thought, even in your own mind. *Anything* you think, will be available to me. I won't bother promising to be nice, but I will point out that I could have done this already on two occasions, and as far as you know, I haven't."

Timmy smiled. "My being here and asking you about it is evidence of a sort, that you've had mental privacy up to now. I already know everything in your past. You would simply be mortgaging your future as well."

"I still don't think," Leonides said cautiously, "that I have enough information to make this decision. I can see that you've gone to quite a bit of trouble, but I can't let that be a deciding factor."

Timmy tilted his head. "Rusty seemed to think he could help you in your work."

"He probably could."

"It's your decision. Your other you wants it, but as you might recall, he could be accused of having a childish viewpoint."

"I do recall that," he said, smiling, "he was having a lot of fun."

"He still is," Timmy said, "but he thinks that a world without sex is a terrible place to be."

"A world without sex?"

"Or booze." Timmy spread his arms. "It's the world inside my head, and I'm stuck on the other side of knowing about sex."

"I'm not touching that subject," Leonides said, "not with you."

"I understand it intellectually," Timmy said, "I have ten thousand books about it in my head. But as I told Rusty, I lack the personal understanding that would allow me to make a quality presentation to my guests. Innocence, and other delights of childhood, are not without their charm."

"Strange," Leonides looked at him, "with all of … us, inside you, how can you maintain any kind of innocence?"

"Maybe I've been lucky, but it seems that people who appreciate the romance and intrigue of the Titanic aren't motivated all that strongly by lust and avarice. It would probably be prudent of me to be a little picky about whom I invite aboard."

Leonides raised his eyebrows. "I'll take that as a compliment then."

Timmy looked at him. "I know you well enough to compliment you."

He smiled. "I like you, Mr. Miller. You're surprisingly forthright and positive about a rather astonishing amount of power."

Timmy nodded. "The steps up the mountain of Olympus are not without effort or peril."

"And you think that I could help guide you in the right direction?"

Timmy smiled. "Yes, I do, and do you mind if I call you Rusty?"

34. The Only Way To Keep Her

The last presentation of "HypNautica!" had nearly as much fanfare as all the others, and its venue was nearly twice as large.

This number of people would have been very difficult to handle at the beginning. For Timmy, laboriously going from one to another of them, through the staged rankings of stadium seating, would have been a nightmare of operational security. In addition to actually putting his head in alignment with the client, he had had to originally shield that action from each individual's neighbors.

In this location, that would have been entirely impossible.

Fortunately, Timmy's abilities had been keeping pace with the show's popularity. It was no longer necessary to walk among them and physically touch each one. Timmy could concentrate on a group of people all at the same time. He could bring each of their minds into individual focus, and do his download and connection procedure, more like a professional photographer getting a group photograph.

It wasn't exactly a "snap", but it was at least possible. Then he merely had to do that same thing a dozen more times.

And *then*, he had to implement the dream scenario for each individual viewpoint, no matter how it twisted and convoluted aboard the imaginary vessel, which was itself being maintained within his ever-expanding imaginarium, and finally, sort out all the various memories of the evening to put back into its proper receptacle and brought into the current-moment framework.

The *easy* part, was what happened in the realm at the end of the show. The mobile audience, astonished and mesmerized, could be released back into the world, to catch their rides, their limousines, and their taxicabs back into the world and their parts in its meanderings.

But those who chose to *stay*, had to be entertained for a longer period, perhaps longer than their original lifetimes.

Of course, this was the meat of Timmy's reward. Originally, he wanted the thinking power, the sheer immensity of brain function that could be brought to bear on any concept, and wrestle it by mass of neuron power alone into docility.

But these select individuals were the ones who wanted to try new things, find new excitements, and be entranced by the mundane miracles that even a lifetime's exposure had neither explained nor made any less astonishing. These were the ones with a sense of wonder, and they were his kindred spirits.

These fifty-six people, sporting purple hair and lovely violet irises, as well as the standard bright-enamel purple color metal bikini wear, walked slowly down the loading ramp of the Locker Room Belle, still clutching at their number plates and looking around at a world that was only beginning to waken their childlike sense of unfathomable awe!

Timmy saw Hanna walking down the ramp with her father, Theo, now merged with Teddy. They were holding hands and chatting like old friends. Timmy smiled to recall Theo's shock, after he found himself in a child's body, to be holding the hand of another child who purported to be his daughter, who was wearing a rather startling outfit even for these standards.

Hannah had delighted in surprising and shocking her father, and in the smooth and debonair way he rolled with it and absorbed the strange world he was mixing into.

Rusty's voice boomed out then, making an announcement for a secondary means of transportation.

"Your attention, please! Announcing the first and final boarding call for the Chemin de Ferris Wheel Transportation System, now accepting passengers for the Library, Sherwood Forest, Camelot, Hannibal, Macomb, Mayberry, Green Town, Cross Creek, and points South."

Up on the grassy slope, a huge Ferris Wheel was taking on passengers, oscillating slightly back and forth like a teenager riding the clutch at an intersection.

Astonished purple-haired children, mostly those traveling together, excitedly got into line for their next thrill and journey of discovery. Timmy assumed that he might see some of them in about a month. Already aboard were quite a few of different hair colors as well. They may have gotten on back at the Library, and simply ridden down here to see what it was like.

Others of the new group began walking up the slope to explore on their own, or were just strolling along the lake shore, enjoying the evening.

"Henry, Alice! It's good to see you! You must be easily entertained, if you find this amusing." Timmy greeted the inveterate sailors, who were picnicking just away from the general assembly area for the tourists.

"They'll be back, eventually." Henry said cheerfully. "Maybe by then they'll want a nice calm lake trip near where it all started. We take a lot of folks out to look down and see the ship."

"Oh, they have such lovely eyes, Timmy! How beautiful they are!" Alice said, clasping her hands together.

With everyone loaded, the Chemin de Ferris Wheel took off, rolling majestically up the slope above the lake, and circling cautiously around to make its way toward Camelot, with a brief stop at the Library again. If there was a control cabin or guidance deck, it wasn't visible from this angle.

Rusty strolled over. Nodding to Henry and Alice, he exuberantly shook hands with Timmy again. "That's going to be a big hit, don't you think?"

"It seems to be already, Rusty." Timmy acknowledged. "I have to admit, you have some very intriguing ideas."

"It's all fun! That's what it's all about. These people thought that this world was lost to them with their childhood. Rediscovering both is going to keep them going long after their thoughts of the Titanic will be seeming passé."

"Childhood, huh?" Timmy smiled. "Sounds like you're getting into the spirit of the place."

"Innocence, merriment, joyful laughter," Rusty smiled. "If that doesn't recharge your batteries, you're pretty much a lost cause anyway."

"I'm going to go look up a friend." Timmy nodded to everyone. "Have a great evening!"

"Bye, Tim!" Rusty said noisily as he squatted down next to Henry. "Did I notice a bottle of bubbly in your basket, old chum?" he murmured rather softly.

"It's not a particularly good year, considering that it's over a hundred years old." Henry said, turning to the picnic basket. "Still, one has to settle for what happens to be available sometimes."

"Well, Teddy. How are things in the Nerve Center?"

Teddy was seated in an office chair, watching a half-dozen monitors of various scenes from the lake to the Library, and from the Promenade Deck of the Titanic to King Arthur's Court and the round table.

Seated beside him was the lovely Hanna, with her shiny protection weaving its way around her svelte body. She also had her feet propped up, and a root beer in hand.

Teddy grinned at him. "You wouldn't believe how tricky all this is to set up! This stuff doesn't even need power, but you have to train it like a puppy dog to get what you want out of it. It can't be programmed. It's something completely different, but we're making progress."

Timmy looked at the various scenes. "I don't see anything from the real world. I guess that's still too difficult, eh?"

"I don't know. We're thinking of trying something involving mirrors. But that's not what you came to see me about. What's up, Boss?"

"How do you like being in two worlds now?" Timmy asked him. "I know how it feels to me, but I thought I'd get your opinion. There may still be a few others I might consider "blessing" in this manner. I'd like your input."

"Oh, my new buddy Theo? He's a great guy. Reminds me of my

father, you know?" Teddy looked over at Hanna. "He worries about a lot of stuff he probably shouldn't."

"Well, on his side, somebody has to, I would think."

"Yeah, I guess." He looked up, "I think he's concerned about a wedding?"

Timmy smiled. "Uh-huh. Now that we've got some money for stuff, it's the social issues that take precedence."

"How can you let your girl marry someone else?" Teddy asked him. Hanna looked up.

Timmy sat down with them. "She's your girl, Teddy. Hannah is *your* daughter."

"Oh, yeah. I forget that." He looked at Hanna. "But what about you? You love her, don't you? How can *you* let her go?"

Timmy smiled, a painful, rueful smile. "The same as you, my dear acquaintance. The only way to keep her is to let her go."

Teddy was watching him. "I may need a bigger brain, or maybe I'm glad I don't have one."

Timmy smiled. "Keep an eye on things, old friend."

Teddy nodded, and watched Timmy disappear.

35. Be Careful What You Wish For

"You wanted to see me, Mr. McMasters?"

"Yes, Tim," Theo looked at the boy. "I don't think I'll need to conduct any more experiments on your capabilities. It will probably be more direct to just ask you."

Timmy smiled and opened his hands.

"That was quite a performance out there." Theo said, "We've gotten used to seeing you either watching from the sidelines, or participating by being inside Hannah or Jeff. It never occurred to me, anyway, that you would … put on muscle, so to speak. What happened?" Theo began packing his pipe for a leisurely bowl.

Timmy smiled and held out his hand, spreading his thumb and forefinger apart. A flame sprang into being as if from a lighter.

Theo raised his eyebrows and leaned in to puff his pipe into ignition. "Thanks! I didn't know you could do that."

"I never did, before."

Theo shook his head slightly. "So, are you showing off or something?"

"No, sir. Not really." Timmy looked thoughtful. "It just never occurs to me to try something until I see an opportunity to do it, and then when I try it, it works." He looked up. "All I do is think about it, but I have to focus precisely on exactly what I'm doing, and with what. The flame, for instance, was a simple butane flame, but I had to generate the butane, will it into existence, and then make a spark to ignite it and so forth."

"This isn't just stage magic, Timmy. You're producing stuff from no one knows where. No human I know of can do that, and the only non-human being with such powers was instrumental in making you what you are."

"I know. It doesn't explain how I do it, partly because we don't know how he did it either. I can't even explain it, other than to say I can produce the butane the same way I would produce a puff of air to blow out a candle. When I think about it, it's just a different kind of air."

"You produced a lot more than air out there. Jeff said you made clothes for him."

"I've been making clothes for a little while. It's a little intense, as I have to twist and wind the fabric together like braiding someone's hair. Actually a lot of thought goes into it. But I've learned to bring as much attention to it as I need, and then compartmentalize putting it all together. Once a pattern is set, it's easy to replicate or modify it."

"If you expanded your body the way you've expanded your mind, you would be huge."

"Yeah. Monstrous." Timmy looked at him and smiled. "I don't see any advantage to doing that. I think the mind expansion and acceleration was a result of absorbing and replicating the thinking processes of hundreds of people. I suspect that I've set up whole networks of parallel thinking minds, and besides duplicating other people; I may be borrowing some of their background capabilities. Harnessing their subconscious routines, so to speak. Most of what our brains do is automatic, once we've trained it to do something. It just doesn't take me very long to train my network."

Theo stared at him. "Probably no sense in trying to establish what your IQ is, then."

Timmy floated over and settled into a chair facing Theo. "It isn't comparable. I think one of the measures for intelligence is how quickly one can deal with a large number of different factors. It's safe to say I can deal very quickly with a very large number. The more challenging a project, the more resources I pull into it. I'm not sure what the limits might be."

"No limits at all?"

Timmy smiled again. "No, I have limits. I'm aware of that. I'm still growing, in many ways, so my current limits may not be permanent. I can't tell at this point what the limits might become, but right now I'm happy to just accept what I can do, and what I may have to put off until later."

"Right now I can do just about anything I want to do. My limit at the moment is of imagination. I don't know what more I might want. Do you know what you want?"

Theo drew another puff. "What do you mean?"

"I'm not a god. Definitely not God." Timmy shuddered. "I'm more like the djinn; what we might call a genie. I don't know what kind of bottle they would use to bottle me up, but apart from that, do you have any wishes?"

"You're granting me a wish? Or three wishes?"

"I didn't say, and I didn't say how many. I just asked if you had a wish, or if you knew what you would wish for." Timmy leaned back and smiled.

Theo leaned back too. He blew some smoke upward.

The smoke started dancing, forming figures and moving around.

Theo blinked. "I didn't know you could do that!"

Timmy shrugged.

"I'm having trouble thinking of anything." Theo looked over at him.

"Maybe you're happy already. That would be a nice thing."

"I may need to get back to you on this."

"I'll probably know it before you do. Be careful what you wish for."

"I've always heard that said. You wouldn't pull a trick on an old man, would you?"

"Sure I would! Remember, I'm trying to figure out what to do next. I might think that would be a fun thing to do!"

Theo smiled. "I do love you, boy. I know I've never said that, and I'm not jealous of Wade. I'm just glad that I came to know you. I'm a very lucky man."

Timmy floated over to him, and ended in his lap. Then he sank into him, disappearing for a moment.

Shortly he came back out again, holding his hand out with a pasty substance in it.

"What's that?" Theo asked.

"You don't need that." Timmy answered. He looked down on the material, as it began vanishing away. It didn't flash into light, but changed into the tiniest dark spots, which then evaporated. In a moment it was gone.

"What was it?"

"I've seen it before. You didn't need it." Timmy gave him a hug, and then flew away.

Theo sat for a while longer, puffing on his pipe.

"Two wishes to go, I guess," he said softly.

✦✦✦✦✦

"So you've come out of the closet, so to speak," Dexter observed.

"I don't use your closet. It's already full. I've got a suit hanging in Hannah's closet."

"I mean that you're finally showing your real strength. I knew you had hidden potential."

Timmy grinned. "You knew more than I did, then. I've only discovered how to do some of these things in the past day or so."

Oliver spoke up. "I think I understand how you could throw and hit the ball. That's just an increase in stuff you could already do. But how did you pick up Hannah and fly around with her?"

"I'd like to know that, myself." Hannah said.

"When I learned that I could produce material things, water, clothing, and stuff like that, I also realized that I could push this material in the direction I wanted. Later that meant I could control my ability to push things in general, with even more force than I ever had before, when I was trying to push with my hands alone."

"So you don't have to touch something to make it move?" Hannah said, "I didn't notice that was happening."

"Right. It makes it easier to concentrate on something if I'm touching it, but I've discovered that I only have to "sense" it to be able to make it move, or manipulate it in other ways. That's why I said I wouldn't be playing any more. The bat I can control more like any of you, but the ball I could make do all kinds of things. It just wouldn't be fair."

"So that's how you picked me up?" Hannah asked.

By way of answer, Timmy just looked at her, and she began rising off the ground.

"So your father was right about the refrigerator?" Hannah asked as she was lowered again.

Timmy nodded. "That kind of thing, I think I can make almost anything move."

Her eyes widened. "Don't you have any limits any more?"

"Your father asked the same question. I told him that I knew I had limits, but I don't know how long they'll be there. I also implied that I could grant him a wish, as if I were a genie. He couldn't think of anything to wish for."

"I could think of something to wish for!" Jeff spoke up quickly.

"I've already thought of something for you, but it's more like something for you to give away," Timmy smiled. He held his hand out toward Jeff, and turned it over. It held a glittering diamond ring.

Hannah gasped. "Is that what I think it is?"

"Nope," Timmy said. "It's only a diamond ring, in your size by the way, but what it becomes depends on Jeff."

"I feel like I'm being pushed into this." Jeff said, taking the ring from Timmy's hand and looking it over.

"You say that as if it's something new for you," Oliver observed.

"You could sell that if you want," Timmy suggested. "I'd bet you would get a very nice price for it. At the moment, it's yours to do with as you wish."

"I can do anything I want with this?"

"Sure! This part of the situation functions as an intelligence test." Timmy replied calmly.

"I know the answer," Dexter murmured.

"Shut up," Jeff said, causing Dexter to raise his eyebrows. "I know the answer too. It's just that I've always thought of myself as not having much. I've never held anything this valuable in my whole life."

"He's talking about presumed monetary value, Hannah. He'll snap out of it in a moment." Dexter explained.

"Why, Dexter, that's the nicest thing you've ever said to me. After all these years, you finally noticed that I'm female, did you?" Hannah smiled.

"Hmm. Noticed that a month or two ago, actually." Dexter responded.

"Hey, give me a minute!" Jeff complained, "I need a car, you know!"

"You're getting a car, remember? Hannah's Dad said he'd take care of it." Timmy reminded him.

"All right! All right! Easy come, easy go. Hannah, I'm sorry. I was just lost in the moment."

"It wouldn't fit you anyway, Jeff." Timmy said.

"Ignore them all, Hannah." Jeff said, getting down on one knee. "Will you marry me?" He held out the ring to her.

Hannah studied the situation for a moment. Then she smiled, and held out her hand to him. "I thought we had this all settled already. Of course I want to marry you! I'll need a father figure for young Timmy, who is so dependent on me."

Timmy smiled and nodded.

Jeff slipped the ring on Hannah's finger, and stood up to kiss her.

"Uh-huh. Getting better all the time." Timmy said encouragingly.

"As long as I don't worry about ever having privacy for anything, at any time, I can handle it." Jeff said, kissing Hannah again.

"I find it hard to believe this kid's related to us, Dex, the way he throws money around."

Dexter looked at Oliver. "I'm not sure I believe *you're* related to me. Have you thought of something to wish for?"

"Hmm. I don't need a diamond ring. I don't have my eye on a girl just yet. How about a decent baseball mitt? It seems all the baseball gloves for left-handed people are made by right-handed people."

"You want one like Dex's, only reversed?" Timmy asked.

"That should work." Oliver said. "You said you liked your glove, right?"

"It's great. I thought yours was okay too."

"It's okay, but it's not great." Oliver shrugged.

"Do you want the letters spelled the right way, or do you want an actual mirror-image?" Timmy asked him.

"A mirror-image! Right out of the Looking-Glass!" Oliver responded with enthusiasm.

"Okay." Timmy went over to one of the equipment cabinets and opened it. Hanging on a hook was a baseball glove. On close examination it looked very much like Dexter's glove, with matching but reversed scuffmarks and scratches. It was already broken in.

Timmy retrieved the glove and handed it to Oliver.

Oliver put it on and his eyes lit up. "This is great! Ready to toss the ball back and forth, brother?"

Dexter looked over at Timmy for a moment. "I think I'll do what Mr. Theo did. I'd like to think about it before I say anything."

Timmy raised his eyebrows and nodded slightly.

Dexter smiled and went out to play ball.

36. His Absence Is Keenly Felt

The church had always seemed empty, except for the occasional use of the choir loft. The church in the Realm, that is.

Teddy had convened as many as possible of those who were fully communicative between the Realm and the real world. Real-M and Real-W, as it were; One upside down with its relationships to the other.

Noteworthy in that regard was Myrtle Stowe, who had been fully communicative for a time, her aging body able to chat and message with her youthful avatar counterpart in a remarkable exchange beneficial to both. But the real life Myrtle, grown quite aged and infirm, resisted any suggestion that she should live longer. And so she had passed.

This, among other developments, had Teddy and others concerned.

"My friends, it has been almost two years since we've had the direct contact with Timmy that we all grew to depend on. For all we knew, he was, and is, immortal. So we never considered what could happen to us if he were not around."

Heads nodded in agreement, but no one chose to interrupt.

"His absence is keenly felt. We don't quite know what to do. Slowly we accrue new activities and patterns. We make discoveries. This is a fascinating world, with wonders around every corner!"

"But it was easier to know what would be happening next when

Timmy was with us. He would simply tell us, or show us. It was delightful and wonderful."

"Now we appear to be on our own, and it is that I wish to talk with you about. We have a report from Rusty, who has been investigating what may have been Timmy's last activities before his disappearance. Rusty?"

"Thanks, Teddy. I have been traveling, which is something I have always done. But traveling in the Realm has a different meaning than it does anywhere else. We know, of course, that instantaneous travel awaits us at the touch of a hip ring, as does communication. But one thing that limits that, is knowing where you want to go."

"Have any of you tried to go someplace that doesn't exist?" He looked around. There were a small number of nods of assent. "It's a little confusing. The system tries to be accommodating, but it can't send you places that aren't mapped for us. So we have learned to state our preferences clearly and distinctly."

"Well, I found a way to stretch that concept rather easily. I simply asked to go somewhere I hadn't been before. That's how I found my way to Key West, where Henry and Alice had gone on a few trips to locate other nautically minded folks."

"But I also discovered, for no discernible reason, that Timmy had been to Europe, Greece, Hong Kong, Hawaii, the Philippines, and Australia. You can all go there too, and I urge you to do so whenever you have the time. One of the things you'll discover is that you will be able to speak and understand the local languages there."

There was a bit of a hubbub over this pronouncement, so Rusty waited for quiet again.

"You know that everything in the Realm is a thought process set up by Timmy, to be ongoing and independent of his active awareness. Apparently when he first visited these locations, he simply tapped into local minds and built his awareness on top of their intrinsic and local knowledge. What else would he do? That's the way he operated. Titanic is here because people knew of it."

Teddy jumped in, "We may speculate about why Timmy went to these places and established operational centers there, but it is clear that he intended them to be somewhat autonomous and that he eventually intended that we in this area be more proactive in our own operations as well."

"Ted, I know that it feels very natural for you to be in charge," Corrie said, "but what is it you think we have to do? Doesn't everything already run itself?"

"Corrie knows that I am father to one of you, father-in-law to another, neighbor and husband, and so forth to the rest of you. She thinks that means I have political ambitions, I guess. It's actually much simpler than that. Somebody has to be watching out for us, and it might as well be me. I'd be trying to do it anyway." He smiled.

"But the main thing I want to bring to your attention is that these other locations have been set up to grow, and we haven't. That, I think, is something we need to fix, and I honestly don't care if I'm the leader in it or not."

"How do they grow, Teddy," Ange asked, "and what does that mean, anyway?"

"They have the ability to bring in new members. So far, we haven't been able to do that."

"But what difference does that make? We have whole cities full of people. Isn't that enough?"

"Not to be indelicate," Teddy responded, "but there's your answer to that." He pointed to Myrtle.

Myrtle left off from re-arranging the flowers in her hair to look around. "What? What do I have to do with anything?"

"Myrtle is still with us here in the Realm, even though out in the real world, her body has passed on. She can be with us here, and we're glad she is, but she can no longer do anything out there."

Myrtle shrugged. "I have a bigger garden here. It's even a tourist site! Not to mention never getting sick or hurting."

"Yes, but if we wait until all of us are in the same condition, we won't be able to have any influence at all out in the real world, and that's when the Realm ceases to have any meaning at all. We would be pinched off from reality, and then it wouldn't matter if we continue or not. We'd be gone."

They were silent for a time.

"Would it really matter? You're talking about fifty years or more from now. We don't have to do anything right away. There'll be plenty of time later on."

"Maybe not. I think it takes a minimum number of specially connected people to induct new members, and we're probably at that level now. If we wait ten or twenty years, we may have waited too long already." He looked around. "And yes, it matters. It will matter to our children, when they are old enough to be inducted, and it will matter to other good people and fine friends, who should be able to join us, because their being here will make it a better place."

They were quiet again.

"Well, Teddy, what would we have to do?" Myrtle asked.

"A lot of the Realm operates automatically. Essentially, you have to announce your intention, in a way that expresses unambiguously what you want to do. When we're ready to bring new members into our group, we have to do the same thing."

"What I saw being done in Europe, on the Mediterranean coast of France," Rusty said, "was a kind of ceremony, more like an introduction or initiation ceremony than a procedure. The inductee would be in the center of a circle of active Realm members, and a similar arrangement would be made on both sides."

37. Replicated In Fancy Style

Hannah had an idea. She drafted Jeff into it, and talked Henry and Alice into joining her.

"You say my boat's off that direction? What are we trying to do here, again?" Henry didn't seem to care for any adventure he hadn't thoroughly charted already.

"She told us, Henry! We're supposed to meet up with our grown-up selves, to see what our "Happy Ever After" turned out like."

"It should only take a minute." Hanna looked across at Jeff, still unchanged from his boyhood avatar, but known to be her husband of at least five years.

He grinned at her.

"You know what to do now, Jeff. Meet me back here with our guests." Hanna told him.

Out in the real world, Mr. and Mrs. Conners, Jeff and Hannah, were escorting their next-door neighbors on a tour of their back yard.

"Now here's our home base, for our baseball games. Please stand right here, Mr. Anderson, and hold my hand. Mrs. Anderson, you hold this hand, and stand over here. Jeff, come on! Join the circle!"

"Everybody ready?" Hannah asked one final time. "Okay, now, close your eyes, and hold them closed."

Hanna said, "All right. Everything is in position now. Everybody concentrate! Make contact with your future self!"

They stood quietly for a moment.

"I'm seeing something." Henry said. "My eyes are closed tight, but I'm seeing something."

"I see something too!" His wife said excitedly.

"Wait …" Henry seemed puzzled.

"Yeah. How come we're all children, and we don't have any clothes on?"

"Keep your eyes closed until we've got a lock, please!" Hannah urged them.

Meanwhile, the young Henry's thoughts were intruding into the older man's brain. It wasn't a comfortable fit. The old man was remembering so much that he should have known too!

Henry took a deep breath. Opposite him, Alice smiled, as if sensing that the connection was being firmly established. Hannah had told her so much about this wonderful gift.

"Alright, Jeff. Let's back away slowly, and let them establish their own connections." Hannah said, releasing hands with her companions, but watching closely on both sides of the divide.

"You know what I'm seeing? Everything is so much brighter! The colors are so vibrant!" Alice said in wonder.

"I think it's working!" Jeff said.

"This seems awfully difficult. However did you discover this trick?" Henry asked.

"I got it from you, or rather, the other Henry, by way of my Dad!" Hannah said. "The other Henry showed us how things will try to work in the Realm, even if you move them. Teddy showed us how to stretch their functions by keeping a link." Hannah explained as she observed, to be sure the current linkage was stable.

"But it wasn't always this tricky." Hannah put her hands down and took a deep breath. "It was always easier when Timmy did it."

"I miss him too, Deary," the diminutive Alice came to Hanna and put her arm around her shoulder. She closed her eyes and seemed to send a thought to Alice.

The older Alice opened her eyes, and turned to Hannah. "We all miss him, you know."

Hannah smiled and took a breath. They all seemed to depend on her. It didn't matter at all that she felt somehow responsible for Timmy's going away.

They knew he wasn't gone entirely, of course. Not as long as the Realm continued anyway.

But she had been talking with Rusty, who was worried. He, perhaps more than any of them, had a lot emotionally invested in the Realm.

"With Timmy missing, we're cut off from new entries." Rusty had said. "We who are in some manner a part of his inner circle, have to find a way to expand the Realm. We have to find a way to bring new candidates into the inner circle, and we have to try to find a way eventually to bring new minds into the Realm."

Hannah knew Timmy wasn't gone. She felt his presence too closely for that to be a possibility. But he was either active in some other inexplicable fashion, or he was inactive for some reason. He just seemed … distant … or distracted, somehow. Maybe in truth he had spread himself too thin.

And so she had come up with this experiment, which at the moment, seemed to have succeeded. Later on, she and Rusty, and others of the "Inner Circle" would put their heads together, probably literally, and see if they could just *will* new candidates into avatar status in the Realm. It was worth a try. Timmy had left them other tools and procedures that ran automatically.

It was worth a try. Who would have guessed that this idea could work?

Hannah smiled. Hanna reached down to her hip, and spoke. "Corrie, how's Emme?"

"She's fine, Hanna. She's just drawing."

"Tell Mom I'll be up in just a minute. We're about done here. Everything worked great! Dad's a genius!"

"You mean Teddy is a genius! I'll tell her."

Alice and Henry still had that dazed look; the confusion from seeing through eyes other than their own. They would be all right now, and their long-awaited cruises could take place in safety, now that they had a new life-line established.

Hannah thought about Alice's curious statement about color brightness. She made a mental note to get Alice's eyes checked at the earliest opportunity. Such things needed the attention of professional and quite real doctors these days.

She glanced at her ring; a gift from Timmy, not to her, but to Jeff, so *he* could give it to her. A diamond ring! An honest-to-goodness diamond ring. Timmy had made that, in that same mysterious fashion that he brought forth all of his beautiful glints and sparkles from between the dimensions.

She had had it appraised, just to be able to get it insured. Her Dad had been insistent about that!

And the jeweler had been quite astonished. "It's flawless, Mrs. Conners. It is absolutely perfect and without any kind of inclusion or discoloration. I will put a value on it. But I have to admit that it is quite irreplaceable. I have no doubt there is no other of its perfection anywhere."

She looked over at Jeff, who was chatting with Henry and pointing out various places in the back yard, and how they oriented to each other in the Realm. In neither world did he need glasses anymore. That was one of the things that Timmy had finally gotten around to doing.

Just another miracle in a very long line of inexplicable things that he had been doing routinely, and now they had to come up with clumsy workarounds, or do without his magic entirely.

Where was he?

No one knew. It seemed the most likely explanation that he was *everywhere*; or at least that small slice of everywhere that he had carved out of reality and replicated in fancy style in his own version of reality. They called it the Realm.

It was still going strong; bigger that ever! That at least was evidence that Timmy was still … somewhere. Maybe he was resting, or sleeping.

Maybe one day he would awaken again, and come to them, or speak to them. To work his miracles again, in modest apprehension that he might be thought to be "showing off". Hannah smiled. His way of showing love; his sharing, his essence.

Yes, he was still around. He was only resting.

Hannah saw that Jeff was walking with the Andersons back to their house. Their house; she smiled.

It had seemed a priority to find a way to get rid of them, by somehow finding out what they wanted.

She shook her head just slightly. What had always been his dream, their dream, was sailing, and enjoying trips of wind and wave.

But what they really wanted was to be a part of a family, like this one. Drive them away? Lure them away? No, they had to be welcomed *in*. They had to be given love, like every other wandering lonely heart they could find, like their dear friend Rusty, who sometimes went on trips with the Andersons, and who sometimes came to visit with them.

Visiting with them in their house, because he couldn't get any closer to the Miller house. Hannah smiled and went inside.

Hannah kissed Angie and Wade and went upstairs to the suite that had been fashioned for her and Jeff.

Oliver and Dexter were always out on adventures, either playing sports or reporting on them. That was their life, and somehow they thought it fitting to be the Millers' representatives to the world. They took pride in being a part of the "most remarkable family in the world", and they would argue the point to exhaustion at every opportunity.

But they wanted the space to go to Hannah, because in those days, if it benefited Hannah, it benefited Timmy. For many years they only spoke the name Hammy, as if they were one and inseparable.

Hannah smiled at her daughter, comfortably ensconced at her drawing table, while her grandmother sat and mended choir robes.

"Hello Emme! How's my little girl?" She kissed her daughter.

"I'm fine, mommy!" She hugged her mother's neck. "I'm just drawing Dreamland, and Grandma is fixing the choir robes. She thinks I'll be able to sing in the choir in a couple more years."

"When the people can see you, dear." Corinne said mildly, holding her hand up about four feet above the floor. She went back to her mending.

"Let's see your drawing, then!" Hannah said. She moved around to Emme's side of the surface and knelt down. The large paper had a very intricate drawing on it, a big ocean-liner with four large, dark tubes rising up above the decks.

"So this is Dreamland!"

Emme nodded her head vigorously. "It's a part of Dreamland. I see it when I dream, most of the time. The men have funny hats. The ladies all have nice dresses." She was pointing out details of her drawing.

"This is the band. It's beautiful music, Mommy. There's always music in Dreamland."

"And what's this up here? Is that an angel?" Hannah asked of a small figure in white.

"He's the singer. I hear him singing all the time when I go to Dreamland."

"Grandma says he used to sing in her choir, but I never heard him there. I only hear him in Dreamland."

"So he's on the boat then?"

"No, not just on the boat. I don't always go to the boat. But I always hear him singing when I go to Dreamland." She looked at Hannah's face. "Is he an angel, Mommy?"

"Sometimes I think he used to be an angel. Some people seemed to think he was *my* angel, before *you* became my angel." Hannah said lightly, kissing the top of Emme's head.

But then something seemed to register and echo in that remark; some kind of accidental truth that had sprung into being. Hannah looked up at her mother, and they shared a look of astonished recognition.

Corinne brought tea to Hannah, and sat down opposite her.

"Thanks, Mom." Hannah watched her mother for a moment. "What?"

"I've been watching you." Corinne replied, "You haven't said anything, but I see you wince every time someone mentions Timmy being gone."

Hannah looked down. The wisps of steam were rising from her cup.

"See! You just did it again! I know what you're thinking, and I think you could be wrong."

"What am I thinking?" Hannah said, bringing the tea to her lips.

"You've been blaming yourself for his disappearance."

Hannah reflected. "The timing is curious. It doesn't feel like just coincidence."

Corinne shrugged. "Sometime coincidence is just coincidence, as Theo might say. But there's another coincidence that occurred about the same time, and I don't think you've considered it at all."

"What's that?" Hannah looked up.

"While you were giving birth, we lost a close friend, Myrtle Stowe. I want you to think about her for a moment. She was another person connected to Timmy in that inexplicable fashion that we all were. But she passed on. Peacefully, as it turns out, but she's the first of our "inner circle" to go away from us."

"That was about the same time?" Hannah said.

"The same day." Corinne nodded. "We think she died just before Emme was born, although no one even dares speculate that it means anything. I just find it … a coincidence, that's all."

"When Timmy … connected … to me, he had to be touching me. At first, that's the only way he could do it. Later, he got better at it, and could apparently do it from way across the room."

She grew quiet for a moment. "I would guess that he could choose to disconnect from someone just as easily, but I don't know what would happen if the connection got terminated in some other fashion."

"When Jeff got hit by the car, I felt it! But we were both connected together through Timmy. I would guess he felt it even more than I did." Hannah looked at her mother. "Maybe when Myrtle died, Timmy was still connected to her, and it stretched him out in a way we might not understand."

"That's what I want you to think about. It may not have anything to do with you or with Emme at all. It could be just bad timing."

"Well, Emme has some kind of connection with Timmy, or at least with the Realm. It may be the most tenuous connection of any of us, showing up only in her dreams. But I can't explain the visions she's been getting otherwise. She never appears in the Realm, but she sees things that are there."

The timing had been … curious. The person-developing process had fascinated Timmy. He had spent perhaps an unusual amount of time in contact with both Hannah and the growing baby.

But he had been doing so many other things as well! He had discovered that he could extend himself for miles; to sense people in trouble who had just arrived in town. People he didn't even know!

He had found a way to manifest his creative hand near anyone with whom he maintained contact. He had produced a car key in the hand of the local family doctor, after he had inadvertently locked his own inside the car. "Now hide this one where you can find it next time!" Timmy had chided the doctor.

And he hadn't even been there! As far as anyone knew, Timmy had been at home, and he hadn't changed position.

Hannah knew that there were other stories that she had not even heard about.

But as her time had grown closer, Timmy's appearances had grown scarce. After the birth had come, no one knew where he was.

No one saw him, or spoke to him again. And yet the Realm went on as usual. Somehow, Emme was aware of things happening in "Dreamland", although she had no avatar in the Realm. Timmy had never made one for her.

But every evening, the party played out on the Titanic, at the bottom of the lake.

If you could get there, you could see it all over again.

If you could get there, like Henry, you could stock your wine cellar.

If you could get there, like Teddy and Rusty, you could steal radio equipment, and try to figure out how to connect it to the real world.

And every day, on the next day, everything went back to the way it should be for an evening to remember.

People out in those quaint childhood adventure towns along the Mythical Mississippi still took crops to market, on riverboats that stayed on top of the water. Strange business dealings were going on with her Dad and with Rusty. That was their business, but she knew it depended on Timmy's automatic functioning.

He was around, somewhere. According to her daughter, he was singing.

Singing, every night, in Dreamland.

Epilog – Advice

Wade was resting in his recliner. It occurred to him that it had been some time since he had conducted a heart-to-heart chat with his "youngest" boy, Timmy.

He passed word for Timmy to come see him.

Presently a very quiet twelve-year old boy approached him, seemingly concerned that he might be sleeping. Wade smiled.

He was dressed in a common appearance for this boy, especially when hurried, for he wore nothing at all. "I came quickly, father. I did not pause to dress."

Wade waved an arm casually, "You don't need that, my boy."

The boy relaxed. No matter that he could never recall his father having raised a hand to strike him, the man's physical presence was intimidating.

"Come and sit with me, Timmy." Wade said.

The boy lifted off the floor and floated weightlessly into his father's lap.

Wade opened his arms to the child and gently embraced him.

"My boy! You are such a delight! That innocent face and shy smile! How can a father ever get enough of that?"

Timmy kissed his father and relaxed in his arms. "I only pretend to be innocent, you know, father."

"Yes, I know." Wade said softly. "You pretend it very well."

"I love you, father. I never pretend about that."

"I know. And I love you too. You have gladdened my heart for many years, even before the changes that made you magical, and even more wonderful. But I don't think I tell you that often enough."

"I know it, father. But I still like to hear you say it."

"I mean it, too! Of all the blessings having a family has meant to me, you are the one that makes my heart want to burst into song!"

The boy smiled. "I'd like to hear that!"

"Not as much as I'd like to hear *you* sing! But that's not why I wanted to see you." He paused, arranging his thoughts. "I guess I'm feeling some mortality. I wanted to share with you some things I've observed, both recently and long ago."

Timmy snuggled even more closely, as Wade idly stroked his smooth skin.

"You have noticed by now, that you are staying the same age, while the rest of us are getting older. That really has only one eventual outcome. There will come a day when we are not around to give you advice and to worry about you." He looked down at the smooth brow of his child. It was serene, untroubled and calm, even after all he had been though.

Wade sighed. "You will find, whatever else you may discover about your remarkable abilities and talents, that there is only one thing worth seeking and securing, and that is the love of those close to you, and the ones you care about. All the rest of it is like daily weather. It comes and goes, and there isn't much you can do about it."

"Your loved ones need your support, and you need theirs. Even if you may be cursed to live for thousands of years, or even longer, you will need the anchor of loved ones to be able to weather emotional tides and storms that come your way."

Timmy looked up at him, his eyes large and wide.

Wade kissed him. "You may not appreciate this right now. Try to save it for the future, maybe. You're more certain to get there than I am. One of these days, you may be tempted to hurt someone; perhaps someone who really has it coming. I've been thinking about that, and I want to tell you now, put that thought aside when it comes around. Just be still, and think your way out of whatever has come up. You, more than anyone else, have to be careful not to hurt someone else, because they will try to hurt you back, and they won't be able to."

He looked down at the innocent face. "That's where the danger will come in. When they start trying to find ways to hurt you. Because they will escalate. They will raise the stakes again and again until they find a way to cause you pain. And eventually they will turn to hurting the ones you care about, and that will hurt you more than any other thing they could do."

Wade shifted his weight, adjusting Timmy's position, though the boy weighed nothing at all. He petted him again, with soothing strokes.

"It frightens me to think what might become of you to have nowhere to turn. To be alone in a hostile world. It makes me weep, for I cannot prevent it. Think about these things, Timmy. If you must, find a place where you can hide, and not be known, when you may find yourself alone. Be safe, and be contented in that place, until you can go out again and be with people you may love, and who will love you."

"That is the only thing I can give to you as a father, my son; that there will always be a place for you to find and share love. For people will always need it, and they will seek it. Be gentle in the world, Timmy. For all its needless pain and hurtful reactions, it is a world of beauty and delight, just like you. You were made to be an ornament for the world, to be its brightest star; the one bright image that proves the world needs, and is filled with love."

He paused, and tears trickled down the lines in his face.

Timmy reached up to touch those tears, as if seeing such things for the very first time.

"You're getting tired, aren't you, father?"

"Yes, I suppose I am. I really wanted to tell you these things, though."

"And now you have."

"Yes. I hope you can remember them."

"I will. I promise I will."

"Then that will have to do."

"It will, father. It will do. You can rest now, father. I will be here with you for a while. I love you."

"Yes. That sounds good. Stay here a while with me, and we will both rest. I love you too."

Epilog – And Consents

"This is how you found him, then?" The Administrator looked annoyed, perhaps wanting to find someone to blame.

"Yes, sir! All things considered, he looks very peaceful."

"When one of our most elderly residents dies, Matson, we don't want him to be unnoticed and alone for hours! This man was a hundred and eight years old!"

"He seemed fine, sir! Only hours before, he was moving his arms and talking." Matson declaimed.

"Talking? Talking to whom?" Maybe there was some hope, after all.

"Well, to no one, actually. He hasn't had a visitor in quite a long time. No one has been seen to enter his room other than the staff at regular intervals. There is a sign-in log, but it remains blank."

"Ah, well. To die alone, and at so advanced an age. Pity."

Matson nodded. "One can die too soon, sir. And one can live too long, as well. But we all die, of course."

"Of course. Well, you know what to do. I'll be handling the paperwork, as usual."

"Yes, sir." Matson said, opening the door, and then locking it behind them. Indeed there were procedures.

After a moment, a naked boy looked out from behind a privacy curtain to see that they were gone. He silently walked over to the old man's body, and placed a single flower from the vase on the sink, on the old man's chest.

He stared for a moment, and then walked out through the wall, into the world.